Holiday Handyman

S.V. Lynn

First edition, October 2025

Cover designed by Kristina Fostovets

ISBN: 979-8-9995636-0-6

Published by: Valle Girl Productions

Holiday Handyman is meant to be a cute small-town romance. Still, there may be some topics that some might find triggering such as:

Explicit sexual content
Cancer
Death of a parent
Infidelity (off page/not MCs)
Incarceration
Alcohol use
Drug use

Please take care as you read, and I hope you enjoy the story.

Hotel Mogul, Roman Spencer, Implicated in $500 Million Embezzlement Scheme

LOS ANGELES, CAL (AP) — Roman Spencer, billionaire CEO of the Spencer Group, which operates 175 properties worldwide, is facing serious allegations in an embezzlement scheme that has allegedly spanned decades. Sources indicate that Spencer and his CFO, Winston Pickering, may have siphoned off nearly $500 million in company funds.

While Spencer's son, Preston, was poised to inherit the family business despite his many personal distractions, the future of the empire is now uncertain.

The Spencer Group has yet to comment, but the FBI is actively seeking information on Pickering's whereabouts as the investigation continues.

This is a developing story. We will provide updates as the situation unfolds.

Chapter 1

Preston

I can't see anything in the complete darkness of the room, but I know I'm not alone. An acrid taste lingers on my tongue, no doubt from the copious amounts of liquor I consumed last night. The consequences of which make themselves known in the form of one of the worst hangovers I've experienced in my thirty-four years on this earth. And my right arm is completely numb.

The specifics of last night are hazy, but what I do remember is the visceral need to expel the rage brought on after receiving an extremely curt email from my father telling me my presence was expected at the seven a.m. meeting with the board.

As the so-called heir to my father's empire, every day he gets closer to retirement, the unbearable weight of that future threatens to suffocate the life right out of me. It's a destiny I never wanted for myself, so last night I responded like I always do—hopping from club to club with my best friend, Alexi, with the single-minded goal of erasing the day's problems with plenty of booze and girls.

Mission accomplished by the looks of it, with a blonde whose head is currently pinning my arm to the bed. Hence, the numbness.

What her name is, I couldn't tell you, nor could I give a shit at this moment as my main concern is getting her the fuck out of my apartment and downing some Advil to cure this massive headache. I wish I could say this is uncharacteristic of me, but the truth is, my life has pretty much been a string of nights filled with excessive drinking and nameless women ever since my father named me his successor. My therapist would say it's pathological avoidance or abandonment issues or unresolved trauma, which is precisely why I haven't seen him in four years.

The last bits of sleep are stolen from me by an incessant buzzing coming from my nightstand. The nightstand that sits opposite of where I currently lay, the blonde blocking my access. I try to reach over her but stop short of ripping my arm out of its socket. The buzzing intensifies as dozens of notifications make their presence known.

It finally occurs to me that I'm supposed be at the office by seven and judging by the beam of sunlight peeking through my curtains, it's much later than that. I glance at the time—9:58. I'm nearly three hours late.

Yanking my arm free, the blonde barely noticing, I grab my phone and am met with a steady stream of news alerts, missed calls, and texts—all from Oliver, my father's assistant. A pit of worry takes hold in my stomach. There's no time to review the news reports when another text comes in, this time from my father himself, stating in no uncertain terms that if I don't get my ass to the office immediately, he's cutting off my black card.

My finger hovers over my phone, poised to respond with some flippant remark but I'm interrupted by an annoyed groan coming from next to me. I nearly forgot about the nameless blonde who still occupies my bed.

She stretches lazily, mumbling a complaint about the early hour while encouraging me to come back to bed. When I don't respond, she tosses the covers over her head in frustration and proceeds to go back to sleep. I let out a loud sigh, wondering to myself, *who the fuck does this chick think she is?*

I walk to the large window and violently rip open the curtains, allowing the harsh morning sun to flood the room. Loudly clearing my throat, I acknowledge her if only to make sure she moves her ass.

"Hey..." I pause, still searching my brain for her name and come up empty, "...you. Time to get your shit and leave."

Oblivious to my impatience, she giggles as if I'm playing around. "Are you sure you wouldn't rather come back to bed?"

In a poor attempt at seduction, she slowly pulls down the sheet, revealing her naked body. Without breaking eye contact, she shoots me a sultry glance, running a finger down the center of her breasts, begging me to give her attention.

And she very nearly hooked me.

Another buzz from my phone jolts me out of that line of thinking. She may be gorgeous, but I have somewhere to be and anyway, I never see a girl twice.

At least not since *her*.

My last public relationship ended in scandal when my engagement to a well-known social media influencer and model ended with her jilting me three days before our wedding. Apparently, my desire to give up the family fortune in favor of continuing my mother's philanthropic work didn't work with her image.

Since then, I've had a strict policy against dating, favoring meaningless sex instead to quell the loneliness. Sure, it's empty and shallow, but a random body warming your bed can't lie, manipulate, or humiliate you, so a win is a win.

"Not interested. I'm getting in the shower. Be gone before I'm done." I forcefully toss her clothes to the empty spot in bed and turn on my heels towards the bathroom.

After a quick scrub to wash away the mistakes of last night, I emerge to discover Nameless Girl obviously took the hint as no trace of her remains.

Making my way downstairs via the penthouse's private elevator, I'm greeted by an abnormal number of paparazzi surrounding the building's entrance and a behemoth of a man clad in black from head to toe. Duane, my father's head of security, waits for me at the door, a barrier already erected allowing me passage from the door to the black SUV parked out front. In my entire life, my father has never once provided an escort to get me to the office. What the fuck is going on? I reach for my phone, but Duane lays a hand on my wrist, shaking his head.

"Mr. Spencer," Duane nods in my direction, "you have to come with us now. It's probably best if you don't acknowledge the press. Your father will fill you in when we get there."

I pull my shades down and the collar of my jacket up,

as if that will protect me from the media circus that awaits. The flash of cameras in my direction is disorienting, the shouting of the paps deafening as I make my way to the SUV.

Once I'm safely in the car, Duane slams the door, drowning out some of the noise. A million thoughts run through my mind as I try to figure out what scandal my father has found himself in now. Usually, it's a tryst with a young actress or some thoughtless social media post, but I can't possibly think of why the press would hound *me* about that.

"I need to know what the fuck is going on. Right now." Duane might be my father's head of security, but as the heir apparent, he is also obligated to me.

"Like I said, I think it's best that I let your father explain this one." We ride the rest of the way in terse silence, exacerbating the anxiety I feel heavy in my chest.

As we pull up to my father's office building, it's pure pandemonium. The crowd outside my apartment seems minuscule compared to the hundreds of paparazzi, onlookers, and news vans that surround the building's entrance. I can't even see the front door through the sea of people, let alone comprehend how we will get through without injuring anyone or ourselves. It's then that I realize we're driving around to the back of the building, a hidden entrance to an underground parking garage I never knew existed until now.

No fewer than a dozen security guards surround the car and escort us to an elevator that takes us up to the top floor where my father's office and the main boardroom reside. We exit the elevator, the doors opening slowly to a scene of utter chaos.

Long time employees of my father's are running around panicked and frazzled, a few of whom are covering their mouths to muffle their sobs. I still have no inkling of what's happening, but it's clear that this is much more serious than my father sticking his dick where it doesn't belong.

Panic fills my chest as I spot a parade of people heading for the exit, all in navy windbreakers clearly marked "FBI," carrying boxes of paperwork and computers. With a somber nod to Duane, one of the security guards swings open the door to the boardroom, directing me to take my place within the sea full of my father's top executives and lawyers, all shouting over one another.

Impeccably dressed in a black striped Italian suit, my father is the perfect picture of restrained rage standing in the eye of the storm. He towers over everyone else, his large stature and presence seeming to envelop everyone in the room like a shadow. Thick lines mar the dark skin of his forehead as he furrows his brow in annoyance as soon as his onyx eyes land on me.

"It's about goddamn time, Preston. Where the fuck have you been?" My father's deep voice booms, overwhelming the room that has now fallen into silence. "You were expected to be here at seven o'clock. I've been calling you all morning."

"You want to tell me why my apartment was surrounded by paparazzi and I was whisked away by your men in black with no explanation?" I ignore his admonition, failing to remove the insolence from my voice. I'm still pissed that no one has told me anything and my head is still fucking pounding. I plop down in the nearest chair, bracing for the verbal lashing I'm sure I've earned.

He lets out a humorless chuckle, shaking his head as he closes the distance between us. "I know you mean *my* apartment that you stay in, rent-free, while you piss away *my* money on booze and parties, right?"

He leans in, slamming both hands on either side of my chair, his eyes staring daggers into mine. "You'll sit up, take off those goddamn glasses, and pay attention because need I remind you that without me, you have *nothing*," he growls through gritted teeth.

Standing straighter, he smooths down his jacket before returning to take a seat at the head of the conference table. He gestures to a short, round man in an ill-fitting tan suit, his head of legal, Stanley Beck, bidding him to address the room.

My father doesn't stop scowling at me until I remove the sunglasses I forgot I still had on. At least he doesn't seem to notice how hungover I am. Deciding to avoid exchanging more barbs with him, I sit up straight in my seat and prepare to listen to Stanley with rapt attention.

"As many of you know, early this morning the IRS froze all of Mr. Spencer's assets as their lawyers work with the FBI to gather their evidence against him and the company." Stanley walks around to the head of the room, looking at my father for approval before continuing.

"It seems that for over the last seventeen years, Mr. Spencer's most trusted advisor and CFO, Winston Pickering, had been siphoning money into a hidden account instead of paying the company's taxes. Unfortunately, Mr. Pickering has fled the country, implicating Mr. Spencer as the sole mastermind behind this embezzlement scheme."

My jaw drops and I have to cover my mouth to suppress a laugh. Here's a man who has always looked out for only himself, now finding himself wrapped up in some cliche, white collar crime. While I cannot say I feel any sympathy for the predicament he finds himself in, I do care about what this means for me, my trust fund, and my so-called inheritance.

My father wasn't wrong in his earlier accusation—he does fund my entire lifestyle from the place I live, to the food I eat, the clothes on my back, and, yes, even the excessive partying I partake in week after week. Of course, he never lets me forget that this money has always come with the caveat that I will take over the company when he finally retires and until then, I'm expected do anything he requires of me to that end.

Pausing, as if for dramatic effect, Stanley takes a long, slow sip of water before continuing. "You're all thinking, 'Well, what does this mean for me?' and that's precisely why we are all here this morning."

He begins walking around the conference table, a smug confidence on his face, seeming to enjoy having everyone's attention trained on him. "As Mr. Spencer is under investigation, his assets have been frozen. We are unsure of the true amount siphoned by Mr. Pickering, but we suspect we may have to sell a few of our properties to repay these debts. Until that time, we've been ordered to cease all operations and cancel all current reservations, effective immediately. Your staff will be furloughed, without pay."

The room descends into chaos as the suits yell in Stanley's direction about stocks, buyouts, and the money they are owed. Stanley is unmoved by the scene before him and looks, I dare say, *bored.* He's always been one of the most ruthless members of my father's staff, so this should come as little surprise, but I thought even he would be more affected by delivering the news that tens of thousands of people just lost their livelihood.

The yelling is drowned out by the ringing in my ears as I slowly begin to understand the implications. My penthouse is an asset. My trust is an asset. My entire future is the company that is now being held by the IRS because my father hired a crook. Or maybe he *was* the crook, but even I have a hard time believing that despite how much he's changed.

My father wasn't always a ruthless, greedy bastard. Before he built his empire, it was just me, him, and my mother living in a small cottage behind their first property, a quaint inn in Vermont. We didn't have much, but we were happy, our home always filled with laughter and love. As much as we were both forever changed by what happened back then, I still cannot believe the man who used to teach me how to maintain the inn with such love and care could cheat people out of millions.

My father clears his throat, snapping me out of my little trip down memory lane as the room starts to clear out. "Preston, we still need to discuss what's about to happen for you. Especially since I could be facing jail time." My father nods to Stanley to take over.

"Right. The penthouse technically belongs to your father and is now a seized asset. We have a team packing your things as we speak," he says without any emotion.

I knew it was coming, but still a laugh of disbelief escapes my mouth. "You're fucking kidding. So I'm homeless now?" I direct to my father, who refuses to even meet my eyes.

"The company does still have one property left,"

Stanley continues. "The inn in Stoney Ridge. As you're aware, its ownership fell to you after...you know. Anyway, the company retained management until you came of age and kept it under your father's purview for ease until you officially take over as CEO, of course."

No. I wasn't aware, but not a part of me is surprised at the revelation that my father hid pertinent information from me. Anger fills every inch of my body, and my fists are balled up so tightly I know there will be little half-moons imprinted on my palms when I release.

I take a deep breath, demanding answers from my father. "You expect me to move back to my childhood home? To do what, exactly? Become a fucking innkeeper?"

"You'll *do* whatever I *tell* you to do," my father finally interjects, shoving his chair backward, slamming his hands on the table as he stands.

"I've funded your aimless life for long enough, so now you're going to do whatever I need you to do. Oliver will arrange your stay, and we'll discuss your role later. You leave tomorrow. I don't want to hear another word."

The venom in his voice leaves no doubt to the level of disdain he has for me in this moment. Without sparing me another look, he storms out of the room, slamming the door in his wake.

I guess I'm moving to Vermont.

Chapter 2

Mia

Sunday brunch is always busy at The Early Bird Inn, but this morning is particularly packed. Not only do we have our current roster of guests, but we have a two-hour wait for walk-ins.

Most people would be stressed with the sight before them, but not me. Serving others at the inn where I spent most of my life is when I feel most like myself.

My mom came to The Early Bird almost thirty-two years ago, a nineteen-year-old Mexican immigrant with a six-month-old baby on her hip and a dream for a better life in her heart. The owners, Roman and Gabriela Spencer, opened the inn four months prior and were in dire need of additional staff.

My mom had never held a job before, but determined to support us, she managed to talk her way into a position, negotiating room and board with her salary. Gabriela, one of the owners, quickly took a liking to us, offering to help watch me so my mother could work until I was old enough to go to school.

Once Mr. Spencer expanded into luxury hotels, he moved his family to LA, trusting my mom, and now me, to run the place in his stead. It may not be the life I had planned, but as I stand there looking around the lively dining room at our happy guests, there's truly no place I'd rather be.

I wander the room, making sure everyone is enjoying their breakfast when commotion coming from the reception desk catches my ear. I dodge the gaggle of children who have turned our dining area into their own personal playground and arrive just in time to see tears threatening to fall from the crystal blue eyes of our newest receptionist, Lizzy.

Mrs. Charlotte Sinclair stands with a scowl on her face, pointing a finger in Lizzy's face, listing off a series of complaints about her room. Today, it seems her shower is on the fritz, causing extremely cold temperatures and leaving her usually perfectly styled bob a tangled mess of frizz. Mrs. Sinclair owns a chain of high-end spas across the Eastern seaboard and regularly stays with us, determined to be a thorn in my side each time. But we can't afford to turn down guests, especially when we need the money to restore and modernize the inn.

"Mrs. Sinclair!" I exclaim in my best attempt to divert attention from her current diatribe against poor Lizzy. I internally curse myself for not preparing her for the inevitable wrath of Mrs. Sinclair. I make a mental note to apologize later but taking the heat off her is something I can do in the immediate term.

"It's so great to see you again! Oh my god, is that a new coat?" I gesture to her, hopefully faux, fur coat, taking her by the arm to seat her at the table I always keep empty for these exact situations.

Glancing over my shoulder, I shoot Lizzy an apologetic smile and continue distracting Mrs. Sinclair with compliments and promises of fresh coffee and a warm breakfast, on the house. Thankfully, this seems to calm her down and she settles in to read the morning paper.

"Oh, Mia? Can we address the issues with my room before you go?" she says with a renewed sweetness and a saccharine, entirely phony, grin.

I grab the seat across from her, matching her smile, and prepare to incur her wrath. "Of course! How can I help?"

"Well, as you know, I always love my time at The Early Bird. But something's changed, and I don't mean to be harsh, honey, but," she darts her eyes around the dining room, leaning in conspiratorially, "it's kind of falling apart, don't you think?"

Yes. Yes, I do think.

Ever since our long-time handyman, Ernie, retired two years ago, the place has fallen into a bit of disarray. I've brought it up with our corporate liaison, but they have yet to approve a job search for his replacement. I do my best to negotiate with local contractors, but I can only do so much with the promise of a free meal.

She continues, "As you might have overheard me telling that new little girl you have up there, my shower was ice cold this morning! I couldn't believe it! And look at the state of my hair as a result." She emphatically gestures to her hair.

"Mrs. Sinclair, I am so incredibly sorry you had that experience this morning. I'll tell you what—our best suite is open for the remainder of your stay. Let me get you moved into that unit, at no charge, after I personally check the hot water situation. Thank you so much for bringing this to our attention," I say with the most sincere smile I can muster as I place a comforting hand over hers.

The tension she held in her shoulders visibly releases and she accepts my offer. I leave her to enjoy her breakfast that was dropped off at her table in record time as I go to deal with getting her items moved and figure out how I'm going to explain a three-day comp for our most expensive room.

Heading back to my office, I can't help but reflect on Mrs. Sinclair's valid criticism. The chipping paint. Light bulbs that have been out for longer than I care to admit. The cracks in the hardwood. The stains on the ceiling, a clear indication of a previous leak. And that's nothing compared to the electrical and aesthetic issues in the individual rooms. It's a far cry from the understated beauty I remember when I lived here as a child.

Gabriela and my mom made sure everything was perfect. Under their watchful eyes, you'd never find so much as an unpolished sconce. I love this place, but I can't help but feel a wave of despair as I worry I'm destroying their legacy.

I pick up the phone, planning to call Mr. Spencer's office and request approval to replace our handyman when Chelsea, our head chef and my best friend, bursts into my office, a solemn look on her face. Standing in her white chef's coat, her golden blonde hair pulled back in two braids that are mostly hidden under her tall chef's hat, she gently shuts the door, turning slowly to meet my gaze, her green eyes already full of apology.

"Hey Chels…what's up?" I say with trepidation, setting the phone down on my desk.

"Okay. So. I have to say it—my kitchen needs new equipment." She flings her arms in resignation before sinking down in the chair across from me.

"The deep freezer is accumulating a layer of frost that could host the winter Olympics. My stove is giving less convection and more 'burn hottest on one spot of each dish,' which means I have to throw out a significant portion of everything I cook. And that's to say nothing of the lack of counter space for all the line cooks we've accumulated last year. We barely got through this morning's service without an international incident. I'm so sorry to be such a complainer, but have we made any headway with the budget?" Her words fall out in one breath, her eyes averting mine.

She knows we're strapped for cash these days and I can tell by the worried look on her face that she does not want to be having this conversation.

Despite being completely booked, it seems that all our profits are going to expenses and paying out The Spencer Group. In addition to the maintenance work, the place is simply out of date. It hasn't changed much in the thirty-two years I've been here and when I try to bring this up to Mr. Spencer, or rather, Mr. Spencer's assistant, I get the brush off. I fear if we don't do something soon, our guests will start to catch on and the inn will lose its reputation.

"It's okay, Chels. I know. Trust me, the kitchen is the first item on the list for renovations. Well, I mean, after the guest rooms, of course. I should hear back from The Spencer Group any day now on the renovation budget. Still, you all knocked it out of the park this morning. I had to fight my way to my office through a sea of happy diners wanting to offer their compliments to the chef."

A wide grin spreads across her face as she swipes an invisible chunk of hair over her shoulder in smug victory. "Okay, good. I didn't want to bring it up because I know how stressful things have been around here lately. The last thing I want to do is add to your worry, especially with everything going on with your mom. How is she?"

"Thanks, Chels. She's doing as well as to be expected. She's back home now. I'm heading over there now to check on her before the staff meeting."

Mom got sick almost two years ago, seemingly out of nowhere. Okay, maybe not completely out of nowhere. When I was twenty-three, she developed breast cancer but fought like hell before finding herself in remission. Her scans had been clear for almost a decade, the very picture of health.

One day she was working marathon days at the inn and the next we were in an oncology office hearing that she had Stage 4 adenocarcinoma, lung cancer. I would have laughed had the doctor not looked so serious. My mom never smoked a cigarette a day in her life. She never drank alcohol. She maintained a balanced, healthy diet, and ran three miles every morning for as long as I could remember.

I moved back from New York where I had been living since college to support her as she fought it for a year with chemotherapy, radiation, and even an experimental drug, but nothing seemed to make much of a difference. She was tired of living in that hospital.

Six months ago, she opted out of treatment as it was making her sicker than the cancer. We agreed that she would come back home to spend what time she had in the place she loved her whole life. Between caring for her, worrying about how much time she has left, and the deterioration of the inn, my stress levels have been through the roof.

Chelsea and I catch up for a few more minutes while I wrap up the agenda for our upcoming meeting. I gather my things and head over to the cottage behind the inn where we live to check in on Mom.

Separated from the main building by the massive courtyard and garden, the cute three-bedroom cottage is where the Spencers lived when the inn first opened. When they moved, Mom and I got to move from our cramped little suite at the inn to the cottage and it's where she wanted to spend the rest of her time.

It's been an unseasonably warm November, and the flowers are still in bloom along the pathway through the courtyard leading up to our home. Before I reach the front door, I hear the voice of Stevie Nicks, her signature raspy voice singing about casting spells, pouring through the open windows of the cottage.

I open the door and see my mom spinning around with a duster in the living room, singing loudly along to the timeless Fleetwood Mac classic, Silver Springs. Her hair, now mostly silver, floats around her with each turn, rich golden skin glowing as slivers of sunlight creep through the window, bathing her in light. I stand in the doorway and allow myself to revel in awe of this woman who raised me as a single mother with nothing and is currently battling a terminal illness yet still manages to find joy in little moments like these.

My mind flashes back to the days we used to dance until we collapsed in our tiny suite at the inn. Back when we were happy, and she was healthy. I snap out of it when I notice her stumble a bit and I race to her side to catch her before she falls, turning down the radio in the process.

"Mamá," I say in my best stern voice, "you know you're supposed to be taking it easy. Where's Glenda? I thought she was coming by today?"

Glenda is the part-time-nurse-slash-housekeeper I hired to help Mom while I'm working. She has been such an immense help, but even she is no match for my mother's stubbornness.

"Oh, she's here." My mom slowly sits down on the couch, catching her breath. "I told her to go relax and I would take care of this today. I wouldn't take no for an answer, so I may have locked her on the porch." She grins and erupts into laughter, inciting a small coughing fit.

My eyes widen in surprise, and I shake my head at her. She's been growing more and more mischievous lately, our poor Glenda being the recipient of the worst of it. I hand her the glass of water that currently sits on the coffee table in front of us, unsuccessfully suppressing the smile that begins to spread across my face. Once I'm confident her coughing fit was routine, I finally hear the pounding on the back door and go around to the porch to let Glenda back inside. It turns out she had been banging on the door for the past twenty minutes, which is when my mother decided to drown out the noise with the stereo. I apologize to Glenda and let her get back to work.

I grab a fresh glass of water and my mother's mid-morning pills and head back to the living room where she is staring out the window smiling from ear to ear.

"Thanks, honey." She swallows the pills I've handed her all at once, pulling a face of slight disgust at the feeling.

I can tell this morning's antics have taken a lot out of her by the dark circles under her eyes.

"Why don't we get you back to bed? You've had your fun, but you really need to rest."

"Mija, you know I love you, but you have to stop worrying so much. I'm fine, I promise. I needed a little dance party today. Staring at those same four walls in that room is going to kill me before the cancer does," she chuckles. She knows I hate the gallows humor, but I resist the urge to guilt trip her today, especially because she's so happy.

"I know, Mom. I don't want you to overdo it, you know?"

"I know, I know. I'll make you a deal. I'll go rest if you promise to cut out early today and we'll cook dinner and blast our music like the old days," she says with a look of childlike excitement in her eyes.

"Deal! Please tell me we can make pozole?"

"Claro! It's your favorite, isn't it?" She winks and laughs, giving me a hug before sending me back to the inn to finish up the workday.

As I turn to close the door, I notice the faintest look of exhaustion on her face as she sips her water. Though I love the inn, I wish I could skip work today and sit with her instead. But the show, as they say, must go on.

⚒ ⚒ ⚒

I ARRIVE AT OUR DINING AREA TO FIND ALL THIRTY-SIX members of my staff waiting for me. This is out of character for them all. I check the time to make sure I'm not late. I'm actually a bit early, but I do notice quite a few news notifications with The Spencer Group in the head-lines. I don't have time to check on it right now, so I shove my phone back in my pocket and turn to greet the team and get started on our holiday kick off meeting.

"Hi, everyone. Thanks for an exceptional breakfast service this morning. I received so many compliments, and it looks like we doubled our turnover!"

The scattered applause is muted for a group who doesn't shy from raucous celebrations for the smallest wins, causing me to worry. I scan their faces and notice they all seem to be sharing the same look of concern. A wave of unease shoots through my body as I try to convince myself I must be imagining things and that they're probably exhausted from the busy morning.

"As you know," I continue, clearing my throat, "we're about to enter our busiest season. For the few of you who are with us through your first winter, The Early Bird is known for our events, spanning Thanksgiving through New Year's. In addition to hosting a Thanksgiving fundraiser for our guests, we also sponsor the town Christmas Festival, which culminates in a Christmas pageant on Christmas Eve held in this very room.

Finally, we host a New Year's Eve party—" I stop speaking as I've noticed more than a few people glued to their phones, somberness plastered on their faces.

"Okay...who died?" I joke. Silence. "Oh god, who died?!"

Chelsea begins walking slowly up to where I stand at the front of the room, staring at her phone in disbelief. "Um, Mia, I think you're going to want to see this." She brings her phone level with my eyes and the blood drains from my face.

HOTEL MOGUL, ROMAN SPENCER, HAS ASSETS SEIZED AFTER BEING IMPLI-CATED IN EMBEZZLEMENT SCHEME SPANNING MULTIPLE DECADES

"Welp. We're fucked," I say as I whip out my phone and see fourteen missed calls from Mr. Spencer's assistant. So much for leaving early.

Chapter 3

Preston

Deja vu hits as I wake up in a pitch black room, arm pinned down under a mass of hair, red this time, a distant banging coming from my front door. I don't bother easing my arm away as I grab my pillow with both hands and fold it over my head in a poor, frustrated attempt to drown out the noise.

I don't know who is at my door at—I look at the nightstand to check the time—four o'clock in the morning, but whoever it is, I hope that if I ignore them long enough, they'll go away.

They don't.

The girl next to me doesn't seem to be phased by the knocking but instead rolls over and lays her head on my chest, but I shove her off with a frown. I don't cuddle.

Tossing the covers off both of us, I pull on my sweats and stomp to the door, throwing it open forcefully ready to rip the head off whomever is fucking with my sleep. Unfortunately, I'm met by the brick wall that is Duane, standing there looking as if he were ready to burst down the door.

"What. The. *Fuck*, Duane? Do you know what time it is?"

"Yes, sir. It's 4:02 a.m." If he's startled by my attitude, he doesn't show it as he stands stoic and statuesque, hands crossed low in front of him.

We stare at each other for no fewer than three minutes when it finally dawns on me why he's here. I'm going to Vermont. As the drug and booze-filled haze begins to lift, I remember everything that happened with my father yesterday. Unsurprisingly, I chose to cope by guzzling an obscene amount of alcohol at the club with Alexi and, apparently, bringing home another random chick.

I check my Instagram to find I've been tagged in dozens of paparazzi photos of last night's debauchery. The captions and comments hold nothing back as they rip into me for being an irresponsible, entitled trust fund douche.

That's a reputation I'd been trying hard to shed. Two years ago, my father made one concession and allowed me to focus on the firm's philanthropic efforts. Since then, I've hosted dozens of respectable galas, raising millions for the Breast Cancer Research fund. Still, I'm not perfect and that old entitled asshole I used to be comes out to play. And I always reap the consequences in the media. Like with last night's fiasco.

"Hotel heir, Preston Spencer, doesn't seem to be bothered as he enjoys a night out filled with booze and women while he and his father are engulfed in scandal," reads the caption of a photo featuring me looking extremely inebriated with a woman on my lap, two on either side of me, and Alexi standing above me, ready to pour two bottles of liquor down my throat. To say it's not a good look would be the understatement of the century.

"I'm not even packed, Duane. As you can see, I got in pretty late last night. And I'm not alone." I nod to the girl still sleeping soundly in my bed, oblivious to what's going on around her, and turn to walk towards the kitchen to brew some much-needed coffee. I leave the door open behind me, a resigned invitation for Duane to follow.

"Sir, Mr...sir." Instead of Duane, I hear the nervous English accent of Oliver, following me into the penthouse. He finally catches up, out of breath, his short stature taking twice as long to match my long strides.

"Sir, it's just that...well, erm, you see, the thing is, your father booked your flight this morning and the movers are on their way to take everything to storage."

I look around at the stacks of moving boxes the packers filled yesterday. It took them one day to pack up my entire life. Thirty-four years of existing and all that remains are a few items of clothing and essentials. Even my coffee maker is gone.

"We have thirty minutes before you need to be at the airport. Why don't you hop in the shower while I pack the rest of your things?" Oliver advises, "I'll grab the essentials, and the rest will be kept safely at your father's storage facility until everything gets sorted. I'm sure you'll be back here in no time," he says with an unconvincing smile.

When I emerge from the shower, I notice the redhead has gone and I no doubt have Oliver to thank for that. He may be a neurotic mess, but he does have a knack for getting rid of problems, I'll give him that.

He barely looks up from his phone to point to the clothing he's left out for me as Duane steps in to take my luggage down to the car. With one final look around the penthouse I've called home for most of my adult life, I close the door and take the elevator downstairs for what I fear may be the last time.

By the time we arrive at the airport, I've been given the rundown of what I can expect in Vermont. I'll have a suite for the duration of my stay, but my father expects me to pull my weight. No partying. No women. No booze. I need to prepare to run the company when he retires. Yadda, yadda. It's all stuff I've heard before. Only this time the promise of running the company isn't holding as much weight with the knowledge there might not *be* a company for much longer.

I step out of the car and walk around to the trunk to gather my two bags; all that Oliver would let me take. Glancing down at my ticket to find my gate, I realize that my morning could get worse after all.

I'm flying coach.

⚒ ⚒ ⚒

AFTER A TWO-HOUR LAYOVER AND NEARLY NINE HOURS in the air, we finally arrive at the Burlington airport. I stop at the gate's exit to stretch my legs after all six foot three of me spent the entire ride crammed into a coach seat while the asshole in front of me reclined into my lap.

Looking around, the place is fairly empty, yet I don't see my driver.

A surly looking attendant sits at the counter in the lobby, her dingy brown hair hanging in limp strands around her face. She's shoving chips in her mouth, mindlessly scrolling on her phone. She doesn't even look up when I ask her for directions to passenger pickup, instead simply pointing to the sign that reads "Rideshare Pickup /

Ground Transportation." Unconventional, I think, but then again, I'm used to flying private.

After waiting for twenty minutes, I have not seen any drivers and realize my bags also haven't been brought around. As a matter of fact, I haven't seen any bags brought around. I head back in to see if I've missed the bag attendant as well.

"Sorry to bug you again." I flash my best smile at the attendant, making sure my dimples pop. Charm has always come easily to me, especially when it comes to women. This woman, however, seems to be unfazed. She barely reacts, save for a small glance to let me know she's heard me, but doesn't particularly care. "Just wondering when you think they're going to bring my luggage around?"

She laughs at me, before realizing I'm serious. "Look, I don't know if this is your first time in an airport, but you pick up your own bag at baggage claim. That way." She snaps her gum at me and points in the direction of the baggage claim signs and goes right back to ignoring me, still chuckling a bit from the interaction.

I manage to find my bag with minimal issue and head out through the exit to hopefully meet my driver. I desperately want to get to my suite at the inn and sleep for at least two days. It's mid-November, but you wouldn't know it with the warm temperature and trees still in full bloom surrounding the exit.

The pickup area is relatively empty, but I'm still unable to locate my driver. Checking the time on my phone, I see my flight got in a bit late, so they really should be here. I fire off a text to Oliver to figure out what's going on.

> **Me**
> Ollie, just arrived at the airport, no car in sight. Can you get in touch with the driver?

> **Oliver Hughes**
> Sorry! No car this time, limited funds and all.

Ignoring his recommendation, I open my rideshare app and punch in the address to the inn. I'm almost surprised I know it by memory after all these years. A notification pops up immediately:

Payment declined. Please enter a new form of payment to continue booking your ride.

Great. Not only am I banished to the middle of nowhere, but I have no money to do anything as simple as get a ride. As I furiously type a text back to Oliver asking how, exactly, he expects me to get twenty miles on foot with two bags in $1,000 Dior Oxfords, a small van pulls up to the door with an "airport shuttle" decal plastered on the side in the most obnoxious green font.

A short elderly man with wiry grey hair and a slight limp gets out to walk around and open the sliding van door, greeting me with a smile so genuine it catches me off guard.

"Hello there, son. Will you be needing a ride today? We're heading to the famous Early Bird Inn up the road. Only accommodation in town for miles."

I'm about to answer him, but my attention is immediately turned to two bickering women, no younger than eighty, pushing their way to the shuttle. They appear to be arguing about the twist of a popular TV show I've never heard of.

"I'm just saying, if they wanted to keep viewers, killing off that Der—oh hi, Vernon! We're back! Can we hitch a ride with you? I'm dying for some of Chelsea's famous chili," the taller one says to the driver, Vernon, apparently.

"Sure thing, ladies. Hop in and I'll take care of these bags."

They smile at Vernon, look at me, then back at Vernon, and to me again before the shorter one runs her hand over my right arm and says, "Oh, why not let this strapping young man help, Vernon? He looks...capable."

Her eyes roam over me in a way that is definitely not appropriate for mixed company. Heat rises to my face at her lecherous gaze, but I reluctantly acquiesce and load our bags into the back of the shuttle before taking my seat in front of the older women. I guess on top of everything else, I'm the baggage attendant today.

The ride is shorter than I anticipated, but a wave of nostalgia rushes over me as I take in the familiar sites from my childhood; the rows of small town shops down Main Street, the beach front off the lake that is no Pacific Ocean, but is beautiful in its own way, the park with the carousel I always went to with my mother and my best friend, Amelia.

Amelia Aguilar, my childhood best friend whom I haven't thought of in years. I remember her mom worked at the inn and they stayed in a modest suite, courtesy of my parents. The memories of better times with my best friend sweep over me and almost help to bury the painful reality of why we left.

Almost.

We pull up to the inn and although it's obvious so much has changed, much has stayed the same. I catch a brief glance of the garden, which appears to still be flourishing, and it's as if I can almost see my father hunched over, tending to the flowers and vegetables with gentle care.

The cottage stands in the background, barely visible, but the sight still makes my heart nearly stop. The cottage where we lived until I moved across the country with my father. The last memory I have of this cottage was the absolute worst day of my entire life.

I blink away the tears threatening to spill at the memory and am jerked back to the present when I notice the main building has fallen into complete disarray. It's probably not as noticeable to guests, but I spent the first part of my life here. The shutters hang loose from the second story windows, the paint is chipping everywhere, and even the sign my mother painted is starting to wear so badly you can barely make out the name.

Anger floods my body as I take in the sight before me. It's not only the fact that I'm now poor, nor the fact that the new caretakers have neglected their main duty to care for the one place that meant so much to my mother. It's all these things combined with the rage that I find myself back here, alone, in the one place I swore I'd never return.

I reach for my phone to text my father asking what I'm supposed to do now that I'm here, stopping short to read a notification that my service has been cut due to nonpayment. I shove the useless contraption into my coat pocket and begin to help Vernon unload the luggage for the rest of the passengers.

By the time I've carried my two bags, plus those of my two shuttle mates, I am sweating profusely. Why on earth is it so warm in Vermont in November?! Admittedly, I'm a bit cranky, in desperate need of a shower and a glass of whiskey or two, so when the overly cheery receptionist informs me that she cannot find a reservation under my name, I'm ready to explode.

"Check again. It's under Spencer. S-P-E-N-C-E-R." The frustration in my tone is unmistakable. She can't be much older than twenty-three and clearly has little business being the face of *our* business. Another strike against the way these people have been running our inn.

Her face turns from concentration to outright panic as she types in my name again. She mutters an "oh no", right before dialing the phone and asking someone, presumably the manager, to come up to the desk.

"Is there a problem?" I grit through clenched teeth.

"There seems to be a slight mix-up. I've called up my manager here to sort this out." She lets out a nervous laugh, plastering a forced smile on her face.

"What kind of mix-up? I've been traveling all day and really need a bed, any bed, and I promise I'll be out of your hair."

"Well, that's not the problem. If you'll let me—"

I cut her off. "Obviously you don't know who I am or who my father is, but think real hard on it, sweetie. Look at my last name. Closely."

As soon as the words leave my mouth, I know how douchey it sounds, but I can't muster up the energy to care. How do you not know the owner of the company for which you work? Still, it's not her fault my father hired a crook and now I'm forced to stay here.

I open my mouth to apologize, but the tears have already begun to fall down her face. I stand there stunned as I watch her run away from the desk, crashing into another woman in the hallway. The woman's back is turned to me, but I watch as she embraces the young girl in an attempt to console her unrelenting sobs. Perfect. Not even twenty minutes at this shithole and I manage to make a girl cry. A girl who, presumably, will be one of my employees. This is off to a great start.

As guilty as I feel, it's not enough to keep me from doing whatever it takes to get to my room. I'm done waiting for them to get their shit together and stride over to where they're standing.

"Excuse me, I need a room and seeing as I own the place, perhaps we can get this accomplished a bit more quickly," I say with no politeness as I tap the woman I assume is the manager on the shoulder.

She whips around, waves of long, wavy dark brown hair wafting the scent of jasmine and citrus my way as she turns to face me. My breath catches at the sight of her. Her rich, mahogany eyes burrow into mine with annoyance and something else. Maybe...recognition? It's there for a flash before returning to red hot anger. But I feel it too, a strange familiarity, though I can't quite put my finger on it.

Even scowling, she's undeniably gorgeous. With golden brown skin, those big doe eyes, full cherry red lips, and a body so curvy poets could write a million sonnets devoted to its perfection, she glares at me, pursing those luscious lips together ready to lay into me.

"Mr. Spencer," she says her sweet voice hiding her disdain, "we've been expecting you. My name is Mia and I'm the manager here at The Early Bird. I understand you're tired from your travels and we want to make sure you have a spot to stay. However, your father contacted us after the suite he wished for you to have was booked. We did try to contact him."

"You cannot be serious. My father sent me here to manage this place, which clearly needs the help," I gesture emphatically around the room point at its extreme disrepair, "surely he would have arranged for my stay."

She resolves her posture and stands straight, as if trying to appear taller than her small stature. "Well, yes, in a manner of speaking, he did. He left a note in the system that you were to have the main suite, but—"

"Great. Key, please?"

"As I was saying before you interrupted, apparently your father didn't check to make sure the suite was available. Unfortunately, it's not and won't be for the remainder of the year. And with this being our busiest time, all the other rooms are fully occupied. Except one, but it's in a bit of a state."

I audibly sigh in frustration, shuddering to imagine how this room looks based on what I've seen so far, but what choice do I have? My credit card and cell phone no longer work, I have no cash, and no backup plan. Plus, the driver, Victor or something, pointed out this is the only accommodations for miles.

"Lead the way," I say with a resigned sigh as she leads me up the stairs to my new room. At least it's at the end of the hall so I can hope for some peace and quiet.

Before she unlocks the door, she turns to me apologetically, and says, "I feel obligated to let you know we had to move a guest from this room as it's in need of some repairs.

I promise to have someone out as soon as possible to fix everything." She offers a tight smile and opens the door.

The light flickers a few times before turning on, emitting a consistent faint hum. I take in the scene before me with abject horror. The wallpaper is chipping, with a few spots completely missing. The acrid air has the faint smell of death and is so heavy I suspect the A/C is one of the many things in need of a repair. I stare at the bed, a single, outfitted with the drabbest plaid comforter I've ever seen. A far cry from the charming inn my parents strived to build.

Right as I open my mouth to protest, Mia's phone goes off and she holds a finger to halt my attempt. Her expression turns to alarm and while I can only hear her side of the conversation, I get the feeling she's urgently needed back downstairs. She apologizes to the other person on the line and promises to meet them in the dining room right away. She stows her phone and sighs.

"Come on. That was your father's assistant. Apparently, they're here and want to speak with both of us. Now."

Chapter 4

Mia

Preston Spencer. That's a name I was sure I'd never hear again. Well, at least outside of the tabloids. I didn't even know he was coming until I saw Mr. Spencer's note in our booking system. Neither of them could have even been bothered to give us a call to alert us to what was going on with the company or that we would need to make space for Preston's stay. I'm not sure what hurt more, how Preston looked at me without so much of a spark of recognition or that the boy who had once been my sweet, carefree best friend has turned into such an entitled prick.

But my god, how he's changed. He must be well over six feet tall, with lines of hard muscle that can only be earned from hours spent in the gym every week. His tight waves lay atop a perfect drop fade and his rich bronze skin glows against those familiar gold-flecked hazel eyes that burned into me as if trying to uncover all my secrets. Of course, I know now that heat had nothing to do with me and everything to do with his rage at being sent here, but I can't silence the part of me that wonders if there is any hint of the boy I once knew behind the playboy facade.

We head downstairs in terse silence to meet his father and his assistant, Oliver. Oliver sounded terrified on the phone, but from all my dealings with him, that just seems to be his normal state. But Preston's apprehensive look has me suspecting whatever is about to happen is not going to be good. Fear takes over as I worry they're here to shut down the inn which would mean not only would I be out of a job, Mom and I would lose our home. And health insurance.

As we enter the dining room, I spot dozens of executives, all of whom are either typing furiously on their phones or yelling incoherently at the person on the other line. The group on their phones move to the far side of the dining room while Oliver and Mr. Spencer take a seat near the fireplace. Mr. Spencer surveys the room, and I don't miss the look of disgust on his face. The inn's a far cry from the cozy elegance it once held, but despite its problems, it has character. Preston and I walk with unease to take our seats across from them and brace ourselves for what is to come.

Mr. Spencer barely resembles the man I remember from my childhood. His formerly warm onyx eyes now seem cold and unfeeling. Where he used to be comfortable in flannel and jeans, he now sits before me in an expensive burgundy suit and shoes that probably cost more than a month's stay at the inn.

He is clearly not a man to bother with pleasantries as he doesn't so much as spare a glance in either of our direction. I guess he doesn't remember me either.

"Preston," he says in a deep baritone laced with disappointment. "I trust you've gotten settled then." It was a statement, not a question.

"Well, actually—" Preston begins, but is quickly cut off.

"Good." His eyes dart around the dining room, his deepening scowl a clear indication of how unimpressed he is with what he sees.

I open my mouth to defend the inn, to explain that I've tried to request budgetary support to fix and upgrade, but the way he's staring daggers at Preston, I realize now's *so* not the time for that and promptly shut my mouth.

"Now, then. I'm sure everyone is up to date on what's happening with The Spencer Group, so I won't bore you with the details. But this is all a misunderstanding that my attorneys assure me will be sorted soon."

Oliver and I exchange a glance of doubt, but he quickly looks away as if he doesn't want to be accused of disagreeing with his boss. Preston looks tense, bordering on indignant, but remains quiet while his father continues.

"When Preston came of age, the board agreed to place the inn in his name. While The Spencer Group has maintained its oversight, we've entrusted the day-to-day operation to you, Miss...uh...?" He searches his brain for my name but comes up short.

"Mia's fine." I'm not sure why I don't give my last name, it's not like he'd recognize it now anyway. Once my mother officially divorced my father, we both shed the Aguilar name in favor of her maiden name, Flores, our final goodbye to the man who never wanted us.

I'm not sure why I don't want Preston to connect the dots. Maybe it's the embarrassment I feel at how easy it was for him to forget me when I've thought about him every day since I watched him walk out of my life all those years ago. Or, maybe it's the way my stomach did a backflip when I saw the commanding, attractive man he's grown into.

"Ah, yes. Mia. Well, I'm sure you've heard the allegations, which are completely false, as I mentioned. But all the same, my assets are frozen until my attorneys are able to clear up this...misunderstanding. To account for this mess, we are no doubt going to have to sell off many of our properties, but luckily the inn has been spared. For now."

Preston looks annoyed and finally cuts in. "And what precisely is this 'job' of mine. What am I doing here?"

"Sorry," I interject, "job?" I brace myself to be told Preston will be taking over the inn while my mom and I are evicted as Mr. Spencer turns to address me, pointedly ignoring Preston's outburst.

"Mia, Oliver has told me you've been requesting a budget for numerous repairs and updates, and by the looks of it, you weren't exaggerating about the state of the place. Firstly, I'm very sorry we have neglected the inn's budget for so long, but despite that, I'm hoping you can help us out here," he says with a forced smile and open palms.

"Help with, what, exactly?"

"Without access to the company funds, we don't have many options to hire help. But since, as I said, the inn was spared from seizures, it's critical in supporting our family through this difficult time. Oliver, could you explain the details?"

Oliver pulls a contract from his briefcase and lays it on the coffee table between us. "Here's what we propose — Preston will stay in the room you've made available for the foreseeable future and in exchange, he will, erm, take over the vacant handyman job. Of course, once this mess is resolved, we will ensure you have a proper budget for the more, erm," he pauses to look around the room, "extensive renovations."

I sit for a moment in stunned silence as relief spreads through me with the realization that I'm not losing my job or my home. But it's short lived when I remember the only help I'll be getting for our busy holiday season is this man sitting next to me in designer clothes, his mouth agape which I take to mean he's also just finding out about this job of his. I scoff and wait for Oliver to say "just kidding" because surely, he can't be serious, but he stays tight lipped.

"Well," I start in my most polite voice, "I truly appreciate the offer but with all due respect, what kind of experience does Preston have with repairs of this magnitude?" I avoid noting if the papers are to be believed, his talents most likely lie elsewhere, between the legs of a socialite.

"Father," Preston pleads, "please think this through. You'll need my help with PR and with planning our next move. Am I to take over the company as CEO or head janitor?"

Mr. Spencer seems ready to explode, his hands clenching into fists in his lap, at Preston's insolence. Though he quickly regains his composure, it's likely for my benefit alone. Mr. Spencer always was a stern parent, but it seems their relationship has grown more strained as the years went on. I can't help but feel a pang of sorrow at the memory of Mr. Spencer teaching Preston the basics of running the inn, all smiles and pride as he prepped him to one day take over. It's a far cry from the look of disdain in Mr. Spencer's eyes as he prepares his retort.

"Preston, you haven't had to work for much in this life, so I know this comes as a surprise. This is what I need from you and you will do as I ask." Preston sinks into his chair, letting the finality of this demand sink in. As Mr. Spencer turns his attention back to me, anxiety causes my spine to straighten.

"Mia, I know this isn't what you'd hoped for, but I'm sure with a little guidance, Preston can handle some of the easier repairs." He again tries to smile at me, but it rings false. I know this is one of those situations where I don't actually have a choice, but he's trying to make it seem as though I'm doing him a favor.

I shoot a glance at Preston and for a brief moment see the little boy I used to call my best friend desperately grasping for his father's acceptance. I can't help but feel sorry for him. He also has no choice in this matter and while I don't have much confidence that he'll be able to make a dent in all the repairs we need, I'll do what I can to help him.

"Of course, Mr. Spencer. We're grateful for the help. I'll see if Ernie, our previous handyman, can swing by and show him the ropes. In the meantime, Preston is welcome to stay as long as he needs."

"Thank you, Mia. I appreciate everything you've done for the inn. We'll be in touch." He stands to leave without so much as a goodbye to his only son.

While I do feel bad witnessing the deterioration of Preston's relationship with his father, the fact remains that I'm now in charge of him and I really do need a lot of help. I can't afford to coddle him when Thanksgiving is a mere two weeks away.

"We have a staff meeting at 5 a.m. I'll get in touch with

Ernie as soon as possible to give you some help. Please don't be late." I give him a sympathetic smile and head towards my office with an overwhelming feeling of dread.

⚒ ⚒ ⚒

I'M FORTY-FIVE MINUTES EARLY TO OUR STAFF meeting after spending the night in a fitful sleep, going through all the possible ways having Preston handle the repairs, upkeep, and renovations at the inn is a bad idea. The most obvious reason? This is the same boy who landed in the ER with sixteen stitches just trying to build a tire swing. I wouldn't trust him to change a lightbulb, let alone handle the sheer mountain of repairs this place needs. Fortunately, Ernie agreed to come back part-time to supervise until Preston gets the hang of things.

The other reasons are more complicated. It's been almost twenty-four hours since Preston first arrived and while I recognized him immediately, he doesn't seem to have a clue that I'm that girl he knew all those years ago. I fear I've waited too long already to pop in with a casual, *"Oh hey, by the way, you were my best friend for the first ten years of my life until you moved and never spoke to me again. Sorry I didn't tell you until now! Let's get to work!"* But I can't continue this lie. For one, I'm an awful liar and I know a slip up is inevitable. Then there's the whole "I'm incredibly attracted to him and can't think straight when we're in the same room" thing.

I shake myself out of these unhelpful thoughts when Chelsea heads into the dining area where I'm sat, hands full with a tray of breakfast treats and a large carafe of freshly brewed coffee.

"My, my you're up quite early. I saw our new guest last night," she says with a sly smile and a suggestive wink.

I ignore her insinuation for the moment. Chelsea is a meddler and for the past few years has been trying to push every mildly attractive man on me, partially because she thinks it's what is missing from my life, but also so she can drag me on double dates with her wife, Katy.

"Couldn't sleep. We have two weeks to get this place in shape for the Thanksgiving dinner and I have no idea how we're going to do it. I mean, all rooms are booked so that doesn't leave a lot of time to get in there and fix things. And that guest you saw? Yeah. That's our new handyman," I say with a look that conveys my utter lack of faith.

She pulls an exaggerated wince before letting out a low whistle. "Well, I bet he looks good in a nice pair of jeans." She chuckles and I roll my eyes.

"Maybe, but I shudder to think of what damage he could do in the meantime. Luckily Ernie is going to come back on part-time to train him, but I feel awful forcing him out of retirement."

Chelsea smiles, laying a hand on my shoulder in a show of support. "Oh you know that crotchety old man is bored out of his mind by now. He was probably a few short weeks away from begging to come back."

She's probably right, but I still feel a little guilty for making a nearly eighty-year-old man come back to bail me out. Ernie was with the inn since my mom took over almost twenty-two years ago. He and his wife, Bea, helped with everything including groundskeeping, repairs, and house-keeping. Bea had a pretty serious health scare two years ago and that's when Ernie decided to retire.

"Is there something more bugging you? You usually

love these early morning meetings, weirdo," she says, taking the seat across from me.

The truth dances on the tip of my tongue and I'm dying to tell her my history with Preston. Maybe letting one person in on this huge secret will be good for me. I look around to make sure no one is within earshot and lean in conspiratorially.

"Okay. You have to swear not to tell a soul. Not even Katy. *No one.*"

She mimes zipping her lips and bids me to continue.

"I know Preston. We grew up together. Until I was, like, ten, he was my best friend and then when he and his father moved, he never spoke to me again."

Chelsea's mouth pops open and then closes as confusion sweeps over her face. "Wait, but you both act like strangers. Did something happen to make him unhappy to see you?"

"So...that's the worst part. I recognized him the second I looked into his eyes, but he looked right through me as if he was meeting me for the first time. And now I feel stupid for not bringing it up yesterday. Maybe I don't have to? I mean, he's not going to be here for that long, I'm sure. And it *would* be easier to focus on work and leave the past in the past, right?"

"That's certainly one way to look at it. But I don't understand why you wouldn't tell him now?"

"What's the point? Clearly, I made more of our friendship than he did, so I figure why add anymore drama during our busiest season? Besides, he made it clear how he felt when he didn't make a single attempt to call or write. I mean, I know we were kids, but he knew how to use a phone. Anyway, I might as well save myself the embarrassment of bringing up the past he so easily forgot."

"Hm. I guess that makes sense." The look on her face suggests she does not, in fact, think it makes sense, but is deciding to give me a pass for now.

"Well, at least he'll make for some excellent eye candy around this place," she says suggestively, wiggling her eyebrows. I roll my eyes with my entire head.

"Ha. Ha. Girl, please. You haven't even looked at a man since you met Katy."

A dreamy look spreads across her face. "You're right. That woman has ruined me for men ever again. Do you think they'll take away my bi card?" She gasps with mock horror, pulling a chuckle from my lips before I shoo her to go take a seat.

I return to my handout, checking over the impossible list of items we need to complete before our first holiday event. Kicking everything off is our annual Thanksgiving feast for the whole town. In addition to serving a multi-course traditional dinner, we raise money for a different charity each year and this year we chose the American Cancer Association, in honor of Mom. As such, there's a lot of work to do and it's an "all-hands-on-deck" situation. Preston has no idea how much I'll need his help with everything. I just hope he's up to the task.

When the rest of the team slowly begins to filter in, everyone is accounted for except Preston. I wait an additional five minutes to begin, uncharacteristic of me, but it's clear he's not coming.

I know I was firm about our start time, but I guess this is what I can expect from the new, not at all improved, Preston Spencer.

Chapter 5

Preston

When I wake, I'm briefly disoriented in the pitch black room. It takes a few moments for me to realize where I am and why I'm here. I've *got* to stop drinking.

I look to the other side of the nightstand to check the time on the alarm clock, but the display is black. When I reach for the lamp and it doesn't turn on, it's clear the power went out sometime during the night. A familiar pounding at the door, my new unwelcome companion, forces me to leave the warmth of the surprisingly luxurious bedding.

"Dammit. Hang on, I'm coming," I shout to whomever is on the other side of the door, though I have a feeling I know who it is before I swing open the door.

Mia looks momentarily stunned, drawing my attention to the fact I'm standing there in nothing but tight, grey boxer briefs that leave little to the imagination. She, of course, looks put together and stunning in her black pencil skirt and baby blue silk blouse. God, this woman is beautiful despite the look of absolute fury painted on her face, aimed firmly in my direction.

"It is ten o'clock," she says with an annoyed emphasis placed on the time. "I asked you for one thing—to be punctual to our meeting, one of the most important meetings of the season. Not only did you miss that, but you missed our entire breakfast rush as well where I could have used your help. There's a leak in the kitchen."

"It's ten o'clock?" I say, confused as I attempt to swipe the sleep from my eyes. Judging by the way she crinkles her nose in disgust as she takes me in, I'm positive she can smell the whiskey emanating from my pores. How much did I drink last night?

She rolls her eyes and pushes past me, the touch of her warm hands on my bare skin setting my every nerve on fire, leaving me in a daze as I watch her walk to the window. She throws open the curtains, letting in an abundance of light so bright it nearly knocks me on my ass.

Shielding my eyes from the harsh light of the sun, I cannot stop myself from staring at her long, dark waves softly bouncing down her back, drawing my eyes to the perfect curve of her ass.

The memory of a dream crawls to the front of my mind. Those glossy waves tangled up in my fingers. Her soft lips parting in a moan as I cover her body in kisses trailing down her neck until I reach her stomach, glancing up at her with a grin.

Nope.

I'm not doing this.

Not trying to get involved with my...boss?

In a panic, I reach for the robe hanging in the closet,

suddenly hyper aware that I am wearing next to nothing, and the evidence of my lust is becoming visible.

Covering myself quickly before she turns, I realize I've paused too long and she's likely expecting me to say something. "Uh. Right. The power went out."

Her brow furrows as she spots the darkened alarm clock, the power outage earning me no empathy as she emits another huff of disdain. "Whatever. Just get cleaned up and meet me downstairs when you're done." She tosses a gray polo at me before storming out the door, letting it slam in her wake.

Since I'm embarrassingly late anyway, I figure there's ample time to take a nice, long, hot shower. After a high squeal accompanied by a few gurgling noises, the shower finally spurts out the tiniest trickle, but the water is ice cold. Even after running for a few minutes, there is no sign of warmth, so I jump into the frigid stream, quickly washing up before the long day. To be honest, I probably could use a cold shower before seeing Mia again anyway.

Staring at the open suitcase on my bed, I once again curse my father for not letting me know what I was getting into. Had I known, I may have packed more appropriately, but as it stands, it looks like I'll be wearing Gucci. I quickly dress, making my way to the kitchen to check out this leak Mia mentioned.

First, I stop by Mia's office, her door slightly ajar, and tap a light knock before pushing the door open further. Without a glance, she holds up her index finger, bidding me to give her a moment to finish whatever she's typing.

"That isn't the polo I gave you," she says by way of greeting with an annoyed sigh.

"It's too small and I don't do polyester. Anyway, you said something about a leak?"

She ignores my question and instead turns away from her computer and proceeds to lecture me. "You completely flaked this morning. I know this is just some kind of punishment for you, but this is my life. My home. We don't have to be friends. Hell, we don't even have to like one another. But we do have to work together. So, I need you to try to do what I ask. Can you manage that?"

Anger simmers under my skin and I have to go to war with myself to avoid laying into this woman. I *own* this place, and she cannot speak to me this way even if I am technically her employee at the moment.

"I don't know what you think you know about me, but I assure you, whatever you've heard is wrong. This inn is my home too—I grew up here. The power went out in my room, so I had no alarm. This isn't my fault."

Her eyes soften as she seems lost to a memory. It's only for a moment, but I can't help but wonder where her mind trailed off to. "You're right. I'll arrange for an electrician to come check it out today. I'm sorry."

She hands me a stack of paper with a list of items to be repair or replaced. There has to be at least ten pages, all double sided. I let out an exasperated sigh and she raises an eyebrow, daring me to challenger her, but I don't take the bait.

"I know this situation isn't ideal for either of us, but I'm hoping we can work together. Despite appearances, the inn is a staple of this town and we're heading into our busiest time of year. I could really use your help."

Part of me still wants to push back, to call her out for

her outburst this morning, but when I look at her, all I feel is a desperate urge to earn her respect.

"I'd like that. When my family and I lived here, my parents basically did everything. My father was the handy-man, gardener, whatever this place needed. I was young, but he did teach me a little, so I'm not completely hopeless. And you said...Edward?...will come teach me the basics, and for the rest, I have Dr. Google." I waive my phone at her before remembering the service had been cut off. Hopefully they have Wi-Fi.

"His name is Ernie and, yes. He'll be here tomorrow at 7 a.m. Sharp." She looks at me pointedly, the heavy implication that I better be on time.

"Great. I look forward to it. In the meantime," I hold up her massive list, shaking it for emphasis, "I'll get started on what I can." I flash her a confident smile. She nearly doubles over with laughter.

"What?" I say, confused.

"In *that?*" she chokes out between giggles as she points up and down at my clothes.

I furrow my brow, embarrassed. "It's not like I have much choice. My father gave me zero information on what my 'job' would be when I got here, so pardon me for assuming it would be a bit more...managerial. It's what I've got."

"You might want to head to town and think about updating that wardrobe to something a bit more durable. Oh, and you better get used to polyester because I require all maintenance staff to be in uniform to maintain the safety and confidence of our guests."

She digs around in her pockets to grab a set of keys and tosses them at me. Caught off guard, I barely catch them between my face and the hand that comes up to grasp them. I shoot her an annoyed glare as she stifles her laughter.

"You can take the catering van out back. Take a look at the list and head to Tucker's and pick up some supplies. And maybe a change of clothes."

I haven't driven myself in years, but there's no way I'm telling her that.

⚒ ⚒ ⚒

It took me forty-five minutes to completely digest everything on Mia's list. I had to Google most of the tasks, but there are a few things that seemed easy enough, so I decide to start with those. I manage to locate a toolbox in the supply closet, but I'm not able to find most of the items I'll need to properly complete the repairs.

I scout the inn for Mia to tell her the news and catch her at the reception desk, a genuine smile on her face as she chats with a tall blonde woman in a chef's uniform. This must be the renowned Chef Chelsea Taylor I've heard about. Some of her recipes have even made it onto the menus in some of our top resorts, but my father never could convince her to leave the inn.

"Hey, ladies," I lay the charm on thick, noticing the way Mia's face loses some of its shine at the sound of my voice. It bothers me more than I would like, but I brush it off, turning my attention to Chelsea, extending my hand for a handshake.

"Hi, I'm Preston. You must be Chef Taylor. I basically spent an entire year existing on little more than your famous lobster tortellini. It's an honor to meet you."

"Good to meet you too, Preston. I've heard so much about you." She shoots Mia a smirk with hidden meaning I don't quite understand before grasping my hand in a firm handshake. "Welp, 'time to make the donuts,' as they say." She turns on her heels and returns to the kitchen.

"What can I do for you, Preston?" Mia asks, a hint of exasperation in her voice.

"I'm about to head over to the hardware store, but I realized I never got directions. Oh, and I'll need the company card to pick up these things," I hand her my own list full of materials. Our hands brush slightly, sending a jolt of electricity through my body. I don't know what it is about this woman, but I've never been more on edge than when I'm around her.

Scanning the list, she winces slightly. "Um. We don't have a company card, per se. Tell Tuck to invoice the inn."

I stop myself from balking against being her errand boy, thinking better of it. I've already made a less than stellar first impression and I didn't miss the way she winced at the mention of needing money for additional supplies. Feeling guilty knowing my family is the source of these financial woes, I give her a nod and make my way to the van and head into town.

Main Street looks almost completely unchanged, though many of the stores are new. The hardware store is nestled in a line of small shops along a charming cobblestone sidewalk. Sandwiched between a bakery and a pet supply stop sits Tucker's Tool Time, a quaint little shop that cannot be more than 350 square feet. I didn't expect chain level fanfare, but I also couldn't have imagined it would be quite this small. I'm suddenly less optimistic that I'll find everything I need to complete these repairs.

I pull open the door and am greeted by the chimes of an old timey bell hanging over the entryway. Behind the counter stands a large man in denim overalls over the top of a red flannel shirt as he hunches over the counter reading what appears to be a sci-fi novel.

"Hey there! What can I do ya for?" He looks up and greets me with a jovial salute, his red, round cheeks sitting high atop a long, bushy white beard.

"I'm helping over at the inn and I need to get a few things." I walk to the counter and hand him my extensive list, the sight of which earns a low whistle from the jolly shopkeeper.

"Looks like you've got your work cut out for you up there!" He chuckles and motions for me to follow him around the store picking up the items on the list. "Helluva project you've got there. That inn has needed a bit of TLC for quite a while now."

"That's an understatement," I mutter. "It's in rough shape now and the new manager is on edge because of it. She's been up my ass all morning and I'd rather not endure another one of her lectures. She kinda scares me."

He barks a bellowing laugh that fills the entire store. "That one is a firecracker! Don't let her size fool you. I've seen her scare the daylights out of the toughest folks. Hell, she's laid into me quite a few times and had me cowering!"

"While you're at it, I'll take any tips for dealing with her too," I say in jest. But I have to admit there's a little truth to the request. I don't merely want to avoid her wrath, but I have this inexplicable urge to avoid disappointing her.

"Well, you know, Mia's got a huge heart, but she's built up a bit of a wall around it. She's always been the light of the town. Helping out whenever anyone needs it and keeping us all in business, frankly. But when her mama got sick, it's like she poured all her focus into that inn and forgot to properly live. I think with her, you just gotta show her you love that place as much as she does, and you'll be right as rain."

"I didn't know she was dealing with that." My shoulders sink as guilt washes over me for being such an antagonistic prick when she's dealing with something like this. Something that hits uncomfortably close to home. I don't push for more information. Tucker doesn't seem like the gossiping type to me and if Mia wanted me to know this part of her life, she would have told me.

"That girl will be there to listen to everyone else's problems, but she's not so great at leaning on us, even though she knows we'd all drop everything to be there for her. Now, hand me that list and I'll give ya some tips."

Armed with new supplies and Tucker's advice, I'm feeling a little more confident as I make my way back to the inn.

Chapter 6

Mia

I can't quiet the worry in my head everything is going to go terribly wrong with Preston here. Disregarding our history for a moment, there's the fact that this inn is my life, and I can't bear the thought of it falling to pieces. Literally, because I am sure Preston won't be able to handle the simplest of repairs and with the company's finances frozen, there's no way we'll be hiring a proper handyman any time soon.

Trying to quell the anxiety brewing in my belly, I decide now is as good a time as ever to check in on Mom. I grab some salad and sandwiches and head over to the cottage.

Panic sweeps over me as I see a familiar sedan belonging to her oncologist, Dr. Sydek, sitting in our driveway. I step into the cottage and see them sitting at the table with Glenda, my mom's hands outstretched across the table to Dr. Sydek as he holds them in a comforting grip. A million thoughts race through my head.

What if my mom's cancer has gotten even more aggressive?

What if she only has days, not months, to live?

What if the troubles with The Spencer Group canceled our health insurance?

I don't have time to run through all my fears as Mom spots me, standing from the table with a wide grin as she pulls me into a warm hug.

"Ah, mi cariño! I'm so glad you're here. Dr. Sydek came by with the most wonderful news," she exclaims, clapping her hands together, the grin not leaving her face. She nods to Dr. Sydek, who joins us in the living room.

"I wanted to come deliver this news in person. I recently applied for a grant to start a clinical trial, and your mother is the perfect candidate." The words fall out in his heavily accented English, exuding a hopefulness I haven't heard from him since she went into remission the first time. He pauses to assess my reaction, whatever he sees giving him confidence to continue.

"Since this treatment is experimental, your mother will need to stay in the hospital under close observation for its duration. This particular trial is at least six months, and we would like to leave this afternoon."

I grip the arm of the chair behind me, my body sinking down while I try to process this information. Six months? In the hospital which is fifty miles away from town. The last time I was separated from my mom for this long was after she slipped into a coma during her last round of chemo. I couldn't bear it, which must show on my face because when I look up, Dr. Sydek is kneeling in front of me, placing one hand on my knee in comfort.

"I know I'm asking you to place a lot of faith in me, but

this is some of the most promising research to emerge in decades. I think your mother has a real shot here. It won't cure her, but it could improve her quality of life and extend that life by years, if not decades." His warm eyes meet mine and he returns a comforting smile peeking through his bushy, black mustache.

Decades. I could have my mom for decades. When her cancer came back, the prognosis wasn't good. With chemo, she could have five years, but she didn't want to go through that again. Without it, maybe three. That was a little over a year ago and I would be lying if I said the thought of losing her wasn't all consuming since receiving the news.

"But aren't there risks? I mean, couldn't she die sooner?" I ask, my voice breaking ever so slightly.

"While I am asking your mother to be part of the first group of patients in my trial, she won't be the first person to undergo the treatment. So far, research has been extremely promising and mortality rates are quite low. But as with any experimental treatment, especially in terminal patients, it is always a possibility that the treatment will accelerate the progression of the disease." My face contorts in worry, and he grabs my hands between his, offering a look of sincere comfort. "Mia, I will do everything in my power to prevent that outcome."

The tears spill down my cheeks and I am unable to find my voice to ask him the millions of other questions I have. My mom places a hand on Dr. Sydek's shoulder and asks him if we can have a private moment. She grabs my hand and leads me to sit beside her on the couch.

"Oh, mija," she says, placing a loving hand on my cheek. "I know this is an awful lot to ambush you with and for that I am sorry."

"I thought you didn't want to continue treatment? Don't get me wrong, I'm thrilled, but what's changed?"

"I never wanted to stop fighting, but the chemo took so much out of me last time. I was bedridden for weeks at a time. After the coma cost me another three weeks, I vowed that I wouldn't continue this fight if it meant losing more time living. And that's what this treatment will give me. More time to live. More time with you."

I think about the things that bring my mother to life. Dancing around the house to her favorite music. Taking long walks in the gardens. Visiting with our friends in town. This illness stole that joy from her and made her too weak to enjoy everything she loved. I want to be supportive, but the fear of losing her is almost too much to bear.

"And I want that for you mamá, but I don't want to be away from you for so long only to lose you." The sob I was trying desperately to hold back escapes and I feel her arms envelop me as she pulls me close to her chest, stroking my hair like she did when I was a child.

"I know, cariño. But I need to be selfish, just this once. I am not ready to leave you. I am not ready to give up watching you become the woman you are meant to be. You've given me so much to be proud of, but I want to be here to watch you find your happiness. And I need to be here to see what happens with the Spencer boy." I can't see her face, but I can hear the smirk as she says those words.

So, she knows Preston is here.

"How did you know about that?" I ask, surprised, as I sit up pulling out of her embrace.

"I have my sources," she asserts, mischief written all over her face.

"Well, I don't know what these sources have to say, but

it's quite boring, I assure you. His family is in a bit of...trouble, so he's sticking around here for a bit. He's even going to help out with some of the repairs around the inn."

"Uh-huh. I remember you two running around here thick as thieves always getting into some kind of trouble. I always wondered what would have happened if you two had gotten to know each other later in life. How are you feeling with him back?"

"Well, he didn't even recognize me, so I haven't bothered to tell him," I say bracing for a lecture on lying.

"I see. Don't blame him for that. I'm sure he doesn't like to think about the sadness from that part of his life. But don't keep this from him. Nothing good ever came from lies."

I'm spared a longer lecture as Glenda and Dr. Sydek return to the living room to let us know they have my mom packed up and it's time for them to get on the road. We say our tearful goodbyes and I vow to visit as much as possible, while she promises to come back for Thanksgiving, pending Dr. Sydek's approval.

After she's gone, I try to muster up some of the optimism they all displayed and head back to the inn to throw myself back into work. She'll be fine, I'm sure of it. But I can't help feeling sorrow as I look around at the cottage that has never felt emptier.

⚒ ⚒ ⚒

ALTHOUGH THE INN HAS BEEN HEMORRHAGING MONEY for months, I managed to shift the budget a bit to hire a proper electrician. It also helps that James is a longtime friend of mine and is willing to let me defer payment.

Another two residents complained of lights flickering and Chelsea swears her warming lamps are turning off and on, resulting in cold food making it to guest tables. We'll have to cut back on some of the more extravagant plans for the holiday events, but it's either that or risk losing more money on comps and cancellations.

"Hi, James," I say as I greet the town's most popular electrician. In truth, he's the town's only electrician, but he's really good at his job. And, if I'm honest, he's not bad to look at, which only adds to his popularity, especially among the older, female contingent.

"Mia! So good to see you, darlin'! It's been awhile." He pulls me in for an embrace after planting a quick kiss on my cheek.

Once upon a time I thought James and I might end up together. He's one of the town's most fawned over bachelors, and for good reason too. Not only is he gorgeous, I mean, the man looks like he stepped out of a lumberjack romance novel, but he's also one of the most genuine and kind people I've ever met. We tried the dating thing for a while, but after six short months, we decided we were better off as friends. Still, I'm grateful for the friendship we managed to hang onto once the awkwardness subsided.

"Okay. Out with it. What's the damage?" I say with trepidation. "And don't sugar coat it, please."

"The good news is, the damage was mostly a few blown out fuses causing the lights to flicker. I went ahead and fixed those, no charge." He averts his eyes and looks down at his clipboard, rubbing the back of his neck as he prepares to tell me the next part, which I can tell is going to cost a pretty penny.

"James, the suspense is killing me. Please, just tell me."

"The room you called about? Well, that's where it gets substantially worse. I'm going to have to get behind the drywall to know for sure, but I think the wiring leading into that room needs a full replacement. My guess is the previous owners never thought to upgrade when they bought the place and it had already been standing for a few decades by that point. That room will be uninhabitable for at least three months."

Of course it would be Preston's room that requires the most work. I can only imagine the drama this is going to cause when he finds out he's lost yet another room. But the more pressing concern is how will I pay for these repairs when our coffers are pretty much tapped, and The Spencer Group's assets are frozen? And then there is the little problem of where I'll put Preston in the meantime.

"And how much is this going to cost me?"

He brushes his long hair back with a slight wince on his face. "I'm not gonna lie. With at least three months of work and full rewiring, plus the fact that we'll have to throw up new drywall and paint as well, I'm afraid we're looking between $10,000 and $15,000 easy."

My entire body slumps and I feel like I'm going to fall over. The inn doesn't have anywhere near that to spare and without the aid of The Spencer Group, there is no way I can swing this repair.

"And what happens if I opt to not do the repairs?"

"I would strongly advise against that, Mia. It's unsafe. If it's as bad as I am anticipating, it's only a matter of time before it causes a fire."

"James, I have to be honest. I'm sure you've heard about the troubles with the inn's owners, The Spencer Group."

He nods.

"Well, the problem is, I can't pay you. A-at least not right now. Everything's such a mess."

My head falls to my hands, and I feel like I'm on the verge of a meltdown when I feel his hand on my shoulder. James crouches down to look me in the eye. "Hey, hey. Don't worry about it. Mia, we've been friends for years, right? I know you're good for it. We'll work out a payment plan and everything will be okay. I'll work with my vendors and try to keep costs as low as possible. I promise, we'll get you fixed up."

Tears stream down my face in disbelief at his generosity. I all but jump into his arms, flinging my body against his in an appreciative hug. "James, thank you, thank you, thank you, so much. You don't know how much this means."

He and I work out a payment plan and timeline, and he informs me the crew will start tomorrow. Unfortunately, that means Preston needs to be out tonight. I flip through our reservations to see if there is any way I can rearrange guests to find a spot for him. We're fully booked, not a vacancy in sight until after the first of the year. There's no way around it. I'm going to have to invite him to stay with me at the cottage.

As I'm considering the implications of this arrangement, Chelsea bursts in, a grin plastered from ear to ear. She sits down across from me and folds her hands together, leaning forward on the desk.

"I see Preston's still here. I saw him taking off in our catering van earlier, right?"

I nod and she sits up excitedly in her seat.

"Oh my god. This is the best news *ever*. You know, I

recently read his feature in GQ. Did you know he was ranked LA's most eligible bachelor? And he's *rich*, rich. He has his own jet, a driver, a penthouse in LA, and there's this rumor he owns a super exclusive nightclub. Oh, but. I wonder how this scandal is going to affect all that? I mean, he's no stranger to scandal, but I hope this doesn't strip his title. He—" she pauses when she clocks the concerned look on my face, "I'm sure it'll be fine, Mia. It's just a silly little superlative!"

"No, it's not that. It's been...a day," I say before bursting into tears. The events of the day finally catch up with me and having my best friend sitting here allows me to finally let down my guard. She pushes up from her chair and comes around to my side of the desk to embrace me in a comforting hug. I bring her up to speed about everything that happened with my mom earlier.

"Oh, Mia. I know being away from her is going to be scary, but it sounds like she and the doc have a plan. This is hopeful news!" When my tears don't immediately subside, she searches my face with furrowed brows. "But there's something else. What is it?"

"James came by today," I say slowly.

She wiggles her eyebrows up and down suggestively. She always rooted for us to get together and still holds out hope we may find our way back to each other, no matter how many times I tell her we only click as friends.

"No, not like that. I had him take a look at some of the electrical issues the guests have been complaining about, and yes, your warming lights. Most of those were blown fuses he fixed up easily, but there is one room that will need extensive repairs. Preston's room. And since we're completely booked up, he's going to have to stay in the spare room at the cottage."

"Oh. My. God! Way to bury the lede! So, you're telling me Mr. 'Most Eligible Bachelor' is going to be staying with you at the cottage? The cottage where you are now staying *alone*? So, you'll see each other at bedtime?"

"Stop! First of all, it's not like we'll see each other that often. With all the work we have to do here for the holidays, I won't be home much. Plus, there is absolutely nothing going on there."

"Uh-huh, sure. Can you imagine seeing him all glistening wet after a hot shower, in nothing but a towel around his waist? I mean, I'm not even that attracted to men these days, but even I would kill to see that in person. Did you see that photoshoot? It's like his abs have abs."

To that I roll my eyes and stand up from my chair, determined to exit this conversation. "Never. Gonna. Happen. Besides, I'm more worried that having some spoiled rich guy handle the massive repairs this place needs is going to be bad for business. I'm legitimately worried he's going to burn the place down. Literally. I mean, you saw the near flood he created trying to fix a simple leak. Ugh. What am I gonna do?"

"It'll be fine. Give him a chance. He's trying," she says, shrugging her shoulders sympathetically.

What I don't say is how despite our many interactions, Preston has still not shown one ounce of recognition. Sure, we were just kids, and he was much easier to recognize being famous and all, but I can't lie that it hurts knowing our time together didn't make as much of an impact on him as it did on me. We were best friends, spending most days together, sharing all our childhood secrets. He was my first crush, my first kiss, if you can call an innocent peck between children a first kiss. The silence after his absence hurt me more than I could ever admit.

I snap myself out of that unhelpful train of thought. It's not like I want to even be his friend, let alone anything more. And it's not like I have time to entertain crushes on impractical men who could quite literally ruin my life. But if that's the truth, why does my breath catch every time I see him? Why am I searching for him in every room? Why does my heart stop when he flashes that smile and those god damn dimples at me?

I shoo Chelsea back to her kitchen and set out to go deliver the news to Preston. I'll head over to the cottage later to get the guest room all set up for him and then I'll push down this silly attraction once and for all. As I step out of the office into the foyer, I see Preston up on a ladder replacing the lightbulbs in the chandelier, loose bulbs and tools resting precariously on the top step. At least he managed to find some jeans and change into the company polo.

He flashes me that damn childlike grin, the one where his dimples threaten to make my knees buckle, assuring me it's much harder than it looks right as the entire chandelier comes crashing down.

Chapter 7

Preston

The chandelier lies under me in a million shattered pieces and Mia has never looked more annoyed. Well, that's not entirely true. When it comes to me, her default setting is annoyed. I can't exactly blame her as my first day isn't quite going as smoothly as I had hoped. I make to move down the ladder and manage to jostle it enough to ensure the other remaining bulbs fall to the ground adding to the mess.

I carefully step over the broken glass and make my way to Mia, a look of appalled disbelief plastered on her face.

"That chandelier was an antique and now it's absolutely trashed," she says, her voice catching as she crouches down to examine the broken pieces of the fixture. Tears threaten to pour down her face and I stand upright in a panic. I don't deal well with crying women.

"Well, it's not like I did it on purpose" I reply, a little more than annoyed that she's acting as though it's my life's goal to ruin her day. I'm not trying to make her life harder, but I also have no idea what I'm doing.

"If you don't know how to do something, please leave it alone, okay? We can't afford to add to the repair log, especially—" she cuts herself off before saying what we're both thinking. Especially since it was my father who fucked up and forced us into this mess.

"Just please, get it cleaned up so no one gets hurt, yeah? Oh, and when you wrap up for the day, could you stop by my office? I need to talk to you about something." Before I have time to respond, she's halfway down the hall.

I try to keep as many of the larger pieces as possible, in hopes I might be able to salvage the broken chandelier. Judging by the look on her face, that chandelier holds significance, and I cannot bear to be the cause of her pain. Trying to unpack that is something I don't have time for with this extensive task list.

But if I did, I might think about how she makes me absolutely crazy trying to earn her approval every time she yells at me. Or how every once in a while she looks at me with softness, as if she sees the man I *could* be, not the pretty boy fuckup whose had everything handed to him. I want so badly to be a better man. To be someone she could be proud to be seen with. *Fuck!* I need to get my shit together and focus on the task at hand, not on impressing a woman I could never have.

If I had a working phone, I'd call my best friend, Alexi for advice. Sure, he's a bit of a fuckup like me, but he always sees to the root of the problem, even when I don't want to hear it. Instead, I turn my attention back to the mess, making sure there are no shards of glass remaining on the ground, and then get to work on the rest of Mia's list.

My plan is to tackle some of the smaller, low-skill repairs and save the bulk of the list for tomorrow when I meet Elijah. I think that was his name. I dig through the supplies from the hardware store and find the spackling, trowel, and smaller scraps of drywall. I decide replacing the minor holes in the dining room shouldn't be too difficult and that's where I'll spend the rest of my day.

Fixing the tiny imperfections barely takes any time at all and I step back to admire my work. Sure, the paint is bit lighter than what's around it, but it's hardly noticeable. Maybe I'll come back and slap a fresh coat over the entire wall tomorrow. I tape up a "WET PAINT" sign and turn my attention to the gaping hole next to the fireplace.

This one is a bit larger and if I'm honest, I'm not entirely sure where to start. Deciding I'm a bit out of my depth, I pull out my phone, connect to the WiFi, and search "how to patch a hole in drywall". Thousands of results appear, but I can't find any videos under fifteen minutes. I'm too impatient for that but there's no way this is that hard. I shove my phone back in my pocket and decide to wing it, nailing up one of the scraps of drywall I found.

A few minutes into my genius idea, I feel a tug at my elbow. I turn around to see a short, round elderly woman with soft silver curls perfectly set behind her ears. I gather she's unhappy with something I'm doing by the annoyed tapping of her foot and the anger smoldering in her eyes. She doesn't make me wait long as she opens her mouth to no doubt tell me everything I'm doing wrong.

"Young man, do you know where you are?" she says with a hint of a transatlantic accent, her tone conveying she's not going to take any nonsense from me or anyone else.

"The Early Bird Inn?" It comes out like a question instead of a confident assertion.

She looks me up and down, assessing me, I suppose. She's not impressed. "Mhm. Mrs. Charlotte Sinclair." She reluctantly offers her hand, which I shake with hesitation, confused by this interaction.

"Preston, the new handyman."

"Charmed." The bite in her tone conveys she's anything but. "Do you happen to notice anything about the room you've chosen to make a racket in, Preston?" When I don't respond, she rolls her eyes and gestures wildly around the room. "The *paying* customers trying to enjoy a peaceful dinner? But here you are, hammering away!"

Still unsure what she expects me to do, I nearly open my mouth to match her energy. First of all, I have a job to do. Second of all, it's 3:30 p.m. Who the fuck eats dinner at 3:30 p.m? The only thing that stops me is Mia. This might be a temporary job for me, but this is her livelihood. I've already gotten off to a rocky start where she's concerned, and I don't want to make it worse if only to avoid making *my* life harder. So instead, I turn on my signature charm, determined to have—what was her name? Cynthia—eating out of the palm of my hand.

I place my hand over my heart, bowing my head in reverence. "I'm so sorry. You're absolutely right, how careless of me. Please let me make it up to you?" I grasp her hand between my own, a plea for her to allow me to try.

She pauses to consider my offer, and I can see I've won the moment her face turns from anger to acquiescence. "Oh all right. What did you have in mind," she says a bit more suggestive than I'm comfortable with, but I guess the charm worked after all. Taking her arm, I lead her over to one of the tables furthest from where I was doing my work.

"Wait right here. I'll be back soon!" I wink and flash her a wide grin, making sure my dimples are visible, and head to the kitchen.

I can already tell she's a woman who likes to be fawned over and who appreciates a free meal. While I know I'm not exactly authorized to be tossing around free items, I technically own the place, so what the hell. I spot the high-end espresso machine, similar to the one that *used* to occupy the coffee bar in my penthouse, and set out to make one of my favorite drinks, a peppermint cinnamon dolce latte, complete with an artistically crafted foam heart. I carefully inspect the pastry counter and find the most perfectly cut slice of the mouthwatering layered almond coffee cake I smelled baking this morning. When I turn to grab a plate, I see Chelsea watching me from where she leans in the doorway.

"First day on the job and you're already pilfering sweets from my kitchen?" she says with a smirk.

"Not quite. These are for Mrs., uh, Sutherland."

"Mrs. who?" she says, her face scrunched in confusion.

"You know. Mrs. Sullivan. Short, elderly, speaks like Audrey Hepburn and complains about everything?"

Chelsea rolls her eyes and laughs. "Oh! You mean Mrs. *Sinclair?*"

"I swear she said her last name was Stewart or something."

"Preston, you've given me at least three different names, and none of them are right. I guess when you grow up the way you did, you don't bother to learn anyone's names, huh?" Her tone is light, but I can't help the sting I feel at her joke that's a bit too on the nose.

"Whatever, names aren't my strong suit, okay? But, yeah, I need to take these to Mrs...uh."

"God, you're hopeless. *Sinclair*," she says the last name slowly and I do my best to commit it to memory this time. "What's her issue today?"

"Ah, so this isn't an isolated incident, I take it?"

"If she's giving you trouble, god no. That woman is a menace, but she's one of our biggest customers, so what're you gonna do? Good luck out there." She turns her attention back to whatever she's working on that's filling the room with a heavenly scent.

When I'm back in the dining room, peace offering in hand, I spot Mia sitting at Mrs. *Sinclair's* table, her face a combination of exasperation and woe. I pick up my pace a bit, eager to take the heat off Mia. She may be the current thorn in my side, but I never could resist a damsel.

Swooping in, I carefully set the coffee and cake in front of Mrs. Sinclair. "My penance, madame." I say with a bow and sly smile.

She giggles and I cannot help but notice the wave of utter disbelief plastered across Mia's face. I give her a cocky wink and turn my attention back to Mrs. Sinclair as her first bite has rendered her speechless, her face conveying her bliss. She takes a cautious sip of the latte and places a hand over her heart. "Oh, Preston, this is divine! Did you make it yourself?"

"Of course. Only the best for you," I say with a bit of flirtation. She giggles again. "It's my special recipe. Everyone loves a good cinnamon dolce, but not everyone knows how much better it is with a bit of peppermint, ginger, and nutmeg to really take it up a notch."

"Well, consider me sold. You can go back to your hammering now. I promise you'll hear not another word from me." She turns her attention back to her treat, ignoring Mia altogether. Mia jerks her head towards her office, and I dutifully follow her, determined not to disappoint her any further. I'll finish up the drywall repair tomorrow.

As we enter her office, she stops short and turns to face me, leaving barely enough space between us to avoid her touch.

"Wow. So, you actually *are* capable of not being a pretentious asshole."

I take a deep breath to avoid saying anything that might have her rethink her new assessment. "What can I say? I know how to handle rich, crotchety old women."

Her only reaction is a terse smile. I guess it won't be my humor that wins her over.

"Listen, Preston, I got some news today." She looks up at me with those big round eyes and I sense a hint of worry. "I'm sorry but your room is no longer available." She moves over to prop herself on her desk.

All previous levity leaves my body. Not only is this inn falling apart at the seams, but they can't seem to even properly handle reservations. I feel myself losing control, the harsh words coming out before I can stop them.

"Unbelievable. So, what? You'll shove me in a shed out back? I don't think so. I'm staying in that room, and you can figure something else out."

She rolls her eyes, ignoring my outburst. "No shed, but you can't stay in that room. I had an electrician come take a look at the power situation because I figured that was a bit out of your depth." She winces at her accidental insult.

"Anyway, evidently the wiring in your room is dangerous and needs to be replaced. They'll need to completely gut the place, and you can't stay there while everything is exposed. I stay in the cottage out a back so you can have the guest room." She gives me two thumbs up and a goofy grin, clearly hoping to get me on board.

My face falls a bit when she mentions the cottage. I must have only been about three years old, but I still remember the look on my mom's face when my father brought us here to tell us he bought the inn for her, showing us the cozy cottage that would become our home. Then a few years later, he was off to New York meeting with investors and building a hotel empire, leaving us back here in that lonely little cottage. Dread fills my every thought at going back to the place where my family imploded, but what choice do I have?

Plus, there's the other thing I've been trying to ignore. I can't stop thinking about Mia. And not just because it seems like she's nagging me every five minutes, but because I cannot deny the attraction I feel towards her.

She's undeniably gorgeous. Not my usual type, but undoubtedly the type of woman I picture being with when I think about the life I could have had if it weren't for the looming shadow of my future. I can't concentrate when I'm around her. The mere sight of her has me fumbling like an idiot, hence the shattered chandelier that currently lives in pieces in a box in the garden shed.

But it's so much more than physical attraction alone. It's the way my mouth ticks up in a grin when I catch her humming and dancing around the inn when she's sure no one's watching. It's the way she meets me with challenge when I'm being a dickhead. It's the way her head tips back with reckless abandon when she's truly happy, making me desperate to become the cause of that laughter one day. Most of all, it's the way my body is begging to reach out and touch her whenever she's near.

There's no way we can be living in a small cottage together. I can tell by the way she looks at me that she feels something too, but my situation is much too precarious to get involved with a girl like Mia. She's someone you have forever with, and I don't do forever.

"Are there no other options?" I finally say, my voice coming out much gruffer than I had intended. Maybe I imagine it, but for the briefest moment, I think I see hurt in her eyes.

"I'm sorry, no. I promise, it's cozy, but not cramped. We'll have to share a kitchen, living area, and bathroom, but otherwise you'll have complete privacy. I mean, we probably won't even see each other that much with how much there is to do at the inn," she says reassuringly.

I have two choices. I can continue my objection which will likely only cause further animosity between us, or I can accept her kindness and try to make however much time I have here as easy as possible. I take a deep breath, deciding the latter will bring me less headache. And perhaps closer to Mia.

"I appreciate it, truly. That place holds a bit of history I wasn't quite ready to revisit."

"You're welcome, and I understand," she says and for a moment, I almost believe it to be true. "Anyway, I'm so glad you agreed because I kind of already had your things brought over," she says with a laugh. "Want to walk over there quick?"

"Lead the way."

I follow her out the kitchen's back door and walk down the path through the garden my mother planted and the cobblestone pathway my father built. I stop short in front of the stairs as I see two sets of handprints in the concrete, one set my own and the other belonging to the best friend who seems to keep popping up in my thoughts now that I'm here. I don't have time to think too much about whatever happened to her and her mom as a wave of nostalgia takes me over the second Mia opens the door to the cottage.

As much as I can feel Mia in this home, there are still remnants of my mother and father everywhere. The wood burning fireplace he built, standing in the center of the room. The pink floral wallpaper my mother picked out, despite protests by me and my father, still lining the walls.

"So this is the living area. There's firewood stacked out back, but I might need your help cutting some more now that it's getting a bit colder," she says, walking me through a tour of my previous home. "I've updated the kitchen, and please help yourself to anything you find in the fridge. Back this way is your room."

She leads me past the living room to the hallway with three bedrooms and bathroom right in the center. The door is shut to the room in the middle of the hall and my body freezes in place. It's my mother's old room and the one place I never want to be in ever again. If Mia notices, she doesn't say anything and walks me towards the door at the end of the hall.

Comically, the spare bedroom I'll be calling home

happens to be my childhood bedroom. I chuckle to myself as I step over the threshold, halfway expecting to see the floor littered with matchbox cars, piles of clothing strewn about, and posters of my favorite athletes and musicians plastered on the wall. Instead, I find a minimalistic room with empty, green walls, a full-sized bed, and a small book-case filled with old paperbacks.

A small chuckle escapes my mouth as I take in some of the titles: *Sinfully His, Rich and Ruthless, Vows in Velvet Chains.* So, our girl is interested in billionaire romances. Interesting.

She clears her throat, cheeks red as she realizes what I've spotted. "Um, I changed the sheets and there are extra towels and blankets in the closet, as well as a few hangers for you to hang up your clothes. I put your suitcases in the corner over there. Oh, and the bathroom is the door on the right."

I nod, clamping down the urge to bring up the fact that this used to be my house. I stand there for a moment, taking it all in. When my father took us to LA, I swore to myself I'd never set foot in this house again. For all the happy memories I have with my family here, they're over-shadowed by the one of my father walking out on us. And no happy memory will ever compare to the deep sadness of what my mother and I endured in his absence.

Mia places a hand on my arm, jolting me out of my memories and back to reality. "Is something wrong?"

"I never thought I'd be back here. I'm sure you know this was my home until I was twelve."

"Not thrilled to be reliving your childhood?"

"Um, you know, family stuff. My father, well you know my father. He's a dick and once he got a taste of a bit of money, he treated my mother like shit, having countless affairs until he eventually walked. Tale as old as time, I guess."

"I never knew he treated your mother so poorly."

"Well, yeah, how could you?" I ask, puzzled by the odd statement.

She laughs nervously, giving me a sympathetic smile. "I'm just surprised, you know? I never knew my father. Guess he was a shit too."

"Cheers to shitty fathers, right?"

"Nah. Fuck 'em," she says with a grin. I can't help but laugh with her at that. "Well, I better get back to the inn for the dinner rush, but please do make yourself at home," she says before turning on her heels, leaving me to fall back into my memories.

Home sweet home.

Chapter 8

Mia

A slight beam of sunlight creeps through the slit in my curtains, gently waking me from sleep. The remnants of a dream dance across my mind, flashes of hands finding their way across every inch of my body. Tender kisses at my neck. Low whispers of promises of forever. I don't remember much, but I know for certain it was about Preston. Having him here in such close proximity is definitely messing with my head.

There was a moment yesterday at the cottage where I almost blurted out our history. Asked him if he truly didn't remember me. But then he started talking about his lying father, and well, I got scared. I don't want to be another liar he's forced to deal with and now that he has to stay with me, I don't want to make things any more uncomfortable than necessary.

With a long stretch, I toss the duvet off my body, and with it, the complicated thoughts I'm having about Preston. I pause for a quick glance in the mirror, checking my hair and the state of my morning breath before deciding to head to the kitchen to start the day. I'm sure Preston is still sleeping, but I'm surprised by how preoccupied I am with my appearance on the off chance he'll see me before I've had time to pull myself together.

I open the door to my bedroom and am immediately hit with the aroma of strong coffee and bacon. I can't tell if I'm more surprised that Preston is awake in time for his shift or that he's cooking breakfast. I round the corner to the kitchen and my breath catches as I take in the scene before me.

Preston is standing in my kitchen, in grey sweatpants and a tank top, leaving his lean muscular body on full display. He's plating two of the most beautiful French omelets I've ever seen, and my mouth waters both at the promise of delicious food and for the equally delicious man standing before me.

He flashes me a grin as he grabs both plates and spins around to take them over to my small dining table. "Morning. Coffee's ready and breakfast is served." He waves a hand over the table as he pours coffee into the cups he's laid out for both of us.

"Wow. I'm impressed," I say as I take the seat across from him, placing a napkin on my lap. "It smells amazing. If you told me last week that Preston Daniel Spencer would be cooking me a gourmet breakfast, I would have laughed in your face."

He shoots me a quizzical look, reminding me he doesn't know who I am and is probably startled that I know his middle name. I smile awkwardly, pushing down the guilt for lying and turn my attention back to my breakfast.

The first bite is so heavenly, I emit a borderline obscene moan, but I can't even seem to care. The fluffiness of the eggs coupled with the creamy Boursin cheese contrasts perfectly with the saltiness of the chips he's sprinkled on top, creating a beautiful symphony of flavors so decadent I swear I never want to eat anything else. Lost in the culinary orgasm dancing on my tongue, I almost forget anyone else is there until a low laugh comes from across the table.

I open my eyes to see Preston, a satisfied grin spreading from ear to ear. "So I guess it's up to standard?"

"This is criminally delicious. Where did you learn to cook like this? I mean, no offense, but I would have never imagined something like this could come from someone like you."

He furrows his brow, and I briefly worry I may have offended him, but his playful tone reassures me he wasn't hurt. "Don't forget my mother was basically the head chef here when we first opened. She taught me a few things before..." He trails off and I notice a deep sadness sweep over him, but it's gone as soon as it arrived.

I open my mouth to offer comfort, but since he assumes I know nothing of his past, I decide to crack a joke instead. "Well, I guess you had to learn how to cook for all the ladies you entertain before shoving them off each morning," I chide, shoving another bite into my mouth. I regret the joke almost immediately when I see the embarrassment on his face. He sets down his fork and sinks back into his chair.

"You know," he continues, "all that bullshit they say about me in the media is...exaggerated. Do I like to go out have have fun? Absolutely. But that's not all that I am.

One day I'm set to take this over, assuming there still is a this to take over, but that's not me. It's not what I want.

What I really want is to focus on the company's charity work. My father's done an excellent job of making sure the media doesn't care about any of that, though. An entitled party boy bouncing from woman to woman is much more interesting publicity."

He pauses, taking a deep breath before starting again. "My mother died when I was young. Once my father met his business partner, he got all these ideas for how he could build an empire. At first, I think it was about providing for us. But somewhere along the way, the money and the acclaim became more important. He took off when I was nine and left me and my mom here to run the inn.

Sure, he provided financially, and I'm grateful for that, but then she got sick. Stage 4 breast cancer. It was so advanced by the time they caught it, she didn't have much time left. And my father couldn't be bothered to come back.

We found out later he had been having an affair with his brand manager, among other women. All the lies he told, all the promises he used to manipulate us into thinking he was doing this for us, it sat with me. I swore I'd never let anyone lie or manipulate me the way he did to my mother.

She died a few years later in that very room." He nods to the center room, and I can see tears pooling in his eyes.

The ache in my gut is screaming at me to tell him who I am. That I understand his loss because I loved her too, as much as if she were my own family. That losing her, and his sudden departure, irreparably changed me. That when she finally succumbed to the disease ravishing her body and he was left scared and alone, I was the one who sat with him until he fell asleep.

But I don't. Not now that he's made it clear how deeply his father's lies hurt him. And selfishly, I don't want him to look at me with that same hateful glare he saves for his father. Instead, I settle on reaching across the table to comfortingly take his hand in mine.

"I'm such an idiot for that wisecrack. Getting to know you these past few days, I can see you are so much more than what's on the surface."

He thanks me with a weak smile that doesn't quite reach his eyes, pulling his hand away to check the time. "I better get this cleaned up and get ready. Don't want to disappoint my boss by being late...again," he jokes with a wink.

"Don't worry about it; I'll do the cleaning. It's the least I can do after you've basically satisfied me more than any man has in a *long* time," I blush, unable to believe I said that.

A smirk spreads across his face, his deep dimples on full display, as he leans in, bringing his mouth to my ear. "Well, then. Consider it my aim to keep you satisfied."

Desire pools low in my belly as he gives me a final wink and pushes himself up from the table. I fling my head back in embarrassment, hiding my face in my hands as I sink lower in the chair, hoping to disappear. I hear his chuckle all the way down the hall until the bathroom door clicks.

⚒ ⚒ ⚒

BACK IN MY OFFICE, I TRY TO DISTRACT MYSELF FROM the wildly inappropriate thoughts I'm having about Preston by finally going over the emails I've let pile up ever since the news broke about the scandal. Understandably, our vendors, most of whom are small and local, are worried about their contracts with the inn. Most of the time, I truly love everything about my job. The one part I never quite mastered was juggling the complex business partnerships. That was more Mom's wheelhouse. Not to mention, my head is in a completely twisted place.

I can't get Preston out of my mind. It's no big secret that he's attractive but seeing him so vulnerable this morning brought back memories of that kind, sensitive boy from all those years ago. I don't know how I managed to fight back my own tears as he recounted his mom's sickness and death.

While we all knew of her cancer, I was a kid back then and didn't fully realize the pain he was going through. I also didn't remember his dad's departure happening so closely to her diagnosis. Part of me feels extremely guilty for not noticing then, but it's nothing compared to the guilt I feel for letting him open up while he still thinks I'm a stranger.

Maybe I could have come clean earlier and brushed everything off as a simple misunderstanding. But after this morning, I'm afraid he might interpret this misunderstanding as willful deceit, like his father seemed to do often, and that is too terrifying to imagine.

Instead, I turn back to my inbox, scrolling through dozens of unread messages. I stumble across one marked urgent from one of our guests who reserved eight of our fourteen rooms for the weekend after Thanksgiving. If they cancelled, we would lose thousands of dollars as it'd be nearly impossible to fill those vacancies on such short notice.

I take a deep breath and double-click the email, realizing it's not from the guest, but their wedding planner, Cecelia. Apparently, the couple couldn't decide on a suitable venue nearby and after seeing photos of our intimate, picturesque location, they want to marry here.

Two weeks from Sunday.

Normally, I would be energized by a wedding. Hosting events at the inn is undoubtedly the best part of my job and it's been a while since we've had a wedding come through here. We typically require at least six months to a year to plan a full-scale wedding, but with the uncertainty of inn's future, how can I turn down the money? This would easily bring in tens of thousands not only for us, but for the vendors in town.

If I can get everyone on board.

In two weeks.

I call Cecelia to assess whether we can even meet their expectations. We have our Thanksgiving event for the town one day before they would arrive, which doesn't leave a lot of time to transform the inn for a wedding. Not to mention the floral arrangements, band, and menu we would have to figure out.

Within a few seconds of the phone call, I'm informed that this isn't just any wedding. This is the wedding of Everett Townsend, former reality star, and Sadie Perkins, Instagram influencer and model.

The Early Bird has had its fair share of celebrities breeze through here, but it's been for a day or two at most and they were usually D-list at best. These two have been plastered all over every gossip magazine, their fairytale romance playing out for all to watch on Sadie's social media. They have extravagant taste and I'm worried that we'll be biting off more than we can chew in such a short amount of time. On the other hand, if we nail this, the publicity the inn will receive might be enough to save us from the backlash of the Spencer scandal.

Normally, I would bring this to Mom. After all, she's still the acting manager since The Spencer Group handed it over to her. Glenda has been sending regular updates and I FaceTimed with Mom and Dr. Sydek a few days ago. Her treatment is going well, but it's taking a lot out of her. The last thing I want to do is burden her with this decision when I assured her I could handle taking over all operations at the inn. I can't disappoint her.

So, I make an executive decision and agree to host the wedding. I hope we can swing it and that Preston can eke out the remainder of the main room repairs before then.

Now all that's left is to convince Chelsea, the rest of the staff, and all our town vendors that this is a good idea. This wedding will either be a turning point for the inn or send us spiraling down in a blaze of glory.

Chapter 9

Preston

This morning's conversation with Mia replays in my head on a loop. I never talk about my mother's death with anyone. If I'm being honest, I'm not even sure my father and I have properly talked out the anger I feel towards him for leaving me alone to watch her die. So why was it so easy for me to open up to Mia, a virtual stranger?

There's something about her I can't quite put my finger on. A familiarity I can't quite place, allowing me to open up to her in a way that took me by surprise. When I look at her, a part of me is reminded of my former best friend, Amelia Aguilar.

It's been years since I've allowed myself to think about the days surrounding my mother's diagnosis and eventual death, but when I let down my guard with Mia, everything came flooding back as if it just happened.

After my mother sat me down and told me what it meant that she had incurable cancer, I couldn't process. Instead, I stormed out of the house, tears streaming down my face, running towards the pond where Amelia and I always swam. I picked up a fallen branch and began hitting the trunk of a nearby willow tree as hard as I could until even that wasn't giving me the release I needed. I tossed the branch aside and began punching the tree with all my might, pouring all my rage into every punch until my knuckles dripped crimson.

Why did my mother have to get sick?

Why did my father leave us?

Why didn't he come back when she was diagnosed?

Why can't I cure her?

Why will I have to be all alone when she dies?

Amelia must have been screaming my name for minutes, but I didn't notice she was there until she tenderly touched my shoulder. She wasn't even afraid as I whipped around, fist still in the air, face contorted with rage and anguish. Even in my worst moments, she saw the best in me. With a pained wail, I collapsed into her arms, and she let me cry, stroking my back gently, until my tears finally ran dry. It was then I knew she would be my best friend forever.

Feeling tears streaming down my face in present day, I think about how Mia provided that same comfort today. Whenever we talk, I'm filled with a similar warmth I always felt with Amelia. If Mia and I can reach even a sliver of the friendship I shared with Amelia, maybe my time here won't be so bad.

Of course, sometimes I want more than mere friendship with Mia. When she pattered into the kitchen this morning in her knee-high socks, scandalously short shorts, and oversized tee, I thought I was going to have a heart attack. Even with no makeup, her hair pulled up in a messy bun, she is the most strikingly beautiful woman I've ever seen.

I have to be on my best behavior with her, though. Not only because she's my boss and we're sharing a home, but because she deserves so much more than the mess of a man I am. But she makes me want to become a better man, the man my mother always wanted me to be.

Before I can spend too much time down this path, I realize it's time to head over to the inn and meet my trainer, whose name I'm pretty sure is Eli, for the day. I don my too tight grey polo and get ready to embarrass myself in front of the inn's former handyman.

The man I assume is my new trainer sits at one of the dining room tables with Mia, laughing together as only old friends could. He must be at least seventy-five years old and looks like he could be my grandfather. His dark skin might be weathered by age, but his mahogany eyes dance with youthful joy. I can't help but let a smile spread across my face as I approach the table.

Mia greets me with a wave and invitation to take the open seat. "Ernie, this is Preston. Preston, meet Ernie. He spent almost twenty-two years with us before he tried to retire, but he couldn't stay away." She nudges Ernie playfully. I could have sworn his name was Evan.

Ernie stands, extending his hand to shake mine. I've always had a difficult time with names, but something tells me I'm going to want to get on his good side, so I commit his to memory. He's larger than I imagined, at least 6'3 and easily 250 pounds, with a grip much stronger than it should be for his age. "Hello, young man. Why don't we sit down to some breakfast and go over this list I'm sure this one has for you," he jokes, taking a seat.

"Well, that's my cue. You boys try not to break anything...else, okay?" Mia says with a laugh as she glides away to her office, my eyes trained on her for much longer than appropriate.

Ernie clears his throat and looks at me pointedly, "You be careful there, son."

"I'm sorry?" I say innocently.

"I've known that girl for most of her life. She's like a daughter to me. Don't think I don't know who you are and how you operate with women. I'm more than happy to help you here, but make no mistake, my loyalty will always be to that girl."

"I assure you, whatever you heard has been grossly exaggerated. But I promise, I'm just here to help and as I'm sure you know, I have little idea what I'm doing."

His eyes glance over to the piece of drywall I haphazardly hung near the fireplace. "That your handy work?"

I lower my eyes in embarrassment. "Yes. I didn't have trouble with the smaller holes, but it looks like a chair or something went through the wall over there and I have no idea how to cover it up."

"Clearly," he shakes his head and chuckles. "Don't worry. Let's start there. You weren't completely wrong. We'll take down what you put up, measure it, sand it, and make sure it properly fits before tossing up a new coat of paint."

"Sounds good. Did you happen to come in through the front, by chance?"

"I did. I take it you have something to do with the missing chandelier?"

I wince. "Yeah, that was my fault. I scooped up as many of the larger parts I could find. Do you think we can try to restore it? It's important to me that we get that put back up. For Mia."

He flashes me a genuine smile for the first time this morning. "Of course. If we can't do it, I know a guy who does antique restoration. I'm sure he can help."

We finish our breakfast and make a plan to go over the basics and check some of the more pressing items off my list. By midafternoon, Ernie has me feeling like maybe I can become something more than the fuckup everyone expects me to be.

⚒ ⚒ ⚒

Before I know it, the day's almost over and Ernie is teaching me how clean and patch up the ceiling, rusty from a previous leak. As I carefully balance on the ladder, I hear a squeal coming from the kitchen and am nearly knocked off as Chelsea barrels down the hallway.

"Ernieeeeeeee!" Chelsea jumps into his arms, embracing him with a bear hug. "It's so good to see you back here!"

Ernie's boisterous laugh echoes through the foyer as she releases him from her grip. "Mia asked me to come by and teach this one here how to be a real handyman." He winks at me and I laugh.

"Oh yeah? Our reformed party boy getting the hang of it?"

"Hey," I say in mock offense, "who said I was reformed?"

She rolls her eyes with a smile. "Well, I better shove off to get dinner service underway. Stop by later, party boy, and maybe I'll take pity on you and fix you a plate.

You too, Ernie," she says before heading off to the kitchen.

We share a laugh, and I see Mia heading our way with a skip in her step. I haven't seen her this happy since I arrived.

"How's our little trainee doing today?" she jokes.

"Surprisingly decent! I'll have him in shape in no time," he says with a laugh.

"Good to hear. Hey, while I have you here, I'm wondering if you and Bea are still planning on being our Mr. and Mrs. Claus this year at the Christmas pageant?"

Ernie *ho ho hos* agreement with a smile plastered on his face that Mia can't help but return. I climb down the ladder, wiping my hands on a handkerchief I shoved in my pocket, and join the conversation.

"You still do it? The pageant, I mean? That's seriously one of my best memories growing up. My mother..." I swallow the lump forming in my throat. Since this morning, I've been lost in the past, barely able to contain my emotions.

Mia places her hand on my shoulder and shoots me a sympathetic look. "We do! If I remember the tale correctly, though, it was your mother *and* father who thought that one up. It's one of my favorite traditions around here too. I promise, we haven't changed much."

"My father? Yeah I can't see him being the mastermind of fun. That was all my mother."

"Hold on, I'll show you." Before I can respond, she's off sprinting towards her office. She comes back with a thick photo album, flipping to a page before handing it over to me. There's a large photo in the center of my parents as Mr. and Mrs. Claus with me on their lap. It's surrounded by photos of my parents putting up decorations, making Christmas cookies, wrapping presents, and setting up the stage for the pageant. They look so happy, so in love. My fingers trace the flyer in my mother's handwriting that sits on the opposite page.

"I had no idea he was such a big part of it." I continue looking through the photos that chronicle the pageant from its first year through the most recent. Seeing my family so happy is like a dagger to the heart as I reflect on the fact that when I lost my mother, I lost my father and myself, too, in a way.

I pause on a photo of my parents sitting on the bench that still sits in the garden. They're surrounded by snow, both in formal wear, but the cold doesn't seem to bother them. My mother sits on my father's lap, her head tilted back in laughter while he stares at her with an adoration I've never seen in his eyes before. It couldn't be clearer how deeply he loves the woman before him. So, then, why was it so easy for him to leave us?

Lost in my memories, I forget I'm surrounded by people. Finally, Mia breaks the silence. "Feel free to take as much time as you need with that. It will be good inspiration for when you get to put up all the decorations this year." She winks and directs her attention to back Ernie.

"Which reminds me...Ernie, I'm so sorry but, um, as you know we're having a bit of a money issue," she pauses, glancing at me apologetically, "with everything going on. I won't be able to pay you in full until after the new year. I completely understand if that means you can't continue to help us out."

Ernie looks at her, incredulous. "Miss Mia," he says sternly, "there's no way you believe I would abandon you in your time of need for something as silly as money. I'm helping."

She jumps into his arms, giving him a grateful hug. "You're really bailing me out! Which brings me to the real reason I came out here. There's a been a bit of a change of plans, so I'll need to adjust your list a bit."

She hands us both a copy of a new list, which is a little shorter than before, but still gargantuan.

"We're now hosting a wedding the weekend after Thanksgiving, so that only gives us about a week and a half to prepare. Plus, we'll have to move fast to transform the inn from Thanksgiving to Christmas because the bride wants a Christmas theme."

Ernie and I share a look that conveys the same thing: Mia must have lost her damn mind. We've made good progress on repairs, but we haven't completed two pages of her first list. To finish that as well as the added work to turn over the decor from Thanksgiving to Christmas in a day or two will be insane. Still, I can't help the excitement pouring through my body at the thought of doing something that might impress Mia.

"I know it's a lot to ask and I'll be here helping wherever I can, but what do you say, ready for some pressure?" she asks, grinning at us hopefully. And it's that damn smile, that cautious yet hopeful glint in her eyes, that ensures I am ready to agree to whatever she asks.

"Sign me up! We got this, don't we, Ernie?" I look at him with an unsure smile, hoping the panic in my eyes doesn't betray me.

"You got it, son." He pats me on the back before turning a reassuring glance to Mia. "Don't you worry, Miss Mia, I'll get Tucker and have him bring in some of the boys from the shop. They need something to keep them out of trouble anyway."

She puts a hand over her heart with a grateful smile. "I can't tell you how much I appreciate this. I feel so much better having you here to supervise," she looks at me sheepishly, "no offense."

"But in the meanwhile," Ernie removes his hat and takes a step closer to Mia, "why don't you tell Miss Chelsea to make sure to save me a plate of whatever she has brewing back there? I can smell it all the way out here!" He pats his belly for emphasis.

"You got it! And I guess I'll get one for you too," she says, glancing in my direction. "You boys let me know if you need anything. Don't work him too hard, Ernie, we wouldn't want him to break a nail." She flashes me a teasing grin and Ernie erupts with laughter.

My eyes stay fixed on her as she saunters off to the kitchen, my heart beating out of my chest. It's then that I know for an absolute fact that I'm in trouble.

Chapter 10

Mia

I'm distracted all day as I try to figure out how to bring up the wedding to Chelsea. It's last minute and I know it's going to add a lot of extra work to her plate, but I'll have to hope she understands how desperately we need this money.

I pop into the kitchen and spot her organizing dinner service, barking orders at her staff with glee. I can't help but beam with pride as she stands there so clearly in her element, a grin spread wide across her face. It's such a far cry from the timid line cook my mother hired and quickly promoted to head chef a few years later.

The kitchen is organized chaos, the smells of roasting meat and vegetables eliciting a loud grumble from my stomach. It appears, once again, I forgot to eat lunch, my mind elsewhere. Specifically, how damn good Preston looked in that tight polo and those jeans. Did I give him the wrong size intentionally? I wouldn't do that, would I? But if I did, thank you, Past Me.

Chelsea catches me standing there and hands her list

over to her sous chef before yelling, "Twenty minutes to service! I want to see perfect plates. No streaks. No mistakes!"

A resounding "Yes, Chef!" fills the room from the cooks in unison as they return to their stations. Chelsea swears she hates that cheer, but her beaming smile tells a different story as she meets me in the doorway.

"Hey, boss! Tonight, we have a classic minestrone with chickpeas, served with a simple arugula salad tossed in my raspberry balsamic. Our main course is a chicken piccata, made with a chardonnay from Pete and Mary's, served over lemon garlic rice, with a side of roasted parmesan asparagus. For dessert, I've made mini limoncello and pistachio tiramisu! We're on time and ready to go!" She gives me a wide grin and two thumbs up to really sell her enthusiasm.

"That sounds absolutely delicious, so I hope you'll save me a plate!" I say, my mouth watering at the smells. My stomach grumbles again. Loudly.

"By the sounds of it, I don't know if you can wait. Let me fix you a plate and I'll bring it to your office so you can tell me whatever it is you're clearly dying to tell me." She laughs and wanders behind the service counter to prepare my plate as I head back to my office.

As soon as I sit down at my desk, Chelsea comes in with a steaming bowl of minestrone and sets it in front of me with an exaggerated impression of a waiter. "Your dinner is served, madame." She bows before sitting down in the seat across from me. "So what's up?"

"So," I start slowly, dreading her reaction, "remember the wedding party we booked for the weekend after Thanksgiving?"

"Yes..." she says with unease.

"Right. Well...um...as it turns out, they haven't found their wedding venue yet and—" I'm cut off as Chelsea holds up a hand, eyes closed in exasperation.

"Let me guess. They suddenly want to host the entire wedding on the premises, right? Ceremony and reception for, what, 150 people? And you need me to come up with staff, plus an entire menu, run it by the bride, bake a whole ass wedding cake, and make sure we have enough liquor for an, I assume, open bar. Is that what you're about to say?"

I wince. I had forgotten how sassy she gets when she's pissed. With a resigned sigh, I place my spoon back down in my soup and fold my hands in front of me on the desk, trying to force my face into a neutral expression.

"Believe me, it's not ideal. But in our current situation, can we really afford to turn away business? I did tell them that due to the short notice, we're going to need a lot more money and all of it upfront to pay for the additional food, liquor, decorations, and staff. Chels, we're talking tens of thousands of dollars in our account. Don't worry about the staff or the liquor. I'll take care of all of that as long as you can make the rest happen."

She makes me wait for longer than is humane but finally tosses me a smile with a shake of her head.

"You're lucky I'm fucking amazing and that I love you. I'll get a tasting menu ready tomorrow if you can swing by to choose. Hey, why don't you bring that new handyman?" She wiggles her eyebrows suggestively and I roll my eyes.

"What? More opinions couldn't hurt. You owe me details, by the way. Like does he walk around the cottage shirtless and in grey sweats? Do you guys accidentally brush hands when you're cleaning up after dinner? Give me something! I'm absolutely living for this real-life forced proximity trope. He's hot as fuck and you haven't gotten laid in a *long* time."

I try to stifle my laugher as I see Preston standing behind her, a satisfied smirk on his face indicating he heard everything.

"He's right behind me, isn't he?" Realization sweeps over her, turning her face a shade redder than the tomatoes she used in this soup.

"Hello, ladies. Hope I'm not interrupting anything," he laughs and the shit-eating grin on his face grows, emphasizing those criminally sexy dimples.

I have no idea why heat suddenly creeps up to my cheeks as if *I* had been the one caught ogling him, but I feel the heat color my cheeks all the same when he trains his eyes on mine. Chelsea clears her throat and gives me a look that conveys exactly what I was thinking, what is going on between me and Preston?

"Seems like you two have a lot to talk about so I'm going to head on back to my cave. Preston, tell Ernie I'll make you both up a plate soon." And then Preston and I are left in my office. Alone.

I shrug nervously. "What can I say? The girl loves her romance novels. What's up?"

He looks at me and points at the chair Chelsea just vacated as if in question. I nod, bidding him to take a seat. He pulls something out of his back pocket and sits down with a nervous sigh.

"I was thinking about the wedding and while I can barely hammer a nail, parties are kind of my thing."

He smooths out a folded piece of paper, turning it to

face me on my desk. It's a detailed sketch of the inn's garden, but transformed into a picturesque wedding alter that any bride would adore. He's sketched an arrangement of chairs, splitting an aisle with a floral arch adorned with poinsettias at the end. Carefully placed around the area are traditional Christmas decorations and twinkle lights strewn throughout the foliage.

"Wow, you did all this? Like, alone?" I ask, trying to keep a normal amount of surprise in my voice. I honestly had no idea he had this level of planning in him. I guess I really have allowed my opinion of him to be influenced by what the tabloids have said.

"I did. I know there will be a lot of work to be done before then and I saw how overwhelmed you were when you told me and Ernie about the wedding. I figured this is an area where I can help. So, let me help," he said with an assertiveness I hadn't seen from him since he's been here.

"This is amazing. You brought to life exactly what I envisioned in my head. How did you do that?"

He grins. "Great minds, I guess." He stands up, ready to leave but turns before going through the door. "Mia, I'm here, you know. Even if you think I'm some spoiled idiot, I can be here for you. Whatever you need."

I ignore the way that statement makes my stomach do somersaults. "Thanks, Preston. And I don't think you're an idiot. I misjudged you and for that, I'm sorry."

"No apologies necessary. I've made some dumb choices in life but trust me, I can do this. I'm going to prove it, to my father and to you." He gives me one last smile before shutting the door behind him.

✻ ✻ ✻

THE WEEK FLIES BY AND WE'VE SOMEHOW MANAGED to nail down nearly all the preparations for the wedding and the Thanksgiving fundraiser tomorrow. There were only a few small incidents, all from Preston, but none requiring major fixes or trips to the ER, so a win is a win. I'm impressed by how quickly he's seemed to find his groove. I stand in the foyer, looking around the inn and exhale with a satisfied sigh, a smile spreading across my face.

Now that dinner service is over and the dining room has been cleaned, the only task left is transforming this room for tomorrow's main event. I grab the box of burgundy tablecloths and other decor from the storage closet before heading into the dining room where I find Preston rearranging the tables, seeming to have ignored my meticulously planned diagram.

I let the box drop to the floor with a thud to get his attention. He looks up at me with a genuine smile, oblivious to the exasperation I'm sure is painted on my face. His face falls when I don't return his warmth.

"Is there a problem?"

I inhale slowly and close my eyes, pushing down my annoyance. I can tell he's really trying, and I don't want to come down too hard on him, but he has to learn to follow directions, especially with the added pressure of the wedding looming.

"Did you forget about the diagram I provided on how to arrange the tables?" I say curtly.

"Nope. It's over there. It was just impractical." His flippant tone threatens to undo my mini meditation and send my anger bubbling to the surface.

"Excuse me? I've been doing this for years and this is

how we always organize the tables. We serve buffet style, and it makes sense to have the buffet over here—" I point to where our buffet table is usually set up only to find a bar in its place. "Where is the buffet?"

"Oh, yeah. We're not doing that this year." He doesn't even make eye contact with me as he begins changing the tablecloths and decorating the tables.

I'm livid. I didn't authorize this change a mere day before the event.

I stomp over to him, hands on my hips. "Sorry, back up. Where did you get this idea without talking to me, you know, the manager of this place?"

He stops what he's doing, standing up to meet my gaze. "I talked to Chelsea this afternoon and, frankly, she agrees. You hold this feast every year in an effort to boost the town's local economy and raise money for charity, right? It should be an exclusive, elegant experience. Chelsea and the rest of the staff agree we should *serve* this meal, not make our guests stand in line to scoop their own food."

"I can't believe you went behind my back to *my* staff and changed something as critical as this. Put it all back. *Now,*" I say through gritted teeth and turn on my heels to storm off to my office. I hear his footsteps gaining on me, so I pick up the pace, barely making it to the door before him.

He catches the door with his hand, slamming it behind him. We exist in heated silence, neither of us wanting to acquiesce and speak first. His gaze burns into me with something more than anger, but I can't seem to place exactly what. Just as I open my mouth to lay into him, he begins to pace, running his hand down his face.

"You're right. I'm sorry. I shouldn't have gone behind

your back." His strained tone lets me know he isn't used to apologizing.

"No. You shouldn't have," I say, my voice surprisingly even, "but you aren't entirely wrong. Chelsea and I have wrestled with this exact change for the past few years, but we never had the time to think about execution. I suppose it's easier to do what we've always done."

"I get that. But, Mia, you have to let people help you. I've only been here for a few weeks and already I can tell you try to shoulder everything on your own and you shouldn't have to do that. I understand that adds a lot of stress, but you also can't snap on those who try to help because you think you know better." There is no cruelty in his voice, only genuine compassion.

I consider his words, coming to terms with the truth in them. The stress of the event and the last-minute wedding preparations has every bit of me on edge and awakens my inner control freak.

"It's been an extremely stressful few weeks. I had no right to speak to you that way and for that, I'm sorry. You've stepped up in ways I could have never imagined." I move closer to him, looking into his eyes with sincerity. "If I haven't expressed to you how grateful I am, I apologize. Thank you, Preston."

We're much closer than I had intended and all I can concentrate on is the smell of his cologne, a mix of smoke and sandalwood, and his warm breath on my face. Electricity fills the space between us as I feel the overwhelming desire to kiss him. He leans closer and I suck in a breath, anticipating his mouth on mine. Instead, he takes my hand in his, a childlike grin spreading across his face.

"Can you come with me for a moment?"

Embarrassed that I misread the situation, I gather my composure and shoot him a suspicious look. "Come with you where? And for what?"

"Mia, I'm not an axe murderer," he chuckles. "Just come with me." He pulls me by the wrist out of my office, down the hall, before stopping in front of the door to the garden. Reclaiming eye contact, he asks, "Do you trust me?"

Every single nerve in my body is vibrating and my stomach does a backflip as his hazel eyes burrow into mine. I have no idea what he's going to do next, but in this moment, I know I would follow those eyes to the end of the earth. My throat is suddenly too dry speak, so I nod instead.

He leans down and whispers in my ear, "Close your eyes."

A shudder runs down the length of my body. I abide and feel his large hand envelop mine, intertwining our fingers, slowly guiding me through the door and down the stairs. The scent of fresh pine and mint are a dead give-away we've stopped in the garden. When he drops my hand, I hear the flip of a switch and the low hum of electricity.

"Now, open your eyes."

Thousands of twinkling lights wrap around every tree and vine in the garden, illuminating the real-life version of the sketch he showed me weeks ago.

White chairs adorned with subtle red, white, and green tulle have been perfectly arranged to part for the cobblestone path which marks the aisle, before veering off to a wedding arch wrapped in poinsettias and more twinkle lights, our garden its backdrop. Surrounding the entire set up are various wire sculptures of reindeer, sleighs, and snowflakes, adding the right amount of Christmas magic to the elegant display before me. My breath hitches in my throat as I meet Preston's eyes, beaming as brightly as the lights before us.

"I know it's a bit early, but I figured if we could get this set up before the guests arrive, it'll be a lot less work to do as we prepare the rest of the inn for the wedding. It should be easy enough to keep the guests from trampling around out here for the next two days. What do you think?"

Placing a hand over my heart, I smile, holding back tears of joy. "Preston, this is beautiful! When did you find the time to do all this?"

He stands a little taller with the compliment and puffs out his chest with pride. It's so adorable and reminds me of when he was a boy.

"Well, I had a bit of help from, uh, Tyler's team."

I bark a laugh as he gets another name wrong. "You mean *Tucker's* team?"

"Right. That's what I said. Tucker."

"You really do have a thing with names, huh?" I'm still laughing when he rolls his eyes and turns my attention back to the display.

"The point is, with five of us, we blew through your list quickly this week and finished the final repairs by noon today. We spent the rest of the afternoon setting this up."

"It's perfect. You really brought your vision to life. I'm impressed."

"Well, you attend enough high society events and something is bound to stick, right? Come on, let me show you the rest." He offers me his arm and loops mine through his as he takes me through the Christmas wonderland they've created throughout the garden.

As we walk the garden path, lit up with Christmas lights and adorned with subtle traditional decor, I stare up at Preston in awe. His eyes meet mine with a smile as he excitedly explains how he and Tucker rigged the lighting system to play in sync with the music. He's beaming with pride, but I can't help but notice it looks as if it's been a long time since he's felt this level of happiness. I open my mouth to tell him it's so good to see him happy again but stop myself as I realize he still doesn't know who I am and that might sound a bit weird.

My mood dips slightly at the thought. I felt the spark of something between us tonight. I don't know what it means, or if it means anything at all, but I know I can't keep lying to him. I have to tell him that I'm Amelia Aguilar, the little girl who lived in the inn.

Chapter 11

Preston

Feeling confident after the transformed garden was a hit with Mia, I can't wait to talk to her this morning about helping with the Thanksgiving dinner. I recall the nerves that ran through my body as I worked up the courage to show her how I brought the sketch to life. An odd occurrence because I can count on one hand how many times a woman has made me nervous. Of course, I owe most of the technical work to Tucker and his crew. I also left out the part where I was nearly electrocuted, saving myself the embarrassment of admitting I still don't have a clue what I'm doing.

I emerge from my room and pad down the hallway, following the smell of freshly brewed coffee. She's awake before I am, and I stop short at the sight of her. Back turned to me, she sips her coffee while admiring the sunrise through the large window. She looks perfectly serene, still in her pajamas, an oversized t-shirt, shorts, and pink, furry slippers, her silky waves falling down her back. She's so lost in thought; I almost don't want to disturb her.

"Good morning," I greet her with a smile as I turn to get my own cup of coffee. "Want some breakfast?"

"Ugh, I wish I could. I have a million things to do today. I should probably head over soon."

"Sit," I say, the sternness in my voice masking my nerves. "I can whip up something fast. You're going to need protein and carbs to get through the day. Plus, I want to talk to you about something."

Shooting me a quizzical glance, she takes a seat at the kitchen counter. "Okay. Maybe something simple."

I turn to the fridge and take out some eggs, strawberries, milk, and the loaf of brioche I swiped from Chelsea yesterday, deciding on French toast. "As you know, I have a bit of experience with parties."

"You mean partying all over LA with rich socialites?"

"Well, yes. But also attending fundraisers with rich, snobby types. Point is, I know how to throw a good party. So, I was thinking, it's not like I can be hammering away while guests are trying to enjoy the party, so let me help with the dinner."

She pops a strawberry into her mouth, considering my offer. "Going to a party and planning a party are vastly different things. And it's not like we're dealing with high society here. It'll mostly be people from around town."

"Right, but like you said, you have a million things to do today. Couldn't you use some help?"

"But how would you help?" I'm almost offended by the doubt in her voice but choose to ignore it and focus on making my case instead.

"Have you ever been to a fine dining establishment?"

She tosses her head back with a cackle. My eyes linger on the length of her neck, wondering what it would feel like to press my lips against her skin. I've got to stop thinking about crossing the line with Mia.

The urge to kiss her last night was all-consuming and I think she felt it too. Around her, it's like I'm no longer the cool, debonair player who has a different girl on his arm every week. Instead, I become a sniveling idiot with hearts in my eyes, unable to keep my pulse from racing at the slightest touch. And the way she looked at me with adoration, as if she could see me becoming a better man before her eyes, she almost had me convinced too.

But I'm not that guy. I'm not worthy of her kindness and affection. I'll never be the man she needs, the kind of man she deserves. So, for now, I'll have to be content with the fact that, at least for now, she doesn't seem to hate me.

"Preston, look around. The finest dining we have in Stoney Ridge is the inn."

"Well, most establishments have a maitre'd who is responsible for greeting the guests and managing their dining experience. They'll schmooze and chat, but also keep an eye on the dining room, alerting the staff of any potential issues before they happen. Plus, and I really don't mean to sound pretentious, it might be good for optics if people see a Spencer on site."

There's a moment where I think she's going to laugh at me or tell me to fuck off. The silence extends longer than I'd like, but I can tell by the expression on her face she's working it over in her head. A grin takes over her face and I feel a wave of relief.

"This a great idea! We'll double team it," her cheeks flush at the accidental innuendo, "wait, no, that sounds dirty. You know what I mean! We'll both be managing the new service plan so no one will get overwhelmed. I like it!"

Her eyes light up and she does a little dance in her chair as she takes the first bite of French toast in front of her. She giggles with a little clap and damn, if that isn't the cutest thing I've ever seen. I grab a plate for myself and lean over the counter, meeting her eyes.

"Thanks. For, you know, taking a chance on me. I know we didn't get off to the best start."

"Oh, because you came stomping in here yelling at Lizzy like you owned the place?" She's joking, but she's not wrong. I wince.

"Not my finest moment, I'll admit. But technically, I *do* own the place." She shoots me a playful scowl, pointing her fork at me. "And I wanted to apologize to her immediately. But yeah. I was being a dick. You didn't make it easy on me either! Acting like I was just going to be a giant fuckup."

"Okay, but you did destroy an entire chandelier your first day." She cracks up at that and I have to laugh along with her because it's true.

"I did do that. You have to admit, I'm getting better, though. You're going to be so sad when it's time for me to leave."

Our faces fall at the thought. Both for the fact that I might lose my inheritance, but also, at least for my part, at the thought of never seeing each other again.

We finish up and our hands brush as we both grab to clean up the plates. With a kind smile, she nods to the sink. "Come on. We gotta get a move on. You wash, I'll dry!"

"Nah, I got this. You go get ready and I'll meet you in the dining room around ten to go over tonight's service." I grab the plates from her hands and start cleaning up as she skips away to get ready for the day.

Something like pride sweeps over me and I can't help

but smile as I do the dishes. Even with all the events I've done for the company, my father never extended trust in me to handle anything on my own. Mia has known me for all of three weeks and already seems to have complete confidence in my follow-through.

When I shut off the water, I hear faint off-key singing coming from the bathroom where Mia is showering. I smile at this beautiful, intelligent, confident, goofy woman who believes in me for some reason. Now I just have to make sure I don't let her down.

⚒ ⚒ ⚒

THE INN IS ORGANIZED CHAOS AS I WALK THROUGH the kitchen to meet Mia in the dining room to discuss this evening's service. The smell of fresh thyme, rosemary, and sage pleasantly fills the room. I inhale deeply, taking it all in and allow myself to remember Thanksgiving with my parents as a kid, waking up to find them buzzing around the kitchen, preparing the day's feast. Back then, we didn't have a lot of guests for dinner, but my mother always made sure we had enough food to feed anyone in town who might not have anywhere to go.

I weave through the staff as they organize canapé trays and table settings for tonight. When I step through the archway of the dining room, I catch Mia sitting at a center table, chewing on a pen cap, her brow furrowed in frustration, as she combs through a stack of papers. The morning sun beams through the large window, engulfing her in a halo of soft, orange light.

"What did that pen ever do to you?" I set my notebook down and slide into the chair next to her.

She removes the pen cap from her mouth and looks at it apologetically.

She waves off my comment and shoves her papers to the side. "Oh, just mountains of paperwork, as usual. So, what's the plan for tonight?"

I open my notebook and point to the sketch I've made of the dining room. "In addition to the normal staff, we've hired three busboys and increased our normal staff to fourteen servers, five bartenders, and eight kitchen staff to support Chelsea. The dry run last night went well, and I think we have all the kinks worked out. Everyone will be mic'd up, and I'll be running point on course delivery."

She holds up the sketch in front of her, nodding with pride. "I didn't think you had it in you, Spencer, but you really do know how to plan a seamless dinner service. The guests are going to go wild."

"You know, I should really be more offended at how you're constantly impressed that I'm not some giant fuck-up." I nudge her shoulder with mine, letting her know I'm only teasing.

Pushing me away at the chest with a scoff, she meets my gaze, and I freeze at the feeling of her hand on my chest. The heavy scent of jasmine and citrus wafts towards me and only then do I realize how close we're sitting together. I'm suddenly hyper aware of the warmth of her thigh against mine, the steady expansion of her chest as she breathes, the tendrils escaping her messy bun lightly grazing her pink cheeks.

My gaze drops to her plump, glossy lips, my thoughts consumed with the desire to lean in and press mine against them. To be honest, it's all I can think of these days, the way her lips might taste, the way her hair would feel tangled up in my fingers, the softness of her skin as I run my hands along every inch, the sounds she might make when I find each spot that drives her wild.

As if she's thinking the same thing, she moistens her lips with her tongue, taking her bottom lip between her teeth and I swear she's leaning in closer. I reach my hand up and tuck a stray strand of hair behind her ear. Today, I'm going to learn if those cherry lips taste as good as they look.

Before I can get any closer, the spell is broken by a loud thud. Mia and I nearly jump out of our chairs as we both slide back away from one another. I look up to see Chelsea staring at us, hands on her hips, and a knowing smirk on her face.

"Oh, hey, guys! Whatcha doin'?" She sits down in the chair across from us, resting her chin on her folded hands, blinking accusations in our direction.

Mia anxiously smooths back her hair as I clear my throat, busying my hands by flipping pages in my notebook.

"I, uh, well, you know, I had to show Mia the plan for tonight's service." I gesture wildly at the schedule Chelsea and I mapped out the day before.

"Uh-huh. Totally what it looked like." Her eyes dart between the two of us and land on Mia. "So, then, Mia, what did you think of our plan?"

To her credit, Mia seems to have gathered her composure rather quickly. She sits up straight in her chair and turns the splayed-out notebook around so it's facing Chelsea.

"As I was telling Preston when you walked in, I'm very impressed by how well thought out everything is for tonight. But what about this part here," she points to the timeline, "where we have almost thirty minutes unaccounted for."

I turn to address Mia. "My mother always liked to get up and take a moment to thank the guests and staff. I thought maybe you'd want some time to do the same before we bring out the first course."

"That's such a good idea! I like that." She places her hand on my knee, and I nearly jump out of my chair, ramming my knee into the table in the process.

"Fuck...ow!"

Chelsea's head flings back with uncontrollable laughter. "You okay there, bud?"

"Yep. Sorry. Just, uh, got a chill and bumped my knee is all."

Chelsea, still stifling laughter, looks between the two of us before shaking her head. Mia still looks like she got caught with her hand in the cookie jar and I'm the very picture of embarrassment, guilt written all over my face. Real subtle, we are. And nothing even happened.

My shoulders drop in relief as I spot Ernie across the room. He looks around, presumably for me to ask for help finishing up a few small tasks before the event. Wasting no time, I push out of my seat and bid both a quick goodbye before walking over to where Ernie stands.

Ernie's beaming with pride as he takes in the transformed dining room before him. I stand next to him, allowing myself to admire my vision for the first time. He places a hand on my shoulder and squeezes.

"You did a good job here, son." I smile and nod my thanks. His smile turns from pride to suspicion. "What's going on with you and Mia?"

I stand up straight, suddenly aware that he suspects me of something, and he may not approve.

"I'm not sure I catch what you mean." I have enough experience with accusations from my father that I ultimately decided feigning ignorance is the best option here. It's not a lie, nothing *has* happened. Yet.

He doesn't buy it for a second as he arches his eyebrows in disbelief at my feeble attempt at deceit. "Now you know I like you, Preston. I can tell you're a good kid with a big heart. But lying is not your strong suit, it would appear. Anyone with eyes can see what was going on with you two over there." He pauses, giving me time to come clean. I keep my mouth shut but give him a knowing nod.

"I just want to see her happy. And since you've arrived, she's been happier than I've seen her in a while. Annoyed, but happy." We share a laugh before he continues. "Still, I'm not oblivious to what the papers say about your dalliances. Now, I'm not one to judge a young man sowing his oats, but Mia isn't a fling, and I don't want you breaking her heart when she already has enough going on right now, you hear me?"

His protectiveness is endearing, and I have to admit, it makes me think. He's not wrong. I've spent my entire youth cycling through women like candy. Sure, I allow my fair share of women into my bed to quell the loneliness, but the majority I've been photographed with were nothing more than a single date arranged by Oliver, for a highly publicized, perfectly curated fake night out. I had an image and my father's team quickly realized having a son who is a cliché is good for business.

I want to ease Ernie's worry and say I would never do anything to hurt to Mia, but if I'm honest, I can't promise that. The truth is, I want her more than I've ever wanted anyone and while I would never intentionally hurt her, I don't exactly have the best track record with relationships. But of course, I can't tell him any of this, so I lie to him as much as to myself.

"Don't worry, Ernie. There's nothing like that happening here. Completely professional." I flash a strained smile and for a second, I almost believe it.

⚒ ⚒ ⚒

Back in my element donning a freshly pressed black Armani suit, I'm ready to work the room. The entire town seems to be in attendance as I take in the packed room before me. I make my way through the crowd, admiring everyone dressed to the nines, as I schmooze and show them to their seats. The general consensus is that they love the decor and are excited to have a proper service this evening. The thought fills me with pride and hope that maybe this will make Mia see me transforming into a man worthy of her attention.

When there's finally a lull, I take a moment to admire the scene before me. My heart fills with warmth as I look around the room, seeing the joy and friendship between the people of this town. Everyone seems to know each other, sharing laughs around the room as our servers expertly weave in and out of the crowd, delivering flutes of champagne and hors d'oeuvres. For a moment, I feel like maybe this forced change was exactly what I needed.

Glancing at my watch, I realize it's time to check in with Chelsea to go over the plan for service and get everyone mic'd up. But as I turn down the hall to the kitchen, I'm frozen in place, utterly stunned by the sight of Mia walking down the cobblestone walkway from the cottage.

She's wearing a form fitting burgundy gown that sweeps along the floor, its scooped neckline low enough to give me the briefest glimpse of her ample cleavage. Her hands, covered in matching gloves that extend to her elbows, hold up her gown in one and a sparkling gold clutch in the other. Her hair falls in delicate waves over her right shoulder, leaving her long neck exposed on one side. The twinkle lights trace her silhouette, wrapping her in an ethereal glow like a goddess I'd gladly get on my knees to worship. My mouth goes dry as she opens the door and greets me with a smile, the scent of jasmine and citrus hitting me like a brick wall.

"You look..." I struggle to find the words, the intensity of her beauty rendering me speechless, "...absolutely breathtaking."

An uncharacteristic shyness has her averting my gaze with a nervous laugh. Her eyes roam over me and I feel heat rise to my face, her timidness vanishing as she lets out a low whistle.

"You don't look so bad yourself, Mr. Spencer. You've been holding out on me if this how you bring it in LA." I roll my eyes with a grin, ignoring the effect hearing her call me "Mr. Spencer" has on me. I offer her my arm to guide her back to the dining room.

We reach the room's entrance, and she stops in her tracks, placing her free hand over her heart, taking in the scene before her. "It looks better than I could have imagined. As much as I hate to say it, you were totally right about rearranging the tables. There's so much more room for everyone to mingle."

I try not to look too smug as I accept the compliment, admiring my work. I hope to get some more time with her, but as soon as she's spotted by eager guests, they descend on us like a swarm. She unhooks her arm from mine and I'm surprised by the sting of its absence. Tossing me an apologetic smile over her shoulder, she allows herself to be whisked away through the crowd.

I'm jolted out of my trance by Chelsea's voice in my earpiece. "Roger, Roger? Can you hear me? Over." I can't help but shake my head and laugh at Chelsea's attempt at trucker speak. Forgetting I meant to check in with her, I sigh in relief. At least she found the mics.

"Go for Preston," I say, keeping up the bit.

"We're ready for service in five minutes. Can you get everyone seated? Over."

"10-4, good buddy. Over and out."

Making my rounds around the room, I guide all our guests to their seats. I catch Mia's glance and nod, giving her the signal to make her way towards the front of the room for her welcome speech.

The chatter hasn't stopped in the room, so when Mia attempts to get everyone's attention, her voice is barely audible. It's then that I remember we set up a wireless mic for this very purpose. Running through the tables, I pick up the mic from behind the bar, switching it on before placing it in her hand. Her gloved hand brushes mine and we both startle at the contact. She clears her throat, and I remove my hand from the mic.

"If I can have your attention for a brief moment." The shake in her voice is nearly imperceptible, but I place a hand on the small of her back in encouragement. My chest tightens at her grateful smile and the room begins to quiet, all attention turned her way, including mine.

"Thank you all for being here tonight. It means so much that you keep showing up year after year for this town. The proceeds from tonight's event are going to the Breast Cancer Federation. With your donations, we can help them make strides to curing this disease." Her eyes glisten with tears as she pauses to allow the applause.

"Tonight, you'll enjoy a symphony of flavors dreamt up by Chef Chelsea Taylor. In a few moments, our waitstaff will begin bringing out the first course, a cranberry-walnut salad drizzled in a sweet, white wine vinaigrette, followed by a butternut squash bisque. For the main course, we have herb crusted turkey with gravy, garlic parmesan mashed potatoes, and roasted Brussel sprouts drizzled with a house made balsamic glaze."

The crowd shares their excitement with a chorale of woos and applause before allowing her to continue.

"Of course, we can't forget the star of the show, dessert! You'll have a choice of pecan or pumpkin pie. And everything is, of course, locally sourced from farms right here in Vermont."

The room erupts in cheers, and I gape at the amazing woman before me, a dopey grin spread across my face. She may shy from the spotlight, but one thing is clear, this town loves her.

"I promise I won't talk too much longer so you can enjoy, but I would be remiss if I didn't thank everyone who helped make tonight happen. To our amazing friends at Tucker's Tool Time and our former handyman, Ernie, for bringing this dining room to life," she pauses for applause.

"To Chelsea and the rest of our impeccable staff for the feast we're about to serve you tonight," she looks at me, placing a hand on my bicep, "and especially to Preston Spencer who has helped out tremendously and is the mastermind behind our new setup and service tonight. Let's give them all a round of applause."

I shoot her a smile before turning to the crowd with a wave and appreciative bow.

"Now, let the feast begin!"

Right on cue, our servers, dressed in white button-down shirts and black slacks, parade out of the kitchen into the dining room and begin delivering the first course. Mia squeezes my hand as we share an excited look, marveling at how the new service is flowing perfectly.

Looking into her eyes, I know I can't keep the promise I made to Ernie earlier. This woman has infiltrated my body, mind, and soul, and I don't know how much longer I can keep these feelings to myself.

Chapter 12

Mia

High off the success of our dinner, I found myself unable to sleep through the night. We raised a little over ten thousand dollars thanks to the town's generosity and most of that was due to Preston's help. He continues to surprise me day after day, shedding his entitled attitude in favor of the sweet, gentleness of the little boy I used to know.

But if I'm being honest, that wasn't the only thing keeping me awake.

Every time I closed my eyes, all I could see was Preston standing before me in his perfectly tailored suit, those hazel eyes burning into mine from across the room. I replayed each time our bodies met, the way his light touch on the small of my back melted away my insecurities and caused a flutter of desire deep in my belly.

I let my mind wander to all of our "almost" moments over the past few days. In the garden, when he brushed my hair out of my face while showing me the Christmas wedding altar he designed. Or each time he would seem to startle at my touch, as if he, too, felt a jolt of electricity. The stunned look on his face when he saw me for the first time last night. And that moment I was sure he was about to kiss me before Chelsea interrupted us. Did I imagine all of this, or is he feeling something too?

Deciding to table those thoughts for now, I focus on today's plan to clear out the remnants of Thanksgiving decor. I gave the staff the day off today, but there's still so much to do before the wedding guests arrive.

I've been in constant contact with their wedding planner, Cecelia, since we agreed to take on the wedding. They're demanding, especially the bride, but I'm confident my staff can rise to the occasion. Still, turning the inn around from Thanksgiving to Christmas will be no small feat.

To my surprise, when I survey the dining room, it looks like the bulk of the Thanksgiving decor had been cleared out last night. I make a mental note to think of a way to thank the staff for their dedication and hard work. Only a few items remain, so it should take me no time at all.

After I've boxed up each of the Thanksgiving centerpieces, I notice a lone scrap of streamer stuck in the corner of the room. With no ladders in sight, I spot a stack of chairs nearby and have the brilliant idea to climb atop those. I kick off my heels and begin my ascent. Once I've stabilized myself somewhat on the top chair, I reach for the streamer which hangs barely out of reach. *If only I had one of those gripper extensions,* I think to myself. My only recourse is to try and stretch my body as long as it will go.

Checking my balance, I extend my right leg to help elongate my body as I rise to the tips of my toes, shifting my weight onto my left foot at the edge of the chair, my tongue pinched in the corner of my mouth, which I somehow believe will increase my concentration. That stretch does the trick and I grasp the scrap in-between my pointer and middle finger, a celebratory shimmy overtaking my body. While I'm considering how I'm going to get down, I hear a familiar voice shouting from across the room.

"Mia! What the hell are you doing?"

I turn slightly, smiling at Preston as he walks towards me. Sudden terror sweeps over me as I feel the stack of chairs begin to wobble. I scramble to right myself, feeling my right ankle twist and throw me off balance. I see Preston's eyes go wide as he sprints towards me just as I begin to fall. I close my eyes, bracing for the hard impact of the floor, except that impact never comes. Instead, I find myself cradled in Preston's muscular arms. He's somehow made it over to me in time and I can't help the dreamy smile that spreads across my face as my eyes meet his.

"My hero," I say as if I'm a swooning damsel and he's my shining knight.

He huffs out an exasperated sigh, rolling his eyes in my direction."That was quite possibly the dumbest thing I've ever seen you do."

He starts to gently place me back on my feet but stops as I yelp like a wounded dog. Pain shoots up from my right ankle through my thigh, so intense I have to grit my teeth to bite back tears. Preston grips me around my waist, shifting my weight back onto him and I sigh in relief.

"Can you stand on your own?"

I shake my head no, the tears threatening to spill now, more out of frustration than pain. Placing my hands around his neck and gripping me under my knees, he scoops me up and carries me to my office, gently setting me down atop my desk. He's in crisis management mode and I have to admit, it's kinda hot.

"Where is your first aid kit?" I point to the cabinet behind him and he turns to rummage through until he finds the kit. He holds up a rolled up athletic bandage in triumph before pulling up a chair in front of me. With the barest touch, he grabs my injured ankle and situates my foot on his chest. He pauses and looks up to me with an uncharacteristic shyness, pink creeping up on his cheeks.

"Um...we should wrap this."

"Do what you have to do, I trust you."

He clears his throat and averts his eyes. "I, um, need you to, uh, remove your tights. I'll just..." He points at the corner before turning around to give me some privacy. Unable to stand, I shift my weight back and forth between each side as I shimmy the tights down my legs. I picked a hell of a day to wear a skirt and tights.

"Um, you can turn around now."

As he turns to face me, his eyes slowly follow the length of my leg, from my ruby red painted toes up to my now bare thighs before meeting my eyes with a tight smile, his hazel eyes uncharacteristically dark. He reclaims his place in the chair, this time slowly caressing my calf before cradling my injured ankle in between his hands. The feel of his soft, warm hands on my bare skin sends a shiver down my entire body. I suck in a breath I hope he mistakes for pain rather than a sign of the unmistakable lust taking over my body.

"Sorry." He stops wrapping and gently sets my leg down as he stands to grab a bottle of water from my mini fridge and empty a few pills in his hand. "It looks like a sprain. I used to play basketball in high school, so I've had my fair share of these. Here, take these for the pain." He drops two aspirin in my hand, passing me the bottle of water before returning to finish wrapping my ankle.

He's gentle and firm all at once, which leaves my mind to wander, imagining how else he might touch me with the same gentle firmness. He secures the wrap and runs his hand up my calf as he sets it out of his lap. I exhale a shaky breath as I realize for the past few minutes, I've been holding it, afraid the slightest movement would release me from his touch.

He stands and clears his throat. "Is it okay if I pick you up again? I'm going to take you back to bed so you can rest." I don't trust my voice, so I offer an affirming nod instead. His face is inches from mine as he bends down and gently places my arm behind his neck before scooping me up again, the feel of his hands on my bare skin setting my body aflame.

The walk back to the cottage feels like miles as we exist in silence. "Couch or bed?" he asks as we enter the cottage and my brain temporarily glitches out before realizing he's asking me where he should take me, not where he should *take* me.

"Couch is good."

He sets me down gently, piling pillows under my ankle. "I'm going to grab an ice pack and make you some tea. You'll need to keep it elevated and stay off it for as long as possible."

I sit up straighter, panic taking over at the thought of being out of commission right before the biggest wedding we've ever hosted. "You're joking, right? I can't just sit here while there are preparations to be made for the wedding that is in two days!"

"Relax. Remember what I said about letting people help you? Chelsea and I got this. Plus, there's not a lot left to do that you can't do from right here. We'll keep you updated on everything, I swear," he pauses for emphasis, shooting me a stern look, "*you* need to rest and let yourself heal, understand me?"

I huff, crossing my arms over my chest to pout, but having little choice, I reluctantly agree to his terms.

"Fine. But can you bring me my laptop so I can at least work on finalizing the itinerary?"

The whistle of the kettle turns his attention back to making me a cup of tea. He brings me a piping hot mug of lavender tea, with honey, before repositioning my leg to allow the ice pack to rest around my ankle.

"Trust me, Mia. I'll make sure everything is taken care of for the wedding." He caresses his hand along my head and bends down to kiss me on the forehead, as if this was something we do all the time. "Call me if you need anything," he says as I sit there stunned, feeling the ghost of his lips on my skin.

⚒ ⚒ ⚒

Laughter from the TV jolts me out of the nap I must have fallen into, and it takes me a moment to reorient myself. I briefly wonder if I imagined the care with which Preston handled me. The forehead kiss, which was probably innocent, but somehow felt charged with something else. He's been such an amazing help these past few weeks, I wonder how I ever managed without him.

Especially since I don't have my mom's support this year.

She was supposed to come back for the dinner, but Dr. Sydek called a few days earlier, explaining her recent round of treatment had taken a lot of out of her so he preferred to keep her at the hospital until she recovered.

When I spoke to her later that day, I could hear the exhaustion in her voice and while it gutted me that she wouldn't be here, I knew she needed to prioritize her health. Dr. Sydek assured me she was still on track to be here for Christmas, but it didn't make me ache any less at her absence. Having Preston's support helped me focus on that sadness a little less.

Ready to turn my attention back to wedding preparations, I spot my laptop on the table in front of me, a sticky note pressed to the top.

> DON'T WORK TOO HARD. REST, MIA. AND TAKE TWO MORE ASPIRIN WHEN YOU WAKE. — P
> P.S. HOW DOES SOMEONE SO SMALL SNORE SO LOUDLY?

"I don't snore," I mutter to myself.

As I'm putting the final touches on the itinerary, my mom's face pops on the screen, alerting me to an incoming FaceTime call. I smooth back my hair and answer the call.

"Hola, mommy!" My bright smile fades slightly at the sight of her. She looks frail and sallow. Her hair hangs in limp strands, some of which have stuck to her face and the dark circles around her eyes let me know she hasn't slept much. "How are you feeling?"

She waves me off. "Oh I'm alright. This treatment is a

bit tougher than I thought, but I've had a lot of support from the doctors and nurses here. And your calls always make my heart warm." She's slipped back into her native Spanish, which confirms she's really exhausted.

"I love our talks too. Everyone missed you at Thanksgiving, but we raised over ten thousand dollars last night!"

"Oh honey, that's amazing! Was everyone...talking about me?"

"No. Not like that, anyway. They just asked after you and sent well wishes is all. I promise there was no gossip."

"Not even Miss Campbell?" She looks doubtful as she references the town gossip.

"Not even Miss Campbell."

"Impressive. How's that boy you have living in my house?"

I'm rendered momentarily speechless. I had no idea she knew about Preston moving into the cottage. I certainly didn't offer that information. Then it dawns on me exactly who has been keeping her so informed.

"You've been talking to Chelsea!" I accuse.

She lets out a bark of a laugh, which quickly descends into a massive coughing fit. A loud beeping sounds in the background as my mom tries to catch her breath, sipping on a glass of water.

"Mamá? Are you okay? What's going on?" My voice comes out in a panic as I watch two nurses come into the room to check her machines.

"I'm," *cough,* "fine," *cough,* "mija," she says, finally seeming to catch her breath. She mutters an annoyed curse at the nurses who fawn over her as Dr. Sydek enters the room.

"Dr. Sydek?" I shout as he turns his head to the laptop. The corners of his mouth turn upward in a terse smile.

"Miss Flores, I'm afraid we're going to have to cut this call short. Your mother's vitals are fine, but she needs her rest, okay? I'll call you later with an update."

Without giving me a chance to ask any further questions, he shuts the laptop, disconnecting our call. Suddenly I'm sweaty all over, panic rising in my chest making it hard to breathe. What if the treatment isn't working? What if she's getting worse? What if that was the last time I speak to her?

My terror turns into intense sobs as a loud plop echos across the room. I look over to find Preston's eyes full of concern, a large brown bag at his feet, as he crosses the room in two long strides. He doesn't force me to speak, just sits next to me on the couch, pulling me into his arms until I gather my composure.

"It's my mom. She's s-sick," I choke out between sobs.

He squeezes me tight against his chest, running a comforting touch down my back, signaling me to continue. After a few steady breaths, I calm down and snuggle deeper into his embrace.

"A few years ago, she was diagnosed with breast cancer. It was tough, but she fought like hell and eventually went into remission. We were sure she beat it, but last year she started feeling crappy and her cancer was back. Lung cancer this time.

Right before you arrived, she was accepted into a clinical trial that can give her literal years, but it requires her to stay at the hospital for six months. When you walked in, our video call ended abruptly when she had a coughing fit. The doctor assured me she was okay, but s-she looked so sick. Preston, what if—what if that was the last time I got to speak to her?"

Sobs rack my body as I can't get the thought out of my head that something terrible is happening and I'm helpless to do anything.

"Fuck, Mia. I'm so sorry. If anything were seriously wrong, I'm sure the doctor would call, right? What can I do?"

"I don't know. I mean, I just, I need to know she's okay, you know? I've been so busy; I haven't been able to break away to visit her and she's been there for weeks. The hospital is about an hour away and now with my stupid ankle, I can't even drive."

He nods, a plan seeming to form in his head. "Well, what about this—Chelsea and the team have the wedding prep covered. Let's take the day and drive up to see her. Would that help?"

The sobs return as I consider his offer, overwhelmed by his kindness. On the one hand, despite his confidence that everything is under control, with me out with my injury, stealing Preston away before the wedding as well seems selfish. On the other, I know if I could just see her in person and know that she's truly okay, I would feel much better.

I realize I'm still snuggled deep in his embrace, covering his shirt in tears. I nod against his chest, hoping he understands.

"Yeah? You'll go?"

I nod more firmly, and he rests his head on mine, squeezing me a little tighter.

"I brought food, it's probably smooshed now, but I'm sure it's still good. I'll let Chelsea know the plan and make sure she's prepared to handle the remainder of the preparations." He exits our embrace to bring over the bag of food, setting it near me on the couch. "Eat up and get some rest. We'll head out tomorrow at nine."

He bends down, placing another quick kiss to my forehead before disappearing through the door. I sink back into the couch trying to process everything that just happened. I'm excited to see my mom, of course, and more than a little nervous about Preston being there. I'm sure he won't recognize her any more than he recognized me, but even the slim chance has me on edge. I want to be the one to tell him my true identity so I can explain why I hid it from him.

Then there's the tenderness and care he's displayed for me over the past few days. The forehead kisses. The comforting caresses down my back. The easy way I fit into his arms. It's all leading me to one, unavoidable conclusion: I might actually *like* Preston Spencer. A lot.

Chapter 13

Preston

I slept like absolute shit last night. Between stressing about leaving Chelsea with virtually no help and the fact I offered to drive Mia fifty miles outside of town despite my lack of recent driving experience, my brain kept going over everything that could possibly go wrong.

I may have oversold how prepared we were to Mia, but I could tell how badly she needed to see her mother and there was no way she would agree to go if she thought it would put the inn at risk. But the pain in her eyes when she told me about her mom spurred me into action and I realized there's nothing I wouldn't do to remove every ounce of pain she felt. And, holy shit, how I did not have time to unpack *that* feeling.

Every day I spend here, I feel more of my old self chipping away as if I might become the man Mia sees in me. I find myself going out of my way to make her smile, searching every room for her presence just to feel her eyes on mine. I'm going out of my mind with the overwhelming urge to claim that kiss I so desperately wanted to take before Chelsea interrupted us. I could use the advice of my best friend right now, but as I pull my phone from my pocket to call Alexi, I remember my service is still cut off. I guess I'll have to figure this one out on my own.

After a quick shower, I head into the living room, finding Mia sitting in the chair by the window, nibbling on her nails, her left leg shaking anxiously.

"Ready to go?"

She nods as I extend a hand to help her up. My chest tightens with worry at the dark circles under her eyes that let me know she, too, had a restless night's sleep.

With a minor struggle getting her safely into her tiny cobalt blue Mini Cooper, we're ready to get on the road. Mia hasn't said much this morning, opting to stare out the window, continuing to chew on her nails instead.

"Should we try some music, or...?" I try to fill the silence, but she only shakes her head, returning her gaze back out her window. "I brought snacks, if you're hungry. And there's coffee. The purple one's yours."

"Thanks." Her voice comes out little more than a whisper.

"Hey. It's going to be okay." I grab the hand that rests on her thigh, squeezing it for comfort.

She offers an unconvincing smile in response, so I decide it's better to leave her to her thoughts. I know what she must feel like with the constant worry whether her mother is going to succumb to the disease tearing through her body, but I don't know the best way to offer comfort. I was only a kid when it happened to me, my father nowhere to be found, leaving me to bury my feelings alone.

We arrive at the hospital in about an hour, but even the long drive did nothing to quell Mia's nerves. She lets out a deep sigh as I come around the car to help her out, placing her crutches in her hand. She stands there, staring at the hospital for a moment, body tense and unmoving.

"Everything...okay?" I ask.

"I-I'm just...scared." Her voice trembles and I can see the tears welling up in her eyes as I notice her knuckles are white from grasping her crutches so hard.

Bending down in front of her to meet her eyes, I place my hands on her shoulders. "I know it's scary, learning your parents aren't invincible. But, Mia, your mother is getting the best possible care and she'll be so happy to see you. I'm here if anything gets to be too much. I got you, always."

It takes a moment, but she finally inhales a shaky breath, giving me a nod as we make our way into the facility.

When we get to her mother's room, it's not what I expected. I braced myself to see her hooked up to machines, tubes connected to her frail body, much like my mother in her final days. Instead, it's more like a tiny dorm room with a bed, couch, TV, and its own en suite bathroom. I notice the tension ease from Mia's body as she sees her mother dancing about, a smile plastered on her face. I notice then how much Mia looks like her mom. That must be why she looks so familiar.

"Oh, mi amor! I'm so glad to see you!" Her mother rushes over, placing her hands on either side of Mia's face before pulling her into a tight embrace. They begin speaking rapidly in Spanish. Even though I'm half Dominican, I don't understand much, but the love and joy emanating from them both is impossible to miss.

"And you must be the man who is currently staying in

my house, *alone,* with mi hija, eh?" She looks over to me with a glare as Mia flashes me an apologetic look over her shoulder.

"Um, y-yes, Mrs. Flores. I'm Preston." The words come out with an uncharacteristic nervousness as I timidly extend my hand to her in greeting.

She looks me up and down, unsure what to think of me. I'm desperate for her approval, knowing how important it will be to Mia if I ever hope to have something more with her.

"Mhm. You may call me Paola. Well, get over here then. Ven acá," she beckons me into a quick hug, turning to Mia when she exits our embrace.

"Cariño, why don't you go you fetch us something to eat, sí? I think Preston and I have some things to discuss."

Mia nods, offering me a sympathetic smile as she exits the room, leaving me alone with her mother who's still looking at me with slight distrust. She extends her hand to the couch, bidding me to take a seat next to her.

"So. How *did* you come to find yourself living alone with my daughter?"

"My father owns the inn, sort of. We're having a bit of a...situation and can't hire help for the repairs needed at the inn right now, so he sent me instead. Unfortunately, my original room experienced an electrical issue, and Mia was kind enough to offer up her guest room until it's finished."

"Hm. I suppose that's reasonable. As long as you *stay in your own room,*" she says, placing an emphasis on the last words.

"Oh, of course, Mrs—I mean, Paola. I-we-I mean, yes.

We're in separate rooms. I would never—we're not—we're just colleagues. Friends, even."

She scoffs, shaking her head with a doubtful laugh. "But you care for her *more* than simple friends or colleagues, yes?"

I'm caught off guard by the forwardness of her question and am unsure how to answer. We've had so many almosts that I cannot deny something's happening between us. And I certainly cannot deny the way my heart threatens to jump out of my chest when she glances my way. But am I ready to admit that to her mother? To myself?

"I've become quite fond of your daughter. She challenges me. Pushes me to be a better man," I look down at my hands, fidgeting nervously, "I'm not sure if you pay attention to the papers, but they haven't been historically kind to me. Frankly, I haven't done much to earn anything different. But I promise you, I would *never* do anything to hurt Mia. She's become...important to me."

"I see." She pauses for a moment, taking one of my hands in between hers, "She's not as strong as she seems. Leaving, even to fight for more time with her, has been hard on her. Knowing that I might not come back, that she might be left alone, well, that has been unbearable. I need to know she'll be okay. I can tell you care for my daughter, so I need you to promise me you will take care of her when I cannot."

The weight of what she's asking is not lost on me. "I understand, more than you realize. My mother passed from cancer when I was young. The difference is, I had no one. I will not let Mia go through this alone, if it comes to that. Trust me when I say I will do anything to ensure your daughter is well taken care of."

She squeezes my hand with a smile, her eyes glistening with emotion. "I am sorry you had to go through that. I am not giving up so easily, but if the universe has other plans for me, I'm glad she has you. She's stubborn, but I see how she looks at you. If you can get her to drop her walls, I think you two could be very happy."

"Sorry, mamá, this is all they had from the vending machine." Before I can respond, Mia interrupts us, holding out a few sandwiches wrapped in plastic, her nose scrunched up in disgust.

I nod to Paola, understanding passing between us, reminding us both of the promise I made, and intend to keep, whatever the cost. "I'll leave you two to catch up," I say as I exit the room.

Stepping out to give Mia some time to visit with her mother alone, I shoot off a few emails to Duane and Natalia, our head of PR, requesting additional security and a press release for the wedding. The WiFi's a bit slow, but I managed to get everything arranged before heading back in.

A few hours pass as we chat and eat dinner together—I trashed the stale vending machine sandwiches in favor of grabbing take out from a diner up the road. By the time we arrive back at the inn, it's late and Mia's happy, but exhausted. I catch her pained look as she attempts to hobble out of the car alone.

"Oh, no you don't," I say sternly as I come around the car to lift her into my arms.

"Preston! What are you doing?"

"I'm carrying you. You've had a long day, and you need

to rest your ankle." She opens her mouth to protest, but I cut her off, sweeping her into my arms in one swift motion. "Deal with it."

She huffs, folding her arms across her chest in resignation. I can't help the smile that spreads across my face at the sight.

I set her down gently in her bedroom suddenly nervous at the thought being alone with her here for the first time.

"I'll leave you to get some rest," I say awkwardly as I turn to exit the room.

She grasps my wrist, pulling me back towards her, her brown eyes filled with what I hope are grateful tears.

"Preston, you don't know how much I appreciate what you did for me today. I don't have the words." She shakes her head, reigning in her emotions.

I place a hand to her cheek, unable to quiet the urge to feel her skin on mine. "You're important to me. I meant it when I said you can count on me for anything you need."

We stand in silence, the only sound our heavy breathing, our eyes locked on each other for what seems like hours. Every nerve in my body is screaming to pull her close and press my lips to hers. But she's had a tough day, and her emotions are all over the place. It wouldn't be right to take advantage of her vulnerability, so instead, I settle for another forehead kiss, my lips lingering on her soft skin for a moment longer than necessary.

"Goodnight, Mia." I make a swift exit before I can do anything stupid. Because one thing is completely clear after today. I would do anything to protect this woman, *be* anything she needs and I'm in far too deep to stay away much longer.

❅ ❅ ❅

Duane arrives early the next day with a team of seven black clad, burley security guards, as promised. Just in time, too, as a steady stream of onlookers and paps have arrived. Natalia emailed over the final press release, my only job to get a few signatures for the photos.

Once I'm confident security is taken care of, I decide to wait by reception to greet the wedding party and ensure they're all checked in. I still don't know precisely *who* they are, but I know low level celebs and how much they appreciate opulence, so I've prepared flutes of champagne to hand them as they make their way to their rooms.

Predictably, the guests all seem to know exactly who I am. I shake hands and make nice with them all, only receiving a few snarky comments from people regarding the company. I don't recognize a single one of them, but nod as if I can recall a party we've attended or an event where we've crossed paths. A limo pulls up and judging by the cheers outside, the bride and groom have finally arrived.

Turning my attention to the door, the fake smile I've plastered on my face for the last thirty minutes drops into a look of utter disbelief. I'd know those long legs and fire red hair anywhere.

"Preston?" Sadie Perkins stands in front of me squealing with excitement as if she didn't lie and manipulate herself into a relationship with me and run out the second she found out I wanted to give up this life, along with the money that came with it.

It's been two years since she ended our engagement on a whim at a New Year's Eve Party.

"*Preston, look. It's been fun and all, but I can't marry a* philanthropist."

I remember the way she spat out the word. *Philanthropist*. As if someone poured piss in her champagne after I confessed I was resigning my position at the firm to focus on raising money for cancer research. It irrevocably messed me up and I haven't seriously dated anyone since.

Dropping her bags in the foyer, she runs towards me and before I have time to react, she's thrown her arms around my neck for a long hug. Unable to move, I simply stand there, eventually clasping my hands around her arms, pushing her away from me. She steps away, hands still on my arms, looking at me with appraisal.

"What on *earth* are you doing here?"

"This is my inn, Sadie. I told you about it millions of times." The words come out sharp and devoid of emotion. Judging by the look on her face, she did not, in fact, remember any of those conversations. True to form, refusing to admit she's wrong, she scrunches up her nose and waves off my comment.

"Hm. I don't think you did. But you know how you always were bragging about your assets; how could I keep them all straight? Anyway, I didn't think you owned anything anymore what with your father's little," she looks around before leaning in with a whisper, her hand concealing her mouth from view, "IRS problem." She winks as if we are sharing some cute secret rather than talking about my family's giant scandal.

"No. *I* own this one and am overseeing operations while he and his lawyers address the mess *his accountant* got us into. Are you here for the wedding?"

She cackles and lightly pushes my shoulder. "Well, I should hope so! I'm the bride, silly."

The bride. This is her wedding. As I stand there searching for the right response, my stomach churns as the man I instantly know is the groom approaches. He looks exactly how I remember from college. His signature slicked back black hair, closely trimmed beard, and mismatched blend of haute and unkempt making him seem unattainable, yet relatable.

He places his hand on the small of her back and bends down for a kiss bordering on indecent for public view. Pulling back, he stares at her with adoration. "My love." Everett Townsend, my former best friend, is marrying *my* ex at *my* inn.

Everett and I met during freshman rush at UCLA. We bonded over the fact we both had shitty dads with deep pockets and all we wanted to do was get out of their shadow. We were virtually inseparable all four years, even after he found moderate fame during a very unsuccessful run on *The Bachelor*. After he was booted from the show in an unprecedented move that cut the season short, I got him a job at my father's company. Until I severed ties when he sold my father out to a competitor, massively undercutting us in a Dubai acquisition that would have been a game changer for our portfolio. All right around the time Sadie dumped me.

"Preston! My guy!" He spreads his arms wide before enveloping me in the bro-iest of bro hugs I've had in at least a decade. "How ya been, man? I guess not so good if the papers are to be believed." He has the nerve to wink at me.

I push out of his grip, a tight smile on my face. "You

more than anyone should know how wrong the papers can be. I mean, if everything they wrote is to be believed, the girls on that show found your goods a bit less than impressive." I bite back before turning to leave.

I storm down the hall to the kitchen in search of a drink. The idea of catering to these two for the next few days is going to be more than I can bear. I'm ready to go off and tell them to get the fuck out when I remember how that would affect Mia.

She's counting on the money from this wedding to keep their books in the black no matter what happens with my father's company. I promised Paola I would make sure her daughter's taken care of and I intend to keep that promise. No, I can't let my need for revenge ruin Mia's life too.

Before reaching the kitchen, I feel the lightest tap at my elbow. I turn and find myself face to face with Sadie. Her porcelain skin is flawless, even in the dim of the hallway.

Two years ago, all I ever dreamed of was seeing her again. Staring into those deep green eyes, inhaling her sweet smell, strawberries with the barest hint of vanilla, but today I look into those eyes and feel nothing. No more desire. Not even anger.

"Preston, I'm so sorry. We had no idea you were going to be here." For a moment, I almost believe the sincerity in her voice, the guilt in her eyes. "You really didn't know?"

"No. I didn't. Like I said, I'm just here temporarily. I had nothing to do with this wedding."

"Oh." She almost sounds dejected. A terrible thought rushes through my brain. Did she choose this location on purpose? I have no idea how she would have known I was here, but it would be just like her to pull some shit like this to rub her perfect life in my face.

"I promise we also didn't know. I would never do that to you."

I don't miss the hint of glee in her eyes, leaving little doubt to how much she's enjoying this. Being the source of drama always was Sadie's speciality. Still, I need to be cordial, if only for Mia's sake.

"It's fine, Sadie. I'm mature enough to handle this professionally."

It occurs to me that whatever is happening between me and Mia could be derailed if she ever found out about me and Sadie. I need Sadie's help with this, whether I like it or not. "And, look, there's no reason anyone here needs to know our history, right?"

She considers for a moment, my breath tight in my chest as I await her response. "Sure. I can keep a secret." She caresses my bicep and flashes a wink that seems more salacious than necessary.

"Thanks. Now, if you'll excuse me, I need to attend to the final details for the wedding. Oh, and if you and Everett could meet me in the dining room in three hours, we'll meet with the head chef to go over the menu and dinner service." I bid her adieu with a strained smile as I turn on my heels and head back to Mia's office.

Chapter 14

Mia

Preston has confined me to the cottage since we came back from visiting my mom, so I've had far too much time to think about *everything*. The way he held me when I was at my lowest and how he somehow *knew* what I needed even before I did. When he carried me to my room, I thought he was going to *finally* kiss me, but he only allowed his lips to brush against my forehead. Again.

There's no denying my feelings are growing for him and the guilt that comes with leaving this lie looming over our heads is heavier than ever. Especially after seeing how easily he got along with Mom and how protective he's been of both my injury and my heart. Without him, I don't know how I would have made it through these past few days.

Tonight's the wedding and it's the biggest event I've hosted on my own. Preston and Chelsea have assured me everything is under complete control and judging by the additional security around the inn, plus the press release I read this morning, I truly believe them.

But my ankle is feeling much better now. It's not swollen, and I can put my full weight on it. Well, almost. Our town doctor, Dr. Kim, stopped by yesterday and she isn't worried that it's anything serious. So today is the day I will be back, no matter what "doctor" Preston has to say about it.

The inn's at 100% capacity now after the bride added some last-minute guests and decided she preferred complete privacy. To clear out the inn, the couple paid a premium, which means I'll be able to pay back all the contractors and even have some left over to maybe get Chelsea a new stove. As long as nothing goes wrong, this wedding is going to keep us flush with cash through January.

I'm all smiles as I sit at the kitchen table with a mug of coffee going over the final itinerary. Chelsea and Preston have thought over every detail and I'm not sure I could have done better myself. With every preparation thought of, I lean back in my chair and gaze out at the morning sun.

I have a perfect view outside our bay window of the garden's elegant display of Christmas cheer. Warmth envelops me like a hug when I think of how this romantic setting was born from Preston's mind. I close my hands around my mug and dream about what it would be like to have a man like Preston planning elaborate events like this for me. But I can't imagine that, not now. Not when I'm still keeping this huge secret from him.

Once it's quiet, I'll talk to Preston. I spent last night tossing and turning thinking of exactly how I will tell him, and I've decided it's best to rip it off like a band aid. "Preston. It's me. Amelia," I'll say.

And he'll either flash me a wide grin, embracing his

childhood best friend, or his gaze will turn to hatred, eyes burning into mine, before he storms off never to be seen again.

No pressure.

I set down the paper and lean back with a sigh, shoving the last bit of my breakfast into my mouth. Preston got in late last night, working on the finishing touches no doubt, so I figured the least I could do is have breakfast waiting for him.

The sunrise is in full bloom now, turning the sky a beautiful mix of tangerine and violet. It must be nearing six a.m. and Preston is still nowhere in sight. We need to be at the inn by seven, so it's weird that he's not awake yet. I decide to take matters into my own hands and hobble over to his room. Only, he's not there. His bed is made so either he's up much earlier than me or he never came home.

I get ready for the day and head over to the inn, hoping to find Preston there. It's the furthest I've walked since my tumble, and while I'm still in a little pain, it's not as bad as it used to be.

Sure enough, Preston is in the kitchen sharing a coffee and laughing with Chelsea.

"Wow you're both here early!"

"Girl, please. I've been here since 3:30 getting breakfast ready! Preston came in about an hour ago to help set up the dining room and even helped prep the buffet. We're like a well-oiled machine!" Chelsea boasts, giggling as she and Preston conduct an elaborate, and *extremely* dorky, handshake, which concludes with a hip bump, finger guns, and an "ehhhh" a la The Fonz. I roll my eyes and move to pour myself a cup of coffee.

I'm a little hurt that they don't need my help, and Preston must see it on my face.

"But we're so grateful to have you back. How's the ankle?" He smiles, intercepting my quest for coffee with a piping hot mug of my own. He must have poured it when he saw me coming.

I stick out my leg triumphantly, hiking up my pants, and moving my ankle in a circle for emphasis. "The swelling is almost completely gone!"

He leans close and grabs my chin, tilting it up to him to make sure I'm listening. "Glad to see it. But don't over do it, okay? We've got your back whenever you need to take a seat."

He holds my face in his hand for longer than necessary, staring into my eyes until I nod in agreement. A shiver travels the length of my body, and I can feel the heat rising to my cheeks...and somewhere else much lower. I can't help but wonder where this would go if we were alone. Which we both seem to realize we are not at that very moment.

He lets go of my chin and clears his throat, stepping back awkwardly. I plaster a goofy smile on my face and envelop them both in a quick, very platonic group hug. "You guys are the best."

Preston exits the embrace first. "Well I better go make the rounds to the wedding party rooms and make sure they're ready for breakfast. Chels, can you get me some coffee mugs, a carafe, and a few pastries?"

I help Chelsea build a basket of breakfast goodies, purposefully avoiding eye contact. The second Preston's out of the kitchen, she grabs my shoulders, shaking me with excitement as a high-pitched squeal escapes her mouth.

"Ohmygod, ohmygod, Ohmygod! Something's going on with you two! That steam could power a boat!" She mocks a swoon, fanning her face with her extended palm.

I roll my eyes. "Nothing is going on between us."

She laughs and points at my face, "You can't fool me, Amelia Inés Flores! That grin on your face tells me everything."

"What grin?" I try, and fail, to wipe the grin from my face. "I promise, nothing has happened. I'm merely appreciative of how he's been helping with the inn and nursing me back to health. And..."

"AAAAAND???"

"He may have driven me up to see my mom yesterday."

She squeals again, her feet alternating back and forth in a little dance. "I *knew* he was planning something when he told me he needed the day off. Now hurry up and close the deal already. You know I'm not a fan of slow burns. Right, Jeremy?"

"Yes, Chef!" her sous chef, Jeremy, asserts without missing a beat.

"Does he even know what he just agreed to?" I ask.

Chelsea laughs. "Nope. I inspire unwavering loyalty in this kitchen."

"Well, we're just friends. *Good* friends."

"Uh-huh. Sure." She rolls her eyes with a grin and turns back to her cooking station as I head out to meet with Cecelia to make sure we keep everything on schedule.

⚒ ⚒ ⚒

THE CEREMONY WAS BEAUTIFUL AND WENT OFF without a hitch. Between Preston and Cecelia, our staff executed the entire thing with military precision. Even the paparazzi behaved themselves and stayed firmly behind the barrier. Though, that was probably more of a testament to Duane and his team than their restraint.

Everyone has filtered into the dining room for the reception when I spot Preston across the room schmoozing with the father of the bride. It's not the first time I've seen him in his formal wear, but today he's in a tux with a violet blazer that's been tailored to perfection. The curves of his biceps flex each time he brings his drink to his mouth, full lips wrapping around its edges, his tongue darting into the glass, causing my mind to wonder what other things he might do with those lips and that tongue.

A gentle hand on my shoulder jolts me out of my very not safe for work daydream. It's the bride, her eyes taking in her happy guests filling the room before her.

"Ellen, I cannot thank you enough for everything you've done. I know this was last minute, but you've done so much with this quaint little inn. It's not what we had planned, but at least it's not as simple as I expected." She smiles at me with oblivious sincerity, and I struggle to bite back my offense at her calling me Ellen, which doesn't sound remotely like Mia, I might add. It reminds me of Preston and his inability to remember anyone's name. Must be a rich person thing.

I mentally chide myself, a reminder that not only is she paying me an obscene amount of money, she also didn't meet with me directly due to Cecelia's involvement and my injury.

"It's Mia, actually. We are so happy to have you here."

"Oops! Sorry, *Mia*. I could have sworn your name was Ellen. Anyway, I bet your little inn never sees this many celebrities here. Don't worry—I'll make sure everyone tags you. Wait does your little inn even have Instagram?"

Her voice, thick with vocal fry, grates on my nerves the more she talks. But I have to be nice, so I suck it up and fake a laugh.

"Of course. I'll make sure to include it on your checkout paperwork."

"How cute! Thank you. So, spill," she nudges me with her elbow, "what's it like having the great *Preston Spencer* around?"

Protectiveness, and a hint of jealousy, floods my body at the way she says his name, as though she's intimately familiar with him.

"Well, he's been instrumental in getting this event planned and executed. He did something similar two days ago for our annual Thanksgiving dinner which raised over ten thousand dollars for breast cancer research. Truth be told, I don't know what we'd do without him. We're lucky to have his support."

She scrunches up her face in disgust. "Ew. He's still wasting his time on charity? Ugh. You know, he could be so much richer if he'd stop worrying about poor people. I was supposed to be marrying him, you know? I mean, I'm *sooooo* happy with Everett, of course. And I couldn't marry Preston when he was about to give up his fortune, you know what I mean? He sure is hot though and *amazing* in bed, but I'm sure you know that." She looks at me pointedly, as if trying to force a confession out of me.

I can't hide my surprise at her words. My eyes drift to him, still talking to her father, his would-be father-in-law, and I can't help but imagine him as Sadie's groom. They certainly fit better than he and I ever could.

Sadie follows my gaze and smiles with smug satisfaction, as if she's uncovered some big secret. "No, I wouldn't know, actually," I say, still unable to tear my eyes away from where Preston stands across the room.

"Huh. I figured you're the prettiest one around here so he wouldn't waste any time finding his way into your bed. Good for yo—oh, shit!" she interrupts herself as she watches Everett walking directly towards Preston, an antagonistic look on his face. "I better go before world war three erupts at my wedding." She hikes up her dress and shuffles over to intercept Everett.

I stand in shock at the new knowledge. I had no idea Preston was engaged, let alone to the bride of our wedding party. I'm a little hurt that he didn't tell me when we've shared so much over the past few weeks, but then again, who am I to talk?

His eyes meet mine, laced with concern as he notices my pained look. I break eye contact and busy myself with other guests, hoping my practiced smile isn't transparent. After a few moments of mingling with various groups, I chance a glance back to where he was standing, but he's gone. I excuse myself from the banal conversation of this season's most coveted handbags and make my way to the solace of my office.

As I round the corner to the hallway, I see Preston and Sadie standing scandalously close for a woman who just married another man. I only see the back of his head, but

Sadie's face is clear and she's definitely enjoying this conversation, whatever it is.

I can't make out what they're saying as I try to hide myself behind a potted ficus, but I hear her loud, flirtatious giggle. She caresses his arm from his wrist up to his bicep and tilts her head up to his, closing the gap between their bodies.

She's going to kiss him!

I'm so startled, I step back on my bad ankle, a muffled, pained yelp escaping my mouth as I stumble into the ficus, knocking it to the ground.

Preston's head whips in my direction, pushing her away from him with both hands. With both of their faces now trained on me and the mess I've made, my face scrunches up in anger at what I just saw. I ignore the throbbing pain in my ankle as I limp towards my office, hearing his voice calling my name as I slam the door behind me.

How could he do this to me?! I mean, okay, it's not like he owes me anything. He can fuck whomever he wants, but she's *married*. I'm not delusional enough to think that when that's the type of high-class woman that he's used to he would slum it with someone like me, but I never thought him to be someone who would cheat. Maybe I don't know him after all.

A banging on my door rips me out of my angry internal monologue. "Mia, let me in," Preston yells from the other side of the door. "Come on, it's not—let me in, okay?"

I hear him snarl, "Get the *fuck* off me and leave me alone, Sadie. Go be with your *husband*." He tries the doorknob, which only rattles, and for once I'm thankful for the broken lock that sometimes clicks on its own.

"Mia, come on. Please," he begs, the last word a deflated plea.

With a reluctant sigh, I move to unlock the door and let him in. I glare at him and turn towards my desk, waiting for him to follow.

"Mia, I promise you that's not what it looked like. *She* was coming on to *me*. I have no idea why."

The blatant lie releases the anger that had been bubbling to the surface at the sight of them together and I unleash. "Oh, you have *no idea* why your *ex fiancée* would be coming on to you? Seriously?"

His face contorts in guilt before turning to anger. "Wait, you *knew*?!"

"I'm sorry," I scoff, "but I know you're not actually angry with me for finding out shit *you* hid from *me* right now."

"Yeah, you know what? I am. You knew and you didn't say anything. Lying and manipulating the situation, just like her. You let me walk on eggshells all night trying to make sure no one told you who she is to me. Who she *was* to me. It's been over for years."

"*Lying and manipulating?* That's a stretch. I only found out seconds before I caught you almost fucking the bride! You realize how much this could damage the inn's reputation, right? Or do you not even care?"

"First of all, we were just talking. No one is fucking anyone, Mia. Second of all, have I not shown you how much I care about this inn?" His words stutter as if he were about to say something else but corrected himself at the last second.

I scoff, stepping back to lean on my desk, giving my throbbing ankle a much-needed reprieve and cross my arms with a scowl. "I know what I saw, Preston. And she was bragging to me earlier about what a good lay you are, so I guess...you know, do whatever you want, but not at the expense of the inn's reputation."

Throwing up his arms in frustration, he growls his anger. "*I don't want to fuck her.* I want nothing to do with her. Our entire relationship was built on lies, Mia. I *loathe* that woman. Do you know she dumped me as soon as she found out I didn't want the money and power? That I'd rather spend my time doing something *good*? That I wanted to be something more than another rich asshole like my father?" He runs a hand down the length of his face with a humorless laugh.

"You know, she orchestrated everything between us from staging a 'chance' meeting to getting me to propose. Everything about us was a lie. If you think I'd ever let someone like that in my life again, a *liar*, you don't know me at all."

A liar. Just like me. I look down, guiltily, as I realize maybe I am as bad as her. He steps closer, balling his fists at his side in frustration.

"She followed *me* into the hallway. *She* came on to *me*. I don't want her. I want..."

"What, Preston? Do you even know what you want? I mean, one day you can't stand me and the next you're being so incredibly sweet, taking me up to see my mom. Then you almost kiss me and now you're trying to make out with your ex. I'm getting whiplash trying to figure out what you want!"

Before I realize what's happening, he shuts the door and closes the gap between us, one large hand twining itself through my hair, resting behind my ear, while the other cradles my back, pressing my body to his.

"You, Mia. I fucking want *you*."

His lips crash onto mine with the desperation of a starved man. He's not gentle with me as he pushes his tongue into my mouth, dancing with mine in a perfect give and take, my body melting into his, giving in to his every demand.

Deepening our kiss, I sink my fingers into his hair and pull his head closer to mine as I try to close every bit of space between us. I know this is wrong. That I should tell him the truth and stop this before we go any further. But the way his hard body feels pressed against mine, realizing every desire I've had these past few weeks, all the good sense I had a moment ago evaporates.

He trails kisses along my jaw, down my neck as he pulls the strap of my gown down, giving him access to plant more kisses on my shoulder, before returning to nuzzle at my neck.

He grabs my face between his hands and stares deep into my eyes. "I've wanted to do this for so long. You fucking consume me, Mia. I think about you every moment of every day. You're in my dreams every night. And, fuck, reality is so much better than I could have imagined."

He claims my mouth again, his kisses hurried and rough as his hands roam the curves of my ass, picking me up and placing me on the desk. His knee slides between my legs, a silent plea to open for him and I feel heat pooling in my center as I grab his hips, pulling him closer to me.

The evidence of his lust presses into the very center of me, the sensation sending need racing through my body. I moan into his mouth, and he answers by granting me the glorious friction of his hardness.

"Mia, I *need* to touch you. Please, can I touch you?" He's nearly undone, pleading with me, driving me crazy at the thought of being the source of his desire.

"Yes," I release the breathy plea before his lips are back on mine, allowing his fingers to run along my soaked panties.

"Fuck. You're already so wet for me," he whispers into my ear before dipping underneath my panties, running his finger along the center of me, coating his fingers in my arousal. He slides two fingers inside, pumping in and out as his thumb moves in gentle circles around my clit. I can't stop myself from bucking my hips into his rhythm, chasing my pleasure.

I'm panting as he works me with his fingers, the filthy words he whispers in my ear driving me absolutely insane. "Your pussy feels like heaven. I need to feel you around my cock. God, Mia, where the fuck have you been all my life?"

I freeze, my body stiffening at his words knowing I'm still lying to him after he *just* told me he'd never let a liar back into his life. I was supposed to tell him I'm Amelia. Instead, I'm on the verge of the best orgasm of my life under false pretenses. He thinks I'm Mia Flores, friendly neighborhood inn wench. Not Amelia Aguilar, former best friend.

Placing a hand to his shoulder, I push him away. "Preston, wait." It comes out little more than a whisper, but he immediately removes his hands from me and steps back, his eyes seeking mine, searching for an answer.

Tears in my eyes, I look at his confused face, hating

myself for letting it get this far. "Preston, I'm so sorry. I can't."

I push myself up from the desk and head towards the door, placing as much distance between us as I can. I'm a coward.

"Mia? Whatever I did, I'm sorry. Don't go, please talk to me."

"I-I can't. I-I have to go," I say as I flee from my office, back to the cottage.

Chapter 15

Preston

Mia leaves me standing in her office, cock rock hard, straining against my zipper, fingers still wet with her arousal, and absolutely fucking dumbfounded. My brain can't even begin to process what just happened. One moment, I felt her pussy clenching around my fingers, begging me for more, and the next she was fleeing the scene as if we'd committed a crime.

My heart's beating out of my chest as my mind wars with itself trying to balance the utter ecstasy of finally touching her with the confusion of what caused her to rip herself away from me so suddenly. I hear a door slam in the distance and move to chase her, presumably back to the cottage.

Confusion stops me in my tracks at the sound of the familiar ringtone I set to alert me when Oliver's calling. I pull my phone out of my pocket, confused at how I'm getting this call when my service is cut.

"Ollie? How is my phone working?"

"Erm, yes, sir, that's partially why I'm calling. Your service has been restored and—"

"Now isn't a great time." My tone comes out more curtly than intended.

"Sorry, sir. I'm afraid this can't wait. They've taken your father into custody."

I sink back onto the desk, panic washing over my body. "What do you mean 'into custody'?"

"Yes, well, evidently, they found some fairly damning paperwork hidden on his office computer during their digital sweep. It seems to suggest he did, in fact, order Winston to embezzle the funds. The authorities have yet been unable to locate Mr. Pickering to refute any of this, so your father has officially been named the primary defendant."

He pauses, more for my benefit than his. I drag my hand down the length of my face in exasperation as my brain wanders to a place I don't really want to dwell—what if it's all true and my father has irrevocably damaged his reputation and this company all for his own greed?

Part of me is sure that he would never stoop that low, but the other part of me, and I'm not sure how large that part is, thinks this sounds exactly like something the ruthless, greedy side of him would do. His image is everything to him and I can't help but worry he would do anything to keep that intact.

I hear Oliver clear his throat on the other end of the call and realize he's waiting for me to react. "What do you need me to do?"

"I'm glad you asked. Before he was arrested, Stanley advised him to transfer full ownership of The Spencer

Group to you. You are, as of now, President and CEO. Because of this, the FBI has agreed to unfreeze our accounts, allowing us to post bail for Mr. Spencer, who will remain on house arrest until his court date a month from now. We'll need you back in LA before then. Three weeks from now, to be exact."

The day after the Christmas pageant. I can't imagine leaving when there's so much to do for the massive New Year's Eve party. But despite everything, how can I abandon my father in his time of need?

Oliver senses my shock and doesn't wait for me to respond before continuing. "You should expect a call from Stanley momentarily. He's advised us to limit your contact with your father until we can clear his name, lest you also be implicated in the process. I'll be in touch. Must go!"

Three tones indicate he's disconnected, and I let my hand drop to my side, clutching my phone for dear life.

President and CEO. The end of the road. Fate coming to collect years before I thought I'd have to deal with it. A million thoughts race through my brain.

Am I ready to handle the livelihood of thousands of employees?

What do I know about running a hotel chain, really?

What about Mia?

Mia. Who ran out as soon as I thought we were finally on the same page about whatever has been brewing between us. Mia, who has poured every ounce of her soul into this inn, caring for it as much as my mother would have. Mia, who I cannot bear to leave. Especially now that we're so close to...something.

I want to go after her, *need* to go after her, but the

sudden vibration I feel in my hand which still grips my phone brings me back to my life's other crisis. I look down to find Stanley's name on my screen like an ominous warning.

"Stanley. What the fuck is happening?"

"So, you know, then? Good." There's not an ounce of worry or concern in his voice as he begins to bark orders at me. "Here's what needs to happen. First of all, you say nothing. Tell no one. No press. No girlfriends. No one is to know you've taken over. My guys are still trying to track down that fucking coward, Pickering, so we can't risk tipping him off.

Second, your father's trial begins in one month. Your presence, and most importantly, display of unwavering support, is nonnegotiable. We'll need you there every day, the very picture of a doting son. Got it?"

"Did he do it?"

He's quiet for longer than I'm comfortable with, leading me to expect the worst. "Your father is a lot of things, but he's not a thief. Winston had free reign and was still making your father a shit ton of money, so no one questioned him. He had every opportunity to pull this off alone and undetected. And I swear to you, Preston, that's what I'm going to prove."

I exhale in relief with renewed hope that the loving man from my childhood still lives somewhere underneath the ruthless businessman he's become.

"Anyway," Stanley continues, "I'll need you to work with Natalia on how we're going to handle any questions from the press. She has a plan to get ahead of the narrative, announcing in due time your ascension to CEO. We're cleared to resume operations, so expect a call from the board. We're going to have to make some tough decisions to figure out which properties we'll have to liquidate to pay back the IRS.

You, of course, have full access to funds now, and Preston, I swear to god, don't fuck this up. That money is not for *you*. It's for the company. Tell me you understand what I'm saying."

Part of me wants to scoff with indignation, but I suppress the urge, realizing my history really doesn't give me much of a leg to stand on. "I understand, Stanley. Money is not mine."

"Good man. Now, I'll leave you with one final reminder—do not talk about anything pertaining to your father, your new position, or the trial with *anyone*."

"Okay, Stanley. I get it."

"And Preston? You can do this. You don't have a choice."

I end the call and sit in the darkness of the office letting it all sink in.

⚒ ⚒ ⚒

I don't see Mia that evening when I'm back at the cottage and by the time I wake up this morning, she's already gone. Despite everything else that happened last night, I'm most concerned with decoding whatever happened between us in her office and figuring out why she ran away and is now avoiding me. I know I wasn't imagining this...thing...between us, whatever it is.

It occurs to me that I have phone service now and can

call Alexi and get his perspective. I notice the thousands of missed texts, most from women I've hooked up with in the past or acquaintances trying to pry information from me about the scandal. When I find my thread with Alexi, I read the series of texts of him trying to get ahold of me.

> **Alexi**
> Bro…pick up. What the fuck is happening?

> **Alexi**
> You good dude? I heard your dad might be going to jail?

> **Alexi**
> Pres, man, I hope you're okay. I saw Natalia today and she said you're holed up in Vermont with no phone. Brutal.

> **Alexi**
> Hey, man. We're heading to fuck around in Patagonia for a few weeks. You probably can't reach me, but text me and let me know you're alive.

Well, fuck. I was really hoping he could help me make sense of what is going on in my head right now.

Every fiber of my being is screaming at me to go find Mia and hash this out, but my phone's calendar alert tugs me in a different direction. I need to meet Ernie about the chandelier I broke. I glance at my watch, debating if I have time to find Mia, but when I see I'm late, I know I don't have the time to get into this with her. With a resigned sigh, I grab the keys to the catering van and head into town.

Following the directions Ernie left scribbled on the back of last weekend's brunch menu, I drive up a long gravel road, nestled between a pasture of grazing cows to my left and an enormous field full of perfectly plowed farmland to my right. At the end of the road stands the most gorgeous farmhouse I've ever seen.

The three-story white house is surrounded by a wrap-around porch held up with elegant, gray brick pillars. The shutterless black trimmed windows provide a stark contrast to the traditional farmhouse facade.

I'm in awe of this architectural masterpiece but cannot help being confused. Ernie said we were meeting his antique restoration guy. I assumed it'd be at a shop in town, not a beautiful mansion ten miles outside of Stoney Ridge. I double check the directions and compare the address. When it becomes clear that I am indeed in the right spot, I head up the short staircase to the front door and prepare to knock.

Right as my hand is about to make contact, the door swings open and I'm greeted by a petite elderly woman with a wide smile. Her silver hair is pulled up in a tight bun, her face prominently lined around the corners of her eyes and mouth, as if she's spent a lifetime in this happy state. I notice small specks of flour adorning her face as she wipes her hands on her apron and pushes open the screen door, inviting me in.

"Oh, you must be Preston! Well, get on in here!" She waves me through and pulls me into an embrace as if she's known me my whole life. It's odd. Normally I'd be annoyed at this lack of respect for my personal boundaries, but there's something so warm about this woman I can't help but chuckle lightly and return the hug.

"Yes, I'm Preston. Nice to meet you...?"

"Esther Wheeler, at your service. Ernie hasn't stopped

talking about you all week! He and Jimmy, that's my grand-son, have been working 'round the clock on that beautiful mess of a chandelier. I hear you really did a number on that one!" She laughs with a shake of her head as she bids me to follow her through to the kitchen.

My head swivels around the home which is as beautiful inside as it is outside. The hardwood must be original, as is the wood burning fireplace in the corner of a cozy living room, but many of the lighting fixtures and accents appear ultra-modern. It's exactly the look I hope to cultivate at the inn when we have the money to fix it up. Although, I guess now I *do* have the money...

"Your home is gorgeous, Mrs. Wheeler. May I ask who you had design it?"

A boisterous laugh escapes her as she holds her hands to her belly. "Oh, honey, *design?* This place is a mishmash of things passed down from my family throughout the years and the fanciful ideas of my late husband, Harold. He and Jimmy always did have an eye for unique. Matter of fact, Jimmy had a hand making most of what you see here."

"We're looking to make some changes over at the inn. Do you think your grandson would be open to talking through some custom pieces?"

"Oh, he would love that! They're out back in the work-shop. Here, why don't you take them out something to drink? They sure must be working up a thirst out there!" She shoves a tray with a pitcher lemonade, empty glasses, and tiny finger sandwiches into my arms, pointing me out the backdoor of the house. Sure enough, I see Ernie and the tall lumberjack who must be Jimmy huddled over a table in the workshop.

I make eye contact with Ernie as I head out to deliver the goodies, bracing for a lecture as I'm almost an hour late. But instead, his eyes beam and a smile spreads across his face. He lifts his hand, giving me a wide wave, Jimmy turning around to do the same.

"Sorry I'm late, but I bring a peace offering!" I set the tray down on the workbench in front of me.

"Ah, I see Grams got ya, huh? How long she keep you hostage in there for?" Jimmy, laughs knowingly, extending a hand. "Jimmy Wheeler."

I answer with a firm handshake and a nod. "Preston. She didn't keep me too long. I can't believe I haven't met her yet. Seems everyone in town swings by the inn for a meal."

"Yeah, you know, since Pops passed, she doesn't get out much. I stay and run the farm now, but I think she doesn't want everyone to fuss over her."

I nod, understanding that feeling more than he'll ever know. That was my mother to a T.

"Anyway, Ernie and me have been working on this here monstrosity," he drags out each syllable so dramatically it becomes *mawn-stross-ih-tee*, "for the better part of the week. We didn't get it exact, the photos Ernie had weren't the best and, frankly, there wasn't much usable glass, but I think you're gonna like what we did." He guides me to the back of the workshop where the chandelier lays in the center of a table.

It looks completely different but for the elegant gold chain that hung from the ceiling. Still, there is no denying its beauty. Similarly to the other fixtures I've seen around the Wheeler house, it has a modern twist that adds to the timeless elegance of old. Where the original featured thin icicle lights, Jimmy has enclosed the salvaged lighting in modern, frosted glass pendants, that hang down in varying lengths. It fits perfectly with the inn and, hopefully, pays enough homage to the original that Mia will be pleased.

"Jimmy, man, you've really outdone yourself here. It's perfect." I pause, because there's really only one opinion that matters here. "I hope Mia likes it."

Ernie and Jimmy exchange a knowing glance and chuckle in unison as Ernie steps forward, clapping the back of my shoulder.

"Uh-huh. Thinking about Mia, eh? Thought that was nothin', son?"

"No idea what you're talking about." I shrug his arm off me at the insinuation, my voice coming out much gruffer than I anticipated. "I broke it, she was pissed, I figured if I got it fixed, she'd be less pissed and get off my back, okay?"

They both erupt in knee slapping laughter as a scowl spreads across my face. I don't know why I'm even fighting the admission so much. Yeah, I like her. And, yeah, I want to do something nice for her. But there's absolutely no way I'm talking about this with these two.

"You know, I don't blame you one bit," Jimmy starts after he's regained his composure enough to speak. "I carried a torch for that woman for years. She never calls me Jimmy though, always James. We dated for a little while, but ultimately, she decided we were better off as friends."

I clench my fists as an unexpected wave of jealousy ripples through my body. Imagining this man with his calloused hands all over her, his mouth claiming hers, her voice calling out his name instead of mine. It's work to push down this reptilian urge to punch him right in his perfectly chiseled jaw.

Jimmy backs away slowly, with both hands up. Guess my rage wasn't as silent as I thought. "Whoa, whoa, man. I got no quarrel with you. That is over. Capital O-v-e-r, over. 'Sides, since you got here, none of the rest of us stand a chance."

"This is a great thing you're doing for that girl, Preston," Ernie interjects. "Her momma picked this out and it was one of the last things she did before she got sick. It's not the same, but it's rejuvenated, much like we all hope for her, and you've been a big part of that. Much bigger than I'd thought, considering I thought we had an understanding."

I wince as I remember I promised Ernie my intentions with Mia were purely professional. "Yeah, about that... we've grown a bit, ah, closer, these past few weeks. I think a part of me always knew I was lying to you, but it wasn't intentional. I was lying to myself too."

"Boy, I knew you'd never be able to stay away from that girl. Your eyes were full of cartoon hearts the second I gave you that warning. But my warning still stands, don't get involved with her if you're not ready."

"My intention is not to hurt Mia, but I'm worried maybe I have. That wedding last night? I didn't know it during planning, but the bride was my ex." I don't know what possesses me to confess to them, but suddenly I could see myself making friends out here. Building a life.

Ernie lets out a low whistle and Jimmy's eyes are as wide as saucers. When they don't say anything, I continue.

"Yeah...and the groom? My former best friend. Most of

the night, it was fine, but then Sadie, my ex, cornered me and tried to kiss me. Right when Mia walked in."

"Well, now, that is quite the pickle. Now, it's not my tale to tell, but what I can say is Mia is particularly sensitive to any hint of infidelity. Let's get this baby hung up and help you untangle the other mess you've made."

"Okay, but can we install it late tonight? I want it to be a surprise for Mia in the morning." All three of us grin as a plan starts to form in my head of how to win Mia back.

We work throughout the night and get the chandelier hung. Despite only getting a few hours of sleep, the next morning, I'm wired and excited to unveil the new chandelier to Mia.

I arrange post-its from her bedroom to the kitchen, pointing her to the fresh pot of coffee and freshly baked pastries I swiped from Chelsea this morning while I head over to wait patiently at the inn.

About thirty minutes later, I see Mia coming up the cobblestone path from the cottage, coffee in one hand, a notebook in the other, and a banana nut muffin grasped between her teeth. I know I'm grinning like an idiot, but I don't even care as her eyes meet mine with a brief look of confusion. At least, I don't care until she quickly breaks eye contact and speeds up her walk.

"Mia! It's so good to see you. How'd you sleep?" I open the door for her, exchanging pleasantries in a voice that is about an octave too high. Who *am* I right now?

She grunts in acknowledgement, and I hope it's more because of the muffin still lodged in her mouth rather than because she's still so angry with me about whatever happened the other night.

I follow her down the hallway, slightly ahead so I can

open each door for her. When we reach her office, she quickly moves to stand behind her desk, setting everything down and freeing the muffin from her mouth so she can finally speak. Silence drags on for a moment as her jaw works to chew the giant bite she took, likely to stall, but I stand there patiently, letting her know I'm not going anywhere until we've talked.

"Preston, it's early and I have a really busy day. I know we need to talk about...things, but can it wait?" She sinks down into her seat, not sounding mad, exactly, but defeated, which is arguably worse. Still, I'm not giving up.

"You're right, we do need to talk, but not right now. Don't worry. This won't take long, but I need you to come with me."

A small, exasperated sigh escapes her lips. "I really don't have time for this. I'm far behind on preparations for the pageant and all the wedding guests check out this morning."

"I promise, it will only take a minute. And besides, I'm helping you with the pageant, so I'm sure we can tackle everything between the two of us."

A torturous pause lingers, but I can tell she's considering it. She slowly stands with a huff and gestures her hands in an impatient circle as if to say "okay, let's go".

My smile grows with victory. "Follow me."

She rolls her eyes at me impatiently but eventually plays along. I guide her out to the foyer where the newly restored chandelier hangs in all its glory.

"Okay stand right there." I back away so that I'm standing directly under the chandelier. "Look up." I point towards the ceiling, watching her eyes follow the direction of my finger.

Her confusion and impatience are instantly replaced with wonder as her eyes travel from my face upwards to the chandelier. Her hand goes to her heart, tears of joy welling up in her eyes, and a grin spreads wide across her face.

"Oh, Preston! It's beautiful!"

And just like that, I think I've won her over, whatever happened last night to make her flee a whisper in the wind.

Chapter 16

Mia

I stare up at the new chandelier hanging from the center of the foyer. It's new, but also familiar. The gold chain and gilded base appear to be the same, but frosted pendants hang down, replacing the dainty icicle lights that hung from the original. It's elegant and modern and somehow more like Mom than the one she worked so hard to pick out before.

The story my mom told me was that before Gabriela passed away, she was obsessed with finding a chandelier to add a quiet elegance to the inn. But she'd been too sick to venture out, confined to her bed while cancer tore through her body. Ever the good Samaritan, my mom jumped at the chance to help her with this request.

Every time my mom told the story, the search for the chandelier became grander and grander. As an adult, I can admit that she was exaggerating for my benefit, but I know there had to be some truth to how she scoured the surrounding towns and called every store within a hundred miles.

But life isn't a fairytale, and things don't always work out. Despite my mom's best efforts, Gabriela passed away before my mom found the perfect adornment, though she never gave up the search. It wasn't until a few years later that she found a small antique shop in upstate New York that held the perfect chandelier that Gabriela would have loved.

I'm snapped out of the memory at the sound of Preston saying my name. The grin previously held across his face begins to fall, disappearing his dimples as concern takes over. I know he's waiting for me to say something, anything, but I'm so overwhelmed, the right words simply won't surface.

What I should do is tell him who I am, at least so he has the full story of the importance of this seemingly inconsequential piece of decor. At least so that he'll know what this means to me, and to the memory of his mother. But he looks so happy and satisfied with himself, I can't bear the thought of breaking his heart right now. This arrogant, immature playboy somehow turned into the most considerate, thoughtful man I've always known he would become. And how do I repay him? By keeping secrets and lying by omission.

Instead, I lean into the emotion and let the tears take over, hiding my head in my hands as I sob. It's only seconds before I feel Preston's strong arms embrace me, pulling me into his warmth as he cradles my head.

"Shh...Mia. I'm so sorry. If you hate it, I can take it down. I thought...I thought this would be a good surprise. I'm so, so sorry."

Realizing he thinks I'm crying sad tears, I lightly push myself away from his chest, locking our eyes together.

"Preston, no. No. I love it. It's perfect. That chandelier was...is...a staple of our inn. You have no idea what this means to me. Thank you."

I refuse to look away, instead staring deeper into his eyes to let him feel how sincerely appreciative I am. If I can't yet tell him the full truth, at least I can let him know how much this means to me.

He stares right back at me, his hands now resting comfortably around my hips, my hand finding its way to rest on his chest. Expectation hangs heavy in the air as my eyes beg him to kiss me again like he did in my office, consequences be damned. I feel his heart racing under my palm, beating as fast as my own, as we unconsciously begin closing the gap between our bodies. I tilt my chin and raise up on my tip toes ever so slightly, hoping he will take the hint and crash his lips to mine. I close my eyes, and the spell is broken as a very loud, very fake, cough clears the silence.

Chelsea stands in the dining room archway, a smug grin plastered on her face. We both push away from each other, knowing we've been caught. I've somehow forgotten what to do with my hands as I fidget uncontrollably, brushing wisps of hair from my forehead, then tucking a few strands behind my ear, before straightening out my shirt, clearing my throat.

"We...um...Preston...uh. We got a new chandelier!" I point emphatically at the new fixture.

"Uh-uh," she says, slowly walking into the room. She's looking at me like I'm a crazy person and, well, who can blame her? I shift my eyes to Preston, pleading for backup, but that traitor gives me a slight shrug, mutters something about having to go help Ernie and scurries off, leaving me to explain to Chelsea alone. Dick.

Chelsea cocks her head to the side, eyebrows raised, a look of expectation on her face. I know without a word that she's waiting for me to tell her everything. And so, with a sigh, I blurt out everything that happened between me and Preston over the last few days.

"You *what? Oh. My. God!*" She excitedly claps her hands in front of her, high on her tip toes in a little happy dance before sing songing, "I kneeew it! I kneeew it!" at me while pointing and moving closer.

"Okay well, not in the way that I actually knew anything concrete, but I have a sixth sense about these things, you know? I'm like, a bloodhound for lust and, babes, you two got it bad. But what are you going to do about, you know, the whole 'you've been lying to him for weeks now about something as basic as who you are' thing?"

I walk into the dining room and plop down on one of the chairs, resting my elbows on the table and dropping my head into my palms. "I have no idea. I like him. Like, *really* like him. This will ruin everything."

"Well, maybe not?" Even her hopeful smile can't convince me.

"Chels, I let him falsely think he confided in me. He opened up to me in a way I know he hasn't to anyone in a long time, if ever. I've had countless opportunities to confess to him. Frankly, I'm surprised no one around town has spilled the beans yet."

"Okay. You're not wrong. But, Mia, people make mistakes. You don't always have to be Miss Perfect all the time. It's complicated and you'll tell him when you're ready." She gives me a sympathetic smile and places her hands over mine with a gentle squeeze.

"No, Chels, you don't understand. He told me about his ex and how much he hates her *because* of her lies. Now I'm just like her. He'll never forgive me for this. Ugh! How do I always get myself into these messes?" I give an unconvincing laugh, but my pity party is interrupted when a tall man in a navy-blue jumpsuit with the words *Gary's Appliances* scripted on his chest walks into the dining room, clipboard in hand.

"Sorry to interrupt, ma'am. I'm looking for the owner?"

Confused, I stand up and begin to walk towards him. I can't exactly tell him the owner's currently in LA on house arrest while he awaits trial for embezzlement, can I?

"Well, um, he's...unavailable at the moment. But I'm the general manager. Can I help?"

"Sign please." He says handing me a clipboard. As I inspect the papers that seem to be an appliance invoice, he begins to waive in a series of men with dollies. They're wheeling in large boxes, awaiting instructions on where to put them. Chelsea and I exchange confused looks, eyes wide at the sheer number of items that are now sitting in the lobby.

"Um, sorry. What is all this? I didn't order anything."

"Right. The owner did. Now, can you point us to the kitchen? We'll get all this set up and be out of your hair in no time."

Chelsea squeals, squeezing the delivery man's bicep with glee before bidding the crew to follow her with a wave and a, "Come on, boys!"

I stand dumbfounded as I read the invoice closer, searching for a name. Panic surges through my body as I realize that I did promise Chelsea a new kitchen, but surely there's no way she would order this without speaking to me first.

I'm about to head into the kitchen to ask her, but another man, this time in a brown uniform, asks me where he should set my deliveries. I shake my head and begin to ask him what he's delivering when yet another man, this one wearing a construction vest and hard hat, asks me where his crew should get started. Get started on *what?* What the hell is going on?

I'm confused and overwhelmed, but moreover, I'm concerned with how we're going to pay for all this. I stammer to both of them that I didn't order these services and can't pay for them. They both look at me like I've grown three heads and say in unison, "It's all paid up, ma'am."

They hand me receipts and I add them to the stack of papers I've accumulated from the appliance guy. In a daze, I manage to direct the deliveries to the corner of the lobby and the construction team into the dining room before heading to my office to try and make sense of what's happening.

My heart rate begins to slow when I comb through the invoices confirming they really have all been paid, but not a single one of them shows *who* paid them. More workers, all from the construction crew I presume, filter in and out of my office, asking me to sign off on this or that as I realize they're here to repair and renovate a large portion of the inn. I scour my email for any confirmation. Nothing. A soft knock on my office door momentarily tears my attention away from the panic brewing in my chest.

"Hey, Mia! Got your check. I knew ya were good for it,

but it was a relief to not have to explain that one to Grams!" I look up to find James standing in my doorway.

"Um...yeah. Sure. No problem." My voice comes out dazed. I still have no idea where all this money came from.

"Well, I'm gonna head upstairs and finish these repairs. You'll be ship-shape in no time! By the way, the chandelier looks great. Preston was in a panic after he broke that one. Man, was that a mess." He shakes his head with a chuckle.

"Oh my gosh, James! *You* rebuilt that?"

"Yes, ma'am. Ernie came to me about the incident, and I've been working on it ever since." He hooks his thumbs through his belt loops, rocking back and forth on his heels, beaming with pride.

"It's beautiful. I've already had a million compliments on it this morning!"

He smiles and puts his hand over his heart in thanks.

"Anyway, I better be off to work. Earn that nice paycheck you sent my way." And with a wink and a smile, he's off.

After the chaos dies down, I pick up the phone and dial Oliver. I need to get to the bottom of where all these deliveries are coming from. The inn's coffers are dry as tinder and I shudder at the thought of going into mountains of debt when we're already so upside down. And while this might seem like a gift, I've been around long enough to know nothing comes without a price.

Chapter 17

Preston

My phone hasn't stopped ringing for the last hour. It's been a week since I've been named CEO and between calls from vendors, the board, resort GMs, and Oliver, I've been busier than ever. I knew my life would be irrevocably changed when I was named CEO, but, fuck, I expected a ramping up period.

Stanley's demand for discretion scared the shit out of me, so out of an abundance of caution, I decided to hole up in a coffee shop about twenty miles outside of town. I have a call with the board in a few minutes and I couldn't risk anyone overhearing anything. Especially Mia. Plus, even though she loved the chandelier, shit's still awkward between us, so instead of talking to her like an adult, I'm choosing avoidance.

A familiar chime indicating an incoming video call emanates through my headphones and I inhale deeply before answering. The truth is, I never wanted this job, and I can't help but hear my father's voice in my ear telling me over and over I'm not ready for this, reminding me what a colossal fuckup I am.

"Preston, hi. Thanks for joining us." Stanley sits at the head of the conference table surrounded by the board, Natalia, and a few others I don't immediately recognize.

"In the absence of a competent CFO," Natalia chimes in, "I've reviewed the financials and compared our situation against the proposed payback efforts from Mr. Pickering's...creative...approach to accounting. To satisfy our payback arrangement with the IRS, I propose we sell ten of our lower performing properties. The board has compiled a list of properties for your review. If you're aligned, we can begin the process ASAP."

She shares her screen, displaying a list of ten of our properties, along with their projected end of year revenues and potential sale prices. I've remained fairly removed from the inner workings of my father's company, so I'm not surprised that I barely recognize any of the property names on this list. As I'm about to agree without further review, trusting in the board, I reach the last name on the list: The Early Bird Inn.

"I was led to believe The Early Bird exists outside of The Spencer Group's main portfolio. This would make it ineligible for liquidation under this agreement, would it not?" I attempt to channel my father's assertive tone but judging by the uncomfortable glances from the team on the screen, it must have not had the same effect.

"Technically that would have been true, but once you accepted the role as CEO, the inn fell back under the purview of The Spencer Group." Natalia continues moving her mouse pointer to the inn's line item. "As you can see here, the inn is hemorrhaging quite a bit of money.

While we recognize this property won't generate a lot of income from the sale, we believe getting rid of it will at least offset some of the loss."

My anger threatens to boil over as I plaster a defiant look on my face, staring directly at the camera. "I've been working with the team at inn for the past month and while perhaps they aren't generating the sort of income we'd expect from a luxury resort, they still manage to break even from what I can see. And with the increased interest generated from the high-profile wedding we recently hosted, they're booked solid for the foreseeable future. With all due respect, you have no idea how much time I have put into renovations and repairs."

Stanley shifts uncomfortably in his chair and clears his throat, glancing at Natalia to indicate he would address me. "Preston, I can appreciate the sentimental value this inn holds for you, but that's clouding your judgement. Your father told me the disarray this place is in after his visit last month. It would take far more money to fix it up than it could ever hope to generate in years."

"Son, you have no experience in business," an older man in a gray suit interjects, slamming his fists on the table. I've never seen him before, but judging by his overpriced suit, I assume he's part of the board. "We're not ignorant to the number of repairs you've done, without our approval I might add, but the fact is, quaint inns are a thing of the past. People want luxury, full-service hotels, not run-down B&Bs."

The entire board nods and hums in agreement. My gentle attempts are clearly not working, so I decide to take a more forceful approach, channeling the scarier aspects of my father.

"I may not have the experience on paper that you'd like to see, but that's irrelevant. This is my company and as the majority stakeholder, this decision isn't yours. I've considered your perspective as a courtesy, but that ends now."

A few of the board members begin to mutter their discontent, but I'm beyond annoyed and decide it's far time to shut this shit down.

"Look," I nearly yell, causing them to stop whatever they were saying and glare at the camera, and me, through the screen. The patrons of the coffee shop shoot me a few annoyed glares, but I stay focused on putting the board in their place.

"Begin the process of liquidating the other nine properties. We will not be touching The Early Bird Inn except to make the necessary renovations to get it back up to standard. This isn't a discussion. This is my fucking company and you all answer to me. Get. It. Done." I exit the call and slam my laptop shut, and within minutes, my phone is ringing again.

"What?" I answer in anger as I see the caller is Stanley.

"Preston, the board is pretty pissed off. They're talking about removing you as CEO," it's Natalia's velvety voice, not Stanley's, that responds.

"I'd love to see them try. I'll get rid of every fucking last one of them." I'm seething with anger and a large part of me knows it's because all I can think of is what losing the inn would do to Mia and her mother. I will not let this money hungry board take this from them.

"Okay, everybody calm down." It's Stanley. "Preston's half-right. They're going to have a hell of a time trying to remove him. The bylaws are fairly ironclad about majority ownership belonging to a Spencer until such time the family relinquishes that right or changes the bylaws."

"Be that as it may," Natalia interjects, agitation weighing heavy in her voice, "they can, and will, absolutely destroy you in the press. A job you've made extremely easy for them with your history of hooking up with randos and allowing yourself to be photographed drinking away your father's money.

I propose we get ahead of this, announcing your new role with all the major outlets, *Forbes, The Wall Street Journal, Bloomberg,* and *The Economist.* You'll do a full press tour, emphasizing the new direction of the firm and your full confidence in turning a new corner. I'll make some calls and can have you on the next flight to New York."

"Absolutely not," I say, my tone leaving no room for negotiation. "I need to be at the inn at least through Christmas, as per my original deal with my father. I cannot be off on some press tour leaving them in the lurch during the most important time of the season. Especially when the board currently has them on the chopping block."

"Preston, I understand, but things have changed. I don't know if we can control the board. If we could at least put out a press release now of your new role, we can do some of the tour remotely, but you can't ignore this and hope it will resolve on its own. This board is ruthless, and I've seen companies taken down by less."

"No. After the holiday, we can announce, and I will go wherever and say whatever you want me to." The truth is, things are so fragile with Mia right now, I don't want to widen into this rift with the knowledge that my company's trying to liquidate her inn.

"My answer is final. Until the new year, no one knows. And there better not be a single leak." I hang up and head back to the inn.

⚒ ⚒ ⚒

DURING THE DRIVE BACK TO THE INN, I'VE HAD TIME to stew in my anger. It's as if a storm cloud follows in my wake. So, when I walk through the doors to see my contractors, who I'm paying collectively over a thousand dollars an hour, standing around flirting with the receptionist, I'm seeing red.

I stomp up to the desk, acid in my veins, and clap my hands together loudly to get their attention. An insincere smile creeps across my face as I prepare to unleash the storm.

"Surely I'm not paying you to stand around and flirt with pretty receptionists, am I?" I say, my tone laced with venom.

To their credit, most of the guys exchange looks of embarrassment and look ready to get back to work, but there's always one asshole. This particular asshole meets my gaze with a scoff and a cocky grin. He stands much shorter than me, but the bulk of him clearly indicates this man is no stranger to the gym.

"What, we're not allowed breaks now?" He turns to the rest of his crew, laughing and earning a few chuckles from them as well.

I close the gap between us, fists balled at my side, my jaw clenching so hard I think I might chip a tooth. "When I tell you to get to work, I mean, Get. To. Work. Do you know who I am?" At this point, my voice barely sounds human as I bite out the words through gritted teeth.

"Yeah, I know who you are. You're that pampered little rich boy whose daddy's about to go to prison for stealing everyone else's money. That about right?" All trace of humor is replaced on his face with a look of challenge, goading me to say or do something. And today, he might just get his wish.

I'd love nothing more than to pummel this guy. To pour all my frustrations about the board, my father, my *future* out as my fist connects with his face over and over. But I'm trying really hard to be a better man. For her.

"Don't fuck with me, kid. Not today. I can have you destroyed like that." I snap my fingers in his face for emphasis.

"Man, it's you who shouldn't be fucking with me. I'll lay your pretty boy ass out on the floor right now," he snaps back, the menace in his eyes telling me this wouldn't be his first fight.

I bring my face close to his, leaning down to emphasize our height difference, fighting the urge to head butt this little prick. "I. Fucking. DARE you." My mouth curves in a smirk, the adrenaline and anger still lingering from my conversation with the board has my fingers tingling, begging for a fight. For now, I settle for pushing him back with one finger, chuckling as I stand upright.

But he's fast.

I don't have time to react as his fist collides with my jaw. The unexpected power behind this kid's right hook doesn't only knock me off balance, it sends me flying backward on the ground. As I fight to gather my bearings, the room erupts in chaos around me.

"Benny, man, you just clocked our fucking boss."

Well, I guess that answers who the fuck this guy is.

His fellow crewmen scramble to hold him back, but they're no match for his speed. He quickly evades their arms and before I know it, he's on top of me, landing blow after blow to my head and stomach. I manage a few strikes straight to his face before two large men finally pull him off me.

Taking a moment to catch my breath, I lay writhing in pain on the ground as Benny continues to shout obscenities in my direction. When I finally gather the strength to sit upright, I wipe away the blood from my lips and can't help the maniacal laughter escaping my mouth. That short asshole can throw a punch but fuck if I'm going to let him win this round. Before I can get up to finish this fight, I hear an angry voice pushing through the chaos.

"*Get out of the way!*" Though I've never heard her quite this panic stricken and pissed, I'd know that voice anywhere. "What did you do?" Mia shoots the crew an accusatory glare as she crouches down next to me.

"Oh my god, Preston! What the hell happened?"

"This rich asshole fucked with the wrong guy, that's what happened," Benny shouts from the other side of the room, still so worked up it takes four of his crew to hold him back.

Mia turns her gaze on him and gives him a murderous look, reaching a hand to help me. My wounded pride won't allow me to take her help so I wave her off with more annoyance than I intended and unsteadily climb to my feet.

"You are *all* fucking fired. Now get the hell out of *my*

inn!" The words come from my mouth, but the voice I hear sounds strangely like my father's.

"Just...hang on." Mia holds out a hand stopping me from approaching the asshat whose head I want to rip off. She glances over to them, then back at me, before turning to walk to where they all stand.

In a low apologetic whisper I can faintly make out even from across the room, she encourages them to pack up for the day, assuring them she'll call them later to realign on the schedule after an interrupted day. They speak too quietly for me to hear the full conversation, but I can absolutely make out the last thing Mia says. She fucking *apologizes* to the asshat who started all this.

Anger burns through my body as she turns on her heel and stomps towards me. All concern for my wellbeing has faded, leaving her own anger to color her usually tan face in a faint red hue.

"Come with me. *Now*," she bites at me, grabbing my wrist forcefully and pulling me towards the cottage. Even though I could easily free myself from her grip, I allow her to drag me behind her. I feel endearment replace a bit of my anger as I watch her stomp up the cobblestone path, never glancing back to spare me a look. She's still so fucking cute when she's angry.

She slams the door behind us with gale-force and stares at me, arms folded, for what seems like an eternity before stomping off to the kitchen. Unsure if she wants me to follow her, I stand awkwardly in the entryway, waiting for instruction. I may find her uncharacteristic display of anger adorable, but even I'm not stupid enough to tempt her wrath.

She returns to me, shoving a bunched-up towel with a handful of loose ice cubes at my chest.

"For your lip. It will help with the swelling." She huffs in annoyance. "You okay?" The kindness still hasn't fully returned to her voice, but I can sense a hint of concern masked by the anger.

"I'll be fine. I had it handled."

She barks out a sarcastic laugh. "Oh yeah. I can see that. What'd you plan to do? Have an all-out brawl in the middle of the foyer? What would that have accomplished?"

"Whatever." I move over to the couch and sink down, wincing as I bring the makeshift ice pack to my lip.

I hear an exasperated *ugh* coming from her direction before she stomps away down the hall. I assume she's trying to put some distance between us but am pleasantly surprised to see her sit down on the coffee table in front of me, bandages and cloths in hand.

Without a word, she rips open an alcohol swab, cradling my head in her hand and swipes at the cut on my brow. I jerk back, sucking in a breath at the sharp pain from the alcohol cleansing my open wound. Mia rolls her eyes, setting her hands and the alcohol swab back in her lap with an exasperated sigh.

"Stop being such a baby. You were macho enough to get in a fight, you can be macho enough to let me clean this up, so it doesn't get infected. You're lucky it doesn't need stitches."

She moves her hand back towards my face to continue her work, muttering something in Spanish, but I catch her wrist in my hand. "You don't have to do this. I can take care of myself."

It comes out harsher than I'd intended, my pride bringing out my inner dickhead. I know she doesn't deserve to get the brunt of my anger, even if she did act all polite with that asshole. She's the only one of us who had their head on straight enough to protect the inn's interests in that moment and considering everything, I should be grateful.

"Preston," the gentleness returns to her voice as she locks her eyes with mine pleadingly, "let me help you."

Reluctantly, I drop her wrists and allow her to continue cleaning me up, sealing my cut with a small butterfly bandage.

When she returns from cleaning up the bloodied cloths and bandage wrappers, she sits down next to me on the couch, handing me a beer, the twin to her own.

"What's really going on, Preston? I've never seen you like this."

Everything inside me screams to tell her the truth. To unburden myself with the knowledge that I'm now CEO and the board is trying to shut down this inn if I cannot convince them it's worth saving. But I know that will do more harm than good, making her worry unnecessarily. It's not like there's anything she could do to prevent what the board decides anyway.

"I had a call with my father's team today. There's a lot going on and a lot that's expected of me while he fights these allegations. And then when I saw those guys, laughing and having fun, not a care in the world, something shattered in me. I guess the old me came through."

She nods sympathetically and shifts her body on the couch to face me. "I can't imagine what you're going through. It must be difficult. But, Preston," she gently places her hand on my thigh, and I struggle to maintain my composure as I focus on the heat of her hand on my body, "no matter how difficult things get, I can't have you assaulting people."

"It won't happen again. You have my word."

Her face softens and she smiles at me like she truly believes me. She gives my thigh two pats before pushing herself to stand.

"Why don't you take the day, stay here and get some rest? I still have a ton to do at the inn, which now includes repairing the damage between you and the only construction crew in town."

I wince knowing I'm leaving her to clean up my mess. "But how about I bring home some dinner later and we go over the final details for the pageant?"

"That sounds great." I stand up, moving towards her to take her hands in mine. "And, again, I am so sorry for my behavior today. It was unacceptable."

"It's okay. It's not *okay*, but, I mean, I accept your apology." She takes her hands from mine and turns to face me in the doorway right before she leaves. "See ya, Preston."

Chapter 18

Mia

As I leave Preston and make my way back to the inn, concern wreaks havoc on my body. I'd never seen him so out of control, every inch of him vibrating with anger that rolled off him in waves. I managed to miss the catalyst for the show of toxic masculinity, but it didn't quite line up with the sweet kid I knew all those years ago or the man I've come to know over these last few weeks. Of course, if the tabloids are to be believed, this wouldn't exactly be out of character for him.

With a sigh, I grasp the door to the inn and head towards my office, dreading the calls I'll have to make to attempt to smooth things over. If I had any other choice, I wouldn't be apologizing. Even though I didn't see what happened, it was pretty clear that Benny was the instigator, at least when it came to the physical blows. But in a small town, Richie's crew is the only contractor for miles and with the pageant coming up I can't afford to leave the dining room unfinished.

"Delany Construction," a deep, gruff voice brought on

by years of smoking comes from the other line. Good, it's Richie, so I don't have to relay the embarrassing reason for my call to anyone else.

"Richie, hi. It's Mia." I pause, my face scrunching as if bracing for him to curse me out. He allows the silence to linger for longer than I'm comfortable, but as I'm about to start my groveling, he speaks.

"Ah, I was wondering when I'd be gettin' a call from you. Fuckin' Benny." His exasperation appears to be directed at Benny rather than me, so I take that as a good sign.

"Listen, I'm not entirely sure what happened. I was in the back and only came out when I heard shouting. By then, the fight was almost over, but I want to make sure you know this is not something I condone from my staff."

"Mhm. From what my boys tell me, Benny here got all puffed up when your new city slicker called him out for flirtin' on the job. Instead of handlin' his business, he went all Rocky IV on the poor guy. The way I see it, any blows he took were well earned and your guy has nothin' to be sorry for."

Wow, not the reaction I expected, if I'm honest. Richie's reputation of being quick to anger has most of the town scared to even glance his way, so the fact that he's already on my side without me saying a word sends waves of relief through my body.

"I appreciate you saying that. I'd hate for this little mishap to damage our long-standing business relationship. I'll, of course, pay your crew for the day and I'd love it if they could continue working, but I'm sure you understand Benny can't come back here." The last words come out more like a question as I'd be lying if I said I wasn't still a little scared of his response.

"Huh. Well, you know, that's fair. That little shit needs to learn to get his temper under control if he's gonna be wearing my logo on his chest. I'll let the crew know and they'll be by bright and early at six a.m. tomorrow. Without Benny."

"Thank you so much, Richie, and sorry again about the drama."

"Don't mention it. It's all good." He hangs up the phone and I finally relax back into my chair taking the first full breath I've had in the last ten minutes.

Of course, that only lasts for about thirty seconds when a niggling thought keeps poking at my brain. *Why?* Why was Preston so incredibly angry that he resorted to violence for something so insignificant? I can't imagine he's into Lizzy. Not because she's not attractive, but she's basically a child and, well, I have reason to believe his interests lie elsewhere.

I bring my hand to my face, grazing my lips gently with my thumb at the memory of the press of his lips on mine. How he moved his deft fingers in and out of me, whispering filthy promises in my ear. Before it was ruined by this stupid lie that overshadows every moment we have together. No, it wasn't jealousy that brought that out in him, but there was clearly *something*.

My phone buzzes with a news alert about The Spencer Group and I swipe up to read the article. Maybe it will shed some light on why Preston was in such a mood.

Early news out of LA this morning confirms hotel mogul, Roman Spencer of The Spencer Group, is officially named the primary defendant in the embezzlement case that has engulfed his company in scandal. Sources report that while he remains on house arrest at his multimillion-dollar estate in LA, the board voted unanimously to strip him of his title and majority stake in the company. We cannot confirm who has taken his place, but with operations set to resume this week, we can assume a new CEO has been named. If true, this could be the first time in its twenty-five year history that a Spencer does not hold a majority stake in The Spencer Group.

So, at least I know what is causing Preston's foul mood. He's officially lost everything. His company. His money. His future. His father. While I still don't condone his violent reaction, I can at least understand why he was out of control. I want to go to him and tell him everything will be okay, but how can I? I don't know if it will be okay. Plus, it seems if he wanted me to know this, he'd have told me, wouldn't he?

Another concerning thought grips me. If Roman and Preston are no longer involved in the day-to-day, that squashes my theory about who's footing the bill for all these deliveries and renovations.

It's high time I get to the bottom of this, and I suspect Oliver will have an idea. Dozens of emails and voicemails to him have gone ignored, so I decide I'll try and force him into a FaceTime call. Not very millennial of me, but desperate times and all that.

To my surprise, he picks up the call before the first ring completes. My screen fills with Oliver's face at the most unflattering angle, his beady eyes magnified through his thick glasses as he holds the phone far below his face. The angle gives him about three chins, and I now have a front row to the unruly hairs in his nostrils. Gross.

"I don't care what that petulant child thinks, we are not continuing to pour money into a losing property! Handle this, Oliver, or we're going to hold a vote. We will not be pushed around!"

I don't recognize the voice of the man shouting in the background, but I can feel his agitation. Terror lives in Oliver's eyes as he appears unsure how to address the criticism. It's clear he isn't aware he's picked up the call, which is confirmed when he finally looks down at his phone and sees my face. I wave and his eyes widen in horror.

"Hi, Ollie! So glad I finally caught you. Do you have a few minutes to chat?" My voice comes out saccharine to butter him up for the questions I have.

"Erm. Oh. Well, Miss Flores, I don't—" His eyes dart around the room and I know he's looking for an excuse to get off this call, but I'll be damned if I let him squirm away after being ignored for days.

"Good! I'll be quick. The craziest thing has been happening at the inn. We've been getting mysterious deliveries and, wouldn't you know it, were suddenly able to hire contractors and proper repairmen. You wouldn't know anything about that, would you, Ollie?"

Oliver is an excellent assistant, but a terrible liar. I can read the deception on his face before he even opens his mouth. "Oh? Contractors and deliveries, you say? Erm, no I've not heard anything of the sort."

"Uh-huh. Well, *I* didn't schedule this work, and we certainly don't have the funds for this. Did I hear that operations are set to resume now that Roman is in custody? Have you appointed a new CEO? I'd love to know who to thank for the sudden interest in the inn's renovation."

The terror written on his face intensifies and I begin to regret how forcefully I'm grilling him. He's always been a good liaison, but if something untoward is going on with money coming into the inn, it also implicates me and my mom.

"I wish I could be of more help, but I'm unaware of any approval for release of funds to the inn, for renovations or otherwise. A-a-apologies."

I sigh in resignation. If he doesn't know, he doesn't know. And if he's been told to lie to me, I'll get nothing more of him over the phone. But maybe in person...

"Okay, well, thanks. Oh, Ollie, one more thing."

"Yes, Miss Flores?"

"We'd love to see you and the board at the annual Christmas pageant this year. It would go a long way to reassuring the team that the firm is committed to the inn." I allow the sweetest smile to spread across my face, hoping to convey sincerity and hide the fact that I'm clearly scheming.

"Erm, yes, well, as you know it's a bit chaotic around here, but we'll try to send someone out." His strained smile tells me that's doubtful to happen.

"You do that. Bye, Ollie." When I end our call, I'm left frustrated as I still have no idea who's playing angel investor. Oliver's performance was less than convincing, and I know he knows something, but refuses to tell me. As much as I want this to all be real, I can't help but worry about the true source of these funds. With all the deliveries, plus the repair and renovation work Richie's team was doing, if we end up being on the hook for even a small percentage of this, the inn will not survive that kind of hit.

Moreover, I can't get what the man in the background said out of my head. *"We are not continuing to pour money into a losing property!"* Is it possible he meant the inn? And if so, what would we do if they decided to shutter the inn for good?

Determined to at least get through the latest invoices and bank statements, I take a swig of my coffee for an extra boost of energy only to find it's gone disgustingly cold. Padding into the kitchen for a warmup, I stop in my tracks as I take in the scene before me. Everything, and I mean *everything* in this kitchen is brand new and state-of-the art. I nearly drop my mug as I mentally calculate what this all must have cost. Chelsea spots me, her face lit up with excitement as she extends her arms, presenting her updated kitchen. When she sees my face, her hands drop to her side, brow furrowing in concern.

"Wh-what *is* all this?" My voice comes out shakier than I'd intended.

"You signed for these, didn't you?" She almost looks guilty as if she thinks it's her fault for accepting the boxes.

"Technically, but I thought they were replacement parts. I don't really have the authority to buy anything of this magnitude..."

"But...don't you own the inn?"

"Well, no, I don't *own* the inn. The Spencer Group still owns—" I stop mid-sentence as realization sweeps over me. No, *The Spencer Group* doesn't own the inn. I hear Roman's voice in my head that day he came to inform me of Preston's new role at the inn.

"When Preston came of age, the board agreed to place the inn in his name..."

"The Spencer Group doesn't own the inn. *Preston* does." It comes out as little more than a surprised whisper, but evidently, it's loud enough for Chelsea to have heard.

"Mia, did you short circuit? You don't look so good..." She places a hand gently on my shoulder, guiding me to lean against the wall.

"Um, I'm fine. Enjoy your new stuff. You deserve it, truly." I give her a tight smile and squeeze her hand before turning to march to the cottage. I know *exactly* where to direct my concerns about our recent influx of cash. Preston.

I know he technically owns the inn and can do whatever he wants, but my mom has run the inn much longer than his family ever had anything to do with it. The audacity that this man would waltz in here, throwing around his money, making major changes without even talking to me about it first is not only maddening, it's utterly disrespectful. He has a lot of explaining to do, beginning with where exactly he came up with this kind of cash. I'll have no part in any of the shady business dealings that now plague The Spencer Group.

I stop short at the door to the garden with an annoyed sigh. It's almost six p.m. and I remember I promised Preston dinner. Reluctantly, I head back into the kitchen to grab two plates of whatever heavenly dish Chelsea has prepared for our guests tonight. He may be the subject of all my ire at the moment, but surely, I can't let the man starve.

⚒ ⚒ ⚒

THE SHORT WALK FROM THE GARDEN TO THE COTTAGE has given me some time to calm down. I feel confident that I've begun to peel back the layers that make up Preston Spencer over these past few weeks and I can't imagine him doing anything that might put the inn at risk. However he came into this money, I have to believe his intentions are in the right place and he knows what he's doing.

Still, he does owe me an explanation and I plan to get that out of him by softening him up with Chelsea's skillet lasagna. But when I open the door to the cottage, I find it covered in darkness, not a hint of anyone else around. Preston has been using our catering van to get around town and I saw it parked around back on my way over, so I'm sure he has to be here.

"Preston? You here?" I shout into the dark room. No answer. "Preeeestoooon, I have delicious foooood," I sing-song as I turn on the lights and head to the kitchen.

"Ooooh, Preston. You better get your ass out here. It took every ounce of willpower I possess to not devour this entire thing on the way over, so you have about thirty seconds before I do!" Still, nothing.

Finally, as I'm plating our dinner, I hear the faint patter of footsteps coming down the hall. He must have been in his room. "Prest—" I stop short, almost dropping the chunk of gooey lasagna I've scooped up as I catch sight of him. Dripping wet, droplets of water glide down his slick, rich brown skin, stopping above the white bath towel which sits precariously on his waist. My mouth hangs open and I swear I must look like the living embodiment of the drooling emoji.

When I'm finally able to tear my roaming gaze from his body, I see why he didn't answer me. Grabbing another towel from the linen closet to dry his hair, he dances around the room, two AirPods snuggled firmly in his ears. Still blissfully unaware of my presence, he begins singing—no, *howling*—the lyrics to a Taylor Swift song. He's terribly off key, but at least he has good taste?

I set down the spoon and stand to face him, arms crossed at my chest, my brows raised in curiosity. I can't help smirking at this display, but my humor turns to something else as my eyes are again caught by the beauty of his form. My gaze borders on lecherous as I take in each curve of his abs, following the faintest strip of black hair leading from his belly button, trailing beneath the towel. I can't stop remembering the feel of him that night in my office as his hardness pressed into me.

It's then his eyes flutter open and he emits a scream much higher than I would have expected possible considering his usually deep, rich voice. Stumbling backwards in surprise, his back rams into the corner of the wall, an "ow, *fuck*" coming from his mouth as he takes the AirPods out of his ears. Hysterical laughter escapes my mouth, my hand clasping over it as I try to regain my composure.

"Fuck, Mia. When did you get here?"

"Oh, probably somewhere around '*why can't you seeee-EEEeee, you belong with meeeEEEeeee*'," I tease, still unable to get my cackling fully under control.

"Ha. Ha. Very funny, but don't deny it. Miss Swift slaps. I've heard you belting her songs from the shower on more than one occasion." He sniffs the air and closes his eyes, a moan escaping his mouth. "Fuuuuck—what *is* that smell?"

"Chelsea made skillet lasagna tonight and as promised, I swiped us a few plates for dinner. I'm warming up some garlic bread in the oven. And, obviously Taylor slaps. She's a god damn musical goddess. I was just surprised to learn you actually have taste is all." I wink as I go back to plating our dinner, struggling to keep my eyes at a respectable height as he moves closer taking in another whiff of the cheesy goodness laid out in front of us.

His eyes land on mine and a faint pink appears at the apples of his cheeks as he seems to remember he is basically naked and wet in front of me. "Oh, uh. I should probably go put some clothes on." He gestures up and down his body with a sheepish grin before turning on his heels back down the hallway, humming more Taylor.

I grab the garlic bread from the oven and put the finishing touches on our dinner. My eyes catch on the stack of papers sprawled out on the table. As I gather them up to clear space for us to eat, I can't help but sneak a glance at their contents. The papers chronicle about a year's worth of financial data on the inn. Preston's thoughts are scribbled in the margins noting things like *"inflated cost"*, *"unnecessary overhead"*, *"discretionary funds"*, and *"devalued rates"*. I scrunch up my nose at the insults. Seems like he's gunning to take a more active role in the inn's operations.

"Here, let me get those." Preston shuffles quickly to the table, lightly pushing me out of the way seeming to try and hide the pages. He flashes a terse smile as he shoves the papers in a briefcase located next to the table. Do I sense... guilt?

I look at him quizzically for a moment before I realize he's not going to expand on what those papers were for. Instead, he rubs his hands together in anticipation. "So, when are we going to town on this amazing smelling lasagna?"

I choose not to explore the suspicious way he handled the papers, tucking away my questions for later. Who am I to judge him for keeping secrets when I've been holding one in since he first arrived? I grab our plates and carry them over to the table as he uncorks the bottle of Chianti I swiped from the wine stash at the inn.

Our first few bites are silent, save for the appreciative moans that escape our mouths. I allow us to enjoy this little bit of edible happiness before I start in about the events of earlier.

"So, I worked everything out with Richie, the lead contractor, and they'll be coming back tomorrow."

He responds with little more than a grunt, refusing to make eye contact as he shovels more of the lasagna into his mouth with a hunk of garlic bread.

"He was pretty pissed. He said he's never had to deal with an actual brawl on site before."

Silence.

I let my fork clatter to my plate in annoyance and let loose an audible sigh, leaning forward on crossed arms as I push away my plate.

"You know, Preston, the least you can do is look at me when I'm telling you I cleaned up your mess. You didn't only embarrass yourself; you embarrassed *me*."

I pause for a moment, allowing him to gather his thoughts. He lightly wipes away some sauce from his lips and sets his napkin and fork down gently before standing up and moving to the chair closer to me.

He scoots impossibly close, so close I can feel the

warmth from his thigh on mine, and trains his eyes on me, grabbing my hand to hold between his.

"You're right. And I want to reiterate how sorry I am. I'm so grateful you resolved the situation. A situation you should have never had to deal with." He moves one hand to cradle my cheek. "What can I do to make it right?"

My eyes soften and I allow myself to melt into his touch. His eyes search mine, pleading for forgiveness. "I- It's okay. You're forgiven." It comes out as little more than a whisper. He could ask me for anything right now and how could I deny him?

His eyes drop to my lips, my body responding with an involuntary urge to lick them, lightly grabbing the corner of my bottom lip between my teeth in response. My breath quickens as I plead with my eyes for him to kiss me again like he did in my office.

His hand slowly moves from my cheek to behind my ear, twining his fingers through the strands of my hair in the process. He leans in, his lips so distractingly close to mine that I almost forget about the papers.

"Why do you have all the financial records from the inn?" I blurt out as he's so close we're breathing the same air.

He releases me from his grip and leans back in his chair, caught.

"Ah. So, you saw that, huh?"

"I did. What I don't understand is why? And right when all these mysterious deliveries are coming in and contractors are suddenly hauling ass on the renovations I've been planning for the better part of a year. I called Oliver today. He said he had nothing to do with it, but the deliveries were marked for 'the owner of the inn,' which, if I'm not mistaken, is you. What's going on, Preston?"

He nods his head at nothing in particular, as if going over his options in his head.

"I need you to not get mad at me and I need to know what I'm about to tell you stays between us. I mean it. You can't tell Chelsea or even your mom. No one. Got it?"

I sit up straight and nod my agreement enthusiastically, dragging my thumb and forefinger across my lips, promising my silence.

"My father was taken into custody and is on house arrest until the trial. It seems as though the evidence implicating him in this whole thing is quite damning. Before they hauled him away, he and his team of lawyers transferred the company to me, making me president and CEO effective immediately. Access to my, and the company's, funds were restored, save for a good faith deposit for the back taxes we owe, and I'm to resume duties in LA next month."

I'm speechless. I open and close my mouth to respond, the words struggling to come to the surface. "So...it *was* you? You arranged all the deliveries and contracts."

"I did. But it was all *you*. When you were hurt, I spent a bit of time in your office. I stumbled across your renovation plan, and it was so well laid out I was able to get everything arranged in a day. I mean, all I had to do was cut a few checks. This was all your vision. I saw how hard everyone works here and how much everyone in town loves this inn, not to mention how vital it is to the tourist economy. I knew I could help, so I did." He lowers his eyes. "How pissed are you?"

"Zero. Zero pissed. But I *am* hurt that you went behind my back."

He nods, bracing for a lecture and my heart aches with the realization that he was probably never allowed to make mistakes with his father. He must be so used to being chastised for not doing things exactly the way others expect that he's genuinely surprised when I don't immediately lay into him.

I pull his hand into my lap and squeeze. "Hey, seriously. I'm not mad. This is such new territory for you. I don't expect you to automatically think of checking in with me. I mean, you should, but I know you're used to running things. Seeing my vision finally being brought to life was amazing. I just wish you had talked to me first, so we could've prioritized all that needed to get done."

"You're right. I was so excited. Once I had access to our accounts, I started seeing the backlog of maintenance requests — the majority coming right from this inn. I was angry my father ignored you for so long, so I guess I was trying to make up for that. But next time, I will come to you with any changes."

He leans closer and I rest a hand on either side of his face. "I really do love everything, Preston. It's everything I could have dreamed of, and you made it happen. I can't thank you enough."

"I'm glad. That's all I ever want, you know? To see you happy."

My heart is ready to leap out of my chest and I'm convinced he must be able to hear its racing beats. I know we need to talk about the other night and this big secret I'm keeping, but I can't wait any longer. I want him. Ignoring the consequences, I crush my lips against his with urgency, my hands grasping the back of his neck, pulling him closer to me.

He reaches a hand between my legs, grabbing my chair and pulling it flush with his. His large hands find their way around my waist, shifting me to straddle him on his chair, sliding down to cup my ass as he helps me find my place atop his lap. I gasp and we both lightly chuckle at the awkward movement. But all humor fades away when I settle on top of him, feeling the evidence of how much he wants this too.

Each kiss deepens with feral urgency, his hands moving up the side of my body until he tangles my hair in one, letting the other splay against my neck. He tilts my head back, gripping a chunk of my hair in his hands before running his tongue from the base of my neck to my jaw where he places urgent kisses until claiming my mouth again and I groan with pleasure.

He returns his kisses back to my neck, his hand roaming down to cup my breast, my body desperately shifting in his lap, seeking friction. "I need you, Preston." It escapes my mouth as a breathless moan.

He brings both hands up to cup my face, and I open my eyes to meet the seriousness I find in his. "Are you sure you want to do this?"

I nod.

"I'm gonna need more than that, Mia. Tell me you want this." He places a hand on my chest, right over my heart, as if insinuating he's asking for more than just my body tonight.

"I want this. I want you."

In one swift motion, his mouth crashes down on mine, standing with his hands cradling my ass as he walks us to my bedroom. I wrap my legs tight around him, hands gripping the back of his neck like a lifeline.

He nearly kicks in the door in a rush to get me into the bedroom before plopping me down on the bed. I prop myself up on my elbows, watching intently as he stands at the foot of the bed, his gaze roving over my body, locking his darkened eyes onto mine.

Grabbing the back of his white Henley by its neck, he pulls it over his head and steps out of his sweatpants without ever breaking eye contact. The moonlight sneaks into my window, casting his naked body in a powerful glow, allowing me to take in every perfectly sculpted inch. *Every* single inch. I gulp and my mouth goes dry at the impressive size of him.

"Come here," he almost growls as he bends down in front of me, hooking his arms around the back of my knees, pulling me to the edge of the bed. As he kneels in front of me, he makes quick work of sliding me out of my jeans, pulling them down with a tug over the ample curve of my ass. Taking one leg in his hands, he places soft kisses from my ankle to my inner thigh. I squirm with anticipation the closer he gets to where my body screams with need.

I let out a frustrated whine when instead of continuing his quest upward, he abruptly breaks contact, turning his attention to my other thigh. "So eager," he laughs into my skin. He stands to lean over me, lowering his face to mine for a soft, languid kiss as he slowly unbuttons my blouse with one hand. I can't help but arch my back to be closer to him. To feel him. To get the parts of him I need closer to me. I reach my hands to his ass and pull him closer as he spreads my blouse open, my nipples hard and visible against my lace bralette.

He lets his teeth scrap the bottom of my lip as he pushes himself up, moving his hips further away from me. "Ah, ah, ah. Not yet, beautiful. I've waited for this for so long. I intend to take my time with you," he whispers in my ear before turning his attention back to my neck and chest, pushing up my bralette and pinching my nipple between his fingers.

An embarrassing groan of pleasure mixed with frustration escapes my mouth as I pout a little, the need intensifying deep in my body. With a soft laugh, he replaces his hand with his mouth, his tongue dancing around my nipple before sucking, releasing it with a pop. I don't recognize the woman I become, muttering pleas between each panting breath, begging for more of him, moaning his name at every single touch.

Leaning forward, I slip out of my blouse and nearly rip my bralette over my head and toss them both across the room. I need to feel his skin on every inch of my body.

His kisses find their way lower and lower, taunting me again at the top of my inner thigh. His eyes lock on mine as he licks me down the center of my soaked panties that have somehow still remained on.

"Do you like that, beautiful?"

I've lost all ability to talk, a low whimper my only response. I lift my hips, bringing myself closer to him. He kisses me softly, once more through my underwear before pulling them off in one swift motion.

And then his mouth is on me, his tongue moving up and down my center, hot and rough, before closing his lips around my clit. Laying an arm down across my stomach, he holds me in place and it's then I realize I was bucking wildly against him, chasing the release of tension building up inside.

I can't control the pleasure building up inside me, screams of ecstasy escaping my lips with each flick of his tongue. I know he can tell it too as I feel two fingers slip inside me, coaxing me over the edge as I shatter under him. His mouth is still on me, tongue moving in slow circles around me as he waits for me to come down.

He pulls himself up, leaning over me with his arms on either side of my body.

"You taste so fucking good when you come." He allows his body to crush down onto mine, taking deep, slow kisses from me. I can taste myself on his tongue and nearly topple over the edge again at the feel of his hardness against my thigh.

I move my hand between us, caressing the thick, hard length of him. His hips thrust forward as I tighten my grip around him, working the tip of his cock with my hand, a sharp inhale escaping him as he bites out my name.

"There are condoms in the top drawer." I nod my head to the side table, and he wastes no time leaning over to rifle through the drawer.

"Oh shit," he says with a surprised chuckle and my eyes widen with embarrassment as he holds up a rather large, bright pink, silicone vibrator. He looks at me with a wanton grin. "Oh we're for sure using this next time." He winks as he finds the box of condoms he was searching for, making fast work of taking one out and rolling it down his length.

He settles back on the bed, hovering over me, resting on his elbows, looking deeply into my eyes with the promise of something much more than just lust. I caress his cheek, hoping to convey with one touch the depth of feelings coursing through my body. "Mia, I—" he says at the same time I reach for him, positioning him right by my entrance.

"Preston, please, I need you…"

He presses into me, slowly at first, a satisfied *"fuuuuuuck"* whispering through his lips as he stretches me to accommodate his thickness. We quickly find our rhythm as if we were made for each other, my hips moving to meet each thrust.

"God, Mia you feel so fucking good."

I feel myself tightening around him, making him tip his head back with pleasure, pushing in deeper. My fingernails scratch down his back as I arch upwards, moaning loudly as I feel another release building up inside me.

He takes the cue and moves a hand in between our bodies, rubbing my clit as his thrusts grow faster and deeper with urgency. "Come for me again, beautiful. I want to look into your eyes when you come." His fingers move in perfect swirls with the perfect amount of pressure, coaxing another powerful orgasm from me as his final thrusts pull a shudder from his body with his own release.

Resting his body on mine for a moment, we lay there cradling one another, gasping for breath as we both ride out the final waves of our orgasms. Searching my face for any hint of regret, he places a soft kiss to my lips, content when he finds none.

He rolls off me to dispose of the condom and I touch my lips, still tingling with the ghost of his. This was so much more than merely crushing the tension that has built up between us over these last few weeks. I felt it when he looked at me. When for a moment, I thought for sure he was going to utter three little words.

He returns with a glass of water for me, climbing back into bed and pulling me into his arms, resting my head on his chest. We say nothing, but the way he cradles me speaks volumes. We've irrevocably altered whatever this is between us, for better or for worse.

But the bliss is ripped from me as the last thing that runs through my mind as I fall asleep to the steady beating of his heart is, "Will this all go away when he finds out who I really am?"

Chapter 19

Preston

Last night was a fucking dream come true. Finally having Mia was better than I could have ever imagined. Obviously, the sex was amazing, the sounds she made, her taste, the way our bodies moved in perfect synchronization. It all drove me absolutely insane, but it was the emotional connection that made me fucking gone for this woman.

And if I'm honest, I don't know how to feel about that.

I could have her every single night for the rest of my life and there's no way I'd ever be sated, which terrifies me. In part because I've never let a woman make me this vulnerable, but also because part of me is holding back, wondering if she's capable of hurting me like Sadie, especially now that I know how bad shit really is with the inn's financial status.

I poured over the last five years of the inn's financial records for hours yesterday to try and find out how they were hemorrhaging so much money. Occupancy has been maxed every day since I've arrived and there's always a wait for breakfast and dinner at the restaurant. I knew something wasn't adding up and after some digging, boy did I find it.

It seems our old pal, Winston, had been skimming off the top in a major way. I dug up the old contract for the inn which promised ten percent to The Spencer Group while the inn would retain the remainder for operating costs and employee salaries. Well, Winny boy was taking *sixty* percent, pocketing the other fifty for himself. I can't wait until they find that lying shithead and make him pay.

Still, even if we recoup every penny he stole, it still might not be enough. The other issue is that they've been grossly undercharging, dating all the way back to when my father walked away from the inn. Their rooms are going for sixty-five percent the fair rate and despite Chelsea being a renowned chef, her menu prices are a third of what they should be. She's at the top of her game and should have earned at least one Michelin Star by now, which would allow them to easily triple their prices.

I know Mia won't like these suggestions as they'll make their prices unaffordable for some of the locals, but we need to present a united front on this if we have any hopes of convincing the board the inn is worth keeping. I stroke her hair as she begins to stir awake, and I vow to tell her as soon as she wakes. She looks up at me, her brown eyes still hazy with sleep, a satisfied grin on her face. Okay, maybe I won't tell her *right* away. I can think of a lot of other ways to spend our morning.

A small moan escapes her as she stretches her limbs out around me. And that's all it takes. A whiff of her scent, jasmine and citrus, the softness of her naked body wrapped around mine, and I'm rock hard and ready for her again. Since Sadie, I've lived by the rule of never fucking the same girl twice, but I can't lie to myself. Mia is not like any other girl and what we're doing is so much more than fucking. Her eyes finally meet mine and a pang of something unfamiliar warms my chest.

"Mmm. Good morning." Her voice is raspy with sleep, and she leans up to place a soft kiss on my cheek as if this is a routine we've done a thousand times. I pull her in for a proper kiss and she pushes me away with a laugh.

"No, no, no! I haven't brushed my teeth and I'm sure I have terrible morning breath!" She moves to get up, presumably to go brush her teeth, but I yank her by the arm, enclosing her within mine.

"I cannot emphasize enough how much I absolutely do not care."

Her hand still pushes out on my chest as she turns her head from me.

"Ew, gross. *I'm* gross."

I hold her steady and lightly grab her chin, tilting her head towards me, ensuring she meets my gaze.

"You're perfect."

Her eyes soften and this time she doesn't fight me when I pull her towards me, my mouth claiming hers. She opens up for me easily after that, our tongues dancing together as if this is what they've always been meant for.

She doesn't break our kiss as she shifts slightly, wrapping her leg over mine, and I can feel the heat from her pussy against my thigh. She's already soaked and I'm desperate to have a repeat of last night.

Glancing at the time, I reluctantly break our kiss. "God dammit we have that staff meeting in forty-five minutes and everything I want to do to you cannot be achieved in that time."

In response, she slides her hand down my abdomen until she reaches my cock, grasping it tight, and leans forward to whisper in my ear, "Is that a challenge, Mr. Spencer?" Fuck, this woman is going to be the death of me.

Her languid, teasing pumps have me ready to do anything she says, but I know she'd never want to miss work for anything, even this. Still, with the way she's grinding against my thigh, desperate for friction, I'm completely at her mercy, willing to give her whatever she needs. I reach between us and run a single finger between her center, stopping at the bundle of nerves at its apex. She gasps my name, and I swear to fucking god I could come at the mere sound of my name on her lips.

I stroke her lightly a few times before commanding, "Get in the shower. I'm going to fuck you against the wall until your knees buckle. And then, tonight, I'll take my time and make you scream my name until you've forgotten your own."

She squeals with delight and hops up from the bed, starting towards the bathroom. I place my arm behind my neck, admiring the curve of her ass and the bounce of her tits as she walks towards the bathroom door. She pauses in the archway, cocking her head over her shoulder and beckons me with a finger to follow her into madness.

⚒ ⚒ ⚒

WE MANAGE TO MAKE IT TO THE MEETING RIGHT ON time despite taking extra time with her in the shower, desperate to taste and feel every part of her body as if it will be the last time. At the memory, I give Mia a sly grin as we walk into the dining room together. She flinches as we both look down at our hands, realizing they've been intertwined this entire time. I meet Chelsea's wide eyes, an excited, knowing grin playing across her face, as Mia and I break apart.

I clear my throat and give Mia a nod, pointing to the other side of the room where I make haste to take a seat. Mia takes her spot at the front of the room and begins going over the final preparations for the pageant tonight. I should be paying attention, but I can't stop staring at her, recalling everything we've done. How her full lips felt around my cock as she dropped to her knees, taking all of me in her mouth this morning in the shower. The filthy things she exclaimed as I drove into her, her body pressed against the shower tile. My cock strains uncomfortably along my zipper at the thought and I will myself to stop this line of thinking as I'm in a room full of people.

I'm jerked back to reality when I hear a familiar voice whisper in my ear, "Omg you two totally did it!" I look over to find Chelsea seated right next to me, grinning from ear to ear. When the fuck did she ninja her way over?

"What? No!" I lie nervously. Mia and I didn't discuss if we were keeping this secret, and I'd rather err on the side of caution. I am technically her employee, or maybe employer now, after all.

"Whatever, Casanova. Tell it to the tent in your pants." Her gleeful cackle reverberates throughout the room as I scramble to cover my growing erection with the notebook I'm holding.

"Shh. Pay attention!" I say, trying to take the heat off me, but she won't stop smiling. Mia looks our way, and her face instantly reddens as if she knows what we're talking about. She only stumbles briefly before regaining her composure and finishing up the meeting.

The crowd disperses to take care of the long list of items we need to complete by day's end. Mia saunters over to us as my heart threatens to leap out of my chest, my body vibrating with the need to touch her.

Whether she does it to torture me or to maintain professionalism, she takes the seat furthest away and barely makes eye contact. We're on our best behavior as we go over the plan for meal service tonight, taking a similar approach as we did for Thanksgiving.

That is, until Chelsea interrupts, slamming her hands down on the table with frustration. "OH MY GOD I DON'T FUCKING CARE! Tell me I'm right. Y'all," she looks around before lowering her voice, "bow chicka bow bow," she sing-songs with an immature grin, her eyebrows wagging up and down lewdly.

Mia rolls her eyes but can't suppress her smile. "Shut up." She looks around to make sure everyone else has gone and reduces her voice to a whisper. "We aren't telling anyone yet. Just...whatever. We'll talk later."

She searches my eyes as if to check for any indication I'm angry at what she's admitted. I flash a wide grin. Of course I'm not upset she told her best friend. I'd shout it from every rooftop if it meant everyone knew she was mine.

Mine.

Fuck.

One night with her and I've already staked my claim. An unfamiliar feeling of dread floods my mind with the possibility that she might not want that. I've never once worried about rejection, but with Mia, something's differ-ent. *I'm* different. I can't shake the idea that I'm fall—

Chelsea claps her hands, squealing with glee at the news of our hook up, jolting me out of my worrying train of thought. Our celebration is cut short when my phone rings and I see Stanley's name pop up.

Mia notices my face drop and she looks at me with concern. I shake my head dismissively and make my exit from the table to take the call. I still haven't told her the board wants to sell the inn, and I dread this call is going to confirm they tried to hold a vote without me. I excuse myself from our little conference and head outside to take the call, hoping no one overhears.

I pick up but Stanley doesn't even wait for me to finish saying hello.

"The board isn't happy. They held a preliminary vote this morning to shutter the inn and take the profits. There's an interested buyer that's willing to pay top dollar."

I swipe my hand down the length of my face with an exasperated sigh as my brain works overtime, trying to come up with a way to avoid this. I lightly punch the wall in frustration, immediately regretting that decision when my fist connects, reminding me it's brick. Shaking my hand to will away the pain, I jump into problem solving mode. "What are my options? We're not selling this inn."

"I thought you'd say that. I've held them off as best I can. Legally, no vote can be final until you've weighed in, but I'm going to be honest with you, they can still try a vote of no confidence to strip you of your position. We're going to have to come up with a way to show them the inn is profitable and will be more so than selling it off to some investment bankers."

"Stanley, Winston was syphoning money from the inn. A *lot* of money. That's the only reason it was losing money, I have the numbers to back this up, dating back at least five years. Probably more if I can get my hands on those records. That fucking piece of shit is not going to steal the last fucking thing that remains of my mother."

"Good, keep working on that and send over what you find. We'll talk soon."

He hangs up and I feel completely sick, thinking of the impact this would have on Mia. Every day, I see this is more than a job for her. This place is her home, literally, and she treats her staff like family. The inn needs this town, and I truly believe this town, and The Spencer Group, needs this inn. I've got to get my hands on those records if I have any chance at stopping this, but first, I need to somehow explain all this to Mia.

Chapter 20

Mia

The next week passes in a blur as everyone works to put the finishing touches on the inn for the Christmas pageant next week. I don't know how we did it, but we've managed to complete repairs and renovate almost every part of the inn. Actually, I know exactly how we did it.

Preston smiles at me from across the the dining room where he and our new maitre-d, Erik, are talking. My heart warms as I reflect on how all of this is possible because of him. Seeing him standing there, confidently instructing our new hire, clipboard in hand, I'm amazed at how much he's changed from the pretentious, entitled asshat who came through those doors a month ago. The sparkle in his hazel eyes reminds me of that little boy I used to call my best friend more each day. I can't help but hope I don't extinguish that light when I confess who I really am.

The guilt I feel over keeping this lie while sharing a bed with him night after night is overwhelming, so I've decided. After the pageant on Friday, I'll tell Preston everything. I know it's wrong to keep him in the dark for this long, but the fear of losing him is more than I can bear, and he's made his feelings on liars quite clear. The thought of being yet another person in his life who has disappointed him is something I don't even want to consider. And anyway, we have a lot of work left to be ready for the festival which kicks off tonight. We need to stay focused on that and talking about us will only be a distraction.

And we can't allow ourselves to be distracted…

My eyes follow Preston as he moves around the room commanding respect. The effortless way he has everyone doing exactly what their told without barking orders like, well, his father, is incredibly sexy. His hunter green button down hugs the muscular curves of his biceps and already has my body responding at the memory of how he felt under my caress.

I shake myself out of this incredibly horny line of thinking and I've been caught. A wicked grin spreads across Preston's face, and he quickly wraps up the conversation he was having with one of the construction guys, pats him on the back, and heads in my direction.

"Hmm…what filthy little thoughts are running through your brain right now, beautiful?" He leans in, the heat of his breath tickling my ear, sending waves of desire throughout my body.

"What? Nothing." The shakiness in my voice does nothing to help sell the lie. "Don't you have work to do?"

"Oh, but how can I concentrate on work when you're fucking me from across the room with your eyes?"

"Pfft. I was doing no such thing! We are *at work*. Try to have some professionalism, Preston, geez." A playful grin spreads across his face.

"Mmmm...never. And don't lie, I can tell by the way your pupils are almost black that you can't stop thinking of me in your bed. Just as I can't stop thinking about how you looked squirming beneath me." He grabs my wrist and pulls my hand to the growing bulge in his pants, pulling a gasp from me. "It's all I ever think about lately."

My face reddens and he breaks away with a chuckle and a wink before walking right past me. "Just try to resist me, Mia. You'll give in by the end of the day," he says over his shoulder. Ah, so he wants to play, huh? Game. On.

We spend the rest of the day locked in a flirtatious volley of who can turn the other on the most without getting caught, and my god is it fun. We've decided not to tell anyone about the new developments in our relationship, aside from Chelsea's nosy ass who figured it out on her own, and I have to admit, the secrecy of it all is such a turn on. I can't remember the last time I've felt this pull towards someone, basking in the absolute joy of simply being around them.

So far, I have to say, I'm winning this battle of wills. Sure, he caught me off guard the first time, but I more than got him back during our lunch rush, when two buttons "accidentally" popped open on my blouse and I had to reach over him where he sat in the kitchen, giving him an unrestricted view of the lacy black bralette that lay underneath.

Though he almost had me stealing him away to my office when he came up behind me later, hands resting on the small of my back as he leaned in to describe in great detail all the filthy things he plans to do to me. I mean, it was right in front the wholesome elderly couple who was wrapping up their checkout paperwork. It took every ounce of professionalism to get through that interaction.

Most of the staff has cleared out for the morning to head into town to set up for the festival. We're left virtually alone, the only sounds of chatter coming from the kitchen staff that stayed back for lunch and dinner service. Preston stands by the fireplace, intently typing on his phone while flipping back and forth between papers in the binder he grips in the other hand. I walk up to him, placing my hand on his chest as I rise up on my toes to give him a languid kiss.

"Hi." My voice a sultry whisper, nearly causing him to drop his phone. I say nothing as I look over my shoulder, making sure we're alone, before locking my eyes on his as I slowly pull my hair up into a loose ponytail. His chest rises and falls, quicker and quicker as his eyes burn into mine. Without a word, I keep eye contact, dropping to my knees in front of him, running my hands along the sides of his muscular thighs, watching his eyes grow wide.

"Oh, fuck. Mia. *Here?* Someone could see us!" His face is a mix of excitement and panic. Maintaining eye contact, I reach for a pamphlet that had dropped from the shelf behind him.

"What," I say innocently as I stand up slowly. "I was just putting this back." I pat his chest as I lean in to whisper, "Why? What did you think I was doing?" With a wicked grin, I turn towards my office, but as soon as I thought I was in the clear, I feel his hand on my wrist, tugging me into the room.

Less than a second after he closes the door, his hands are everywhere. Fisting my hair, moving along my jaw as his lips desperately claim mine, moving lower until he grips my ass, pulling my body flush with his, pushing his hardness into me.

"I can't believe you did that. You see what you do to me, Mia? I wonder what I do to you?"

"I...I...*oh god.*" All intelligible thoughts escape my brain as his hand slips under my skirt, a finger lightly grazing my soaked panties. A light chuckle turns into a feral growl as an obscene moan escapes my mouth.

"Fuck, woman, those sounds you make are going to be the death of me." He brings my knee up to his waist, turning me so that my back is against the door before pushing my underwear to the side and slipping two fingers inside me. I gasp his name, locking my arms around his neck to steady myself, his fingers curving to press against my inner walls just the way I like.

"Please...Preston...I need you." I've turned into a mad woman, begging him to fuck me, not even caring that the kitchen staff outside this door can probably hear everything.

His rhythm slows and he leans his forehead against mine, breathless. "I want you too, but not when everyone can hear." Despite his words, his fingers are still working inside me, his thumb moving languidly around my clit as I struggle to find a single coherent thought.

"I can be quiet." My hand reaches between us, stroking the hardness of him that is currently straining to get out of his tight khakis. "I promise."

"Fuuuuck," he groans into my mouth. Just as I'm about to unclasp the button I've been working at, he grabs my wrist, stopping any progress, earning a look of confusion from me.

"What I want to do to you, I don't want anyone to hear.

And, trust me Mia, you're going to be loud." He removes his hand from under my skirt, setting my leg back down and backs away. With his eyes still locked on mine, he takes his fingers in his mouth, the same fingers that were just inside me, and sucks with a moan. He leans past me, brushing his lips against my ear as he grabs for the door, shifting me to the side. "Mmm. You taste like the sweetest fucking honey." He leaves me standing against the wall, trembling with my mouth agape, panting for more.

⚒ ⚒ ⚒

Downtown has been completely transformed into a magical winter wonderland. The windows of the shops along Main Street have all been decorated and lights are strewn around every tree. The carnival style game and food stalls are being erected in the town square for the festival, all circling the massive twenty-five-foot tree that will be the focal point of the lighting ceremony.

Emotion sits heavy in my chest as I approach our booth where we'll sell Christmas-themed baked goods and hand out coupons for discounts on stays at the inn. Every festival since I was little, my mom has run this booth and this will be my first time running it without her. Dr. Sydek assures me she's responding well to treatment and will be here for the pageant, so at least she'll get to see the town transformed for her favorite holiday. Still, her absence stings.

The boxes I've packed with Tetris-like precision mock me from the trunk of my car. Sure, I was able to shove everything *in,* but now I'm not quite sure how to get anything *out.* With a shrug, I go for the topmost center box, tugging on it forcefully finding it won't budge. I struggle with it a few more tries as I feel it dislodge suddenly, sending me stumbling backwards. I expect everything to come crashing down, but nothing happens.

"Whoa, let me get that for ya." James appears behind me just in time, grabbing the box that hangs precariously out of my trunk.

"Oh my god, thank you. I assumed I had it, but, well, you know what happens when you assume." A self-deprecating laugh escapes my mouth as we work together to empty my trunk.

"Gettin' all set up for tonight, I see? Damn, do I smell Chelsea's peppermint mocha brownies?" As if to emphasize, he takes a deep inhale, sniffing the box he's placed on the booth's counter.

"That you do! Tell ya what, go ahead and swipe one for your help." A grin fills his face as he rifles through the box in search of his prize.

"Why thank you, Miss Mia. Hey, do you need any help getting this all set up?"

"Oh my god, that would be amazing! I mean, only if you have time. Usually, Mom and Chelsea help with the booth but..." I stop short of talking about Mom's illness and all of the drama surrounding the inn. Fortunately, James is perceptive enough to understand my meaning and doesn't force the topic.

"It's no problem, really. I was wrapping up the last of the twinkle lights on the smaller trees and Tuck, as usual, is too protective of the tree to let me, or anyone, help." He rolls his eyes in exasperation as he begins unloading the boxes, carefully placing our baked goods into the display cases I've set out.

"Well, I appreciate it. Chels went a bit overboard this

year. That new kitchen has unleashed her creativity, and she spent all night last night thinking up all of these Christmas-themed goodies."

"Sounds about right. Hey, remember that year she cooked up some atrocious fruitcake themed cheesecake and no one had the heart to tell her how awful it was?"

I toss my head back, cackling at the memory. "Yes! You know, I think that's when she knew she was in love with Katy. Everyone else pacified her with fake praise, but not Katy. She hated it so much, she spat it out right in Chelsea's face."

"Oh, man. I almost forgot about that part. That was a good year." He goes quiet for a moment, as if lost in the memories. That was the year we spent together as a couple. We weren't together long, only six months, but things were just getting started between us during the Christmas festival. We're definitely better off as friends, but sometimes, like right now, I worry that maybe he isn't as over us as I had thought.

"It really was a great year." I place my hand on his, comfortingly, "I'm so glad to have you as a friend, James."

"I didn't mean. I mean, I didn't mean like it was great because of *us*. I just mean, it was great period. I'm not still carryin' a torch for you or anything, if that's what you're thinkin'."

"Oh! Of course not! I didn't think you meant, I mean, *obviously*." The awkwardness is palpable as we both share a strained laugh.

"But now that we're on the subject...I gotta ask—what's up with you and Preston?" He knocks his shoulder lightly against mine with raised eyebrows and a knowing grin.

I feel all the blood rush to my cheeks as they turn

bright red. I hope he mistakes the blush for my reaction to the cold as I dart my eyes around, feigning ignorance. "I don't know what you mean?"

"Pfft. You know *exactly* what I mean. That man is head over heels for you. I just—I don't think he's as tough as he makes himself out to be."

"Okay...sure. But there's nothing going on. Swear." I feel bad lying, but Preston and I decided to keep things quiet for now.

"Uh-huh. I mean, back then, I thought, well, I guess you know I thought I was falling for you."

"James, I—"

"No, Mia, it's okay. I'm not sayin' any of this to guilt you. Our friendship is something I'm grateful for every day. My point is, when we were together, it's like we were in two different relationships. I was falling hard, but you were barely there. And when you realized my feelings were getting intense, you pulled away fast. And since then, it seems that's been your pattern with anyone who tries to get close."

"In my defense, after my mom got sick and I took over the inn, I really didn't have time to be a good girlfriend. And then there's the whole Geoffrey thing. But, James, I'm really sorry, I didn't mean to treat you like you didn't matter."

Ugh. Geoffrey. The name tastes like poison in my mouth. Shortly after graduating from NYU, I landed a marketing internship at one of the top restaurant groups in Manhattan. That's where I met Geoffrey Freedman. He was everything I thought I wanted at the time. Successful, mature, ambitious, and *painfully* gorgeous, with the kind of piercing arctic blue eyes that seemed to look straight into your soul. He made junior partner at his law firm at only twenty-five and he wanted *me*. I couldn't believe it.

Our romance was the very definition of whirlwind. After a few dates, we jumped headfirst into a serious relationship, declaring our love within a few mere weeks. Three months later, I'd moved into his high rise, and we quickly fell into a comfortable, if a bit boring, routine.

He was my rock the first time Mom got sick, but once she recovered and things got less intense, it's as if he lost interest completely. And when she got sick the second time, he couldn't seem to find the time to support me.

I tried to be understanding. By this point, he was up for senior partner, and I knew that was going to take up a lot of his time, so I commuted back and forth to Vermont every weekend alone. The second week I came back, I caught him in bed with his assistant like a horrible cliché. As I'd come to find out later, they'd been sleeping together for months. I heard through the grapevine they married last year.

I'm brought back to the present when James weighs in. "Yeah, well, from what you told me, Geoffrey was a dick. But Preston isn't Geoffrey."

Chewing on my bottom lip, I consider that. I've seen Preston grow so much in these last few weeks, but he wasn't always like that. In fact, he was much more like Geoffrey than I care to admit.

"Isn't he, though? When I met Geoffrey, he was a player. He had an entire roster before we started dating. If you'll recall Preston's *many* appearances in Page Six, he always had a new girl on his arm every night. I guess I don't want to be another temporary stop."

James considers this for a moment, stroking his nonexistent beard. "So what if you're temporary? Maybe that's okay. With you and I, well, there was a lot of expectation there. It didn't help the entire town was deeply invested and had no qualms about sharing their opinions."

"True. My god, why do we put up with these people?"

"They're family. What can ya do?" We share a chuckle as he shrugs, shaking his head. "What I mean is, we were doomed from the start. Our chemistry was always more friendly, and I think we tried to force something that wasn't there because we both wanted the marriage and picket fence thing. With Preston, maybe that's where you go, but maybe not. Maybe opening up to someone, without pressure, is exactly what you need."

"It's not that simple with me and Preston though."

James looks utterly perplexed, and I realize I haven't shared the truth with him either.

"Why? Because his family owns the inn and their company's engulfed in scandal? Who cares? It's not like either of you can control that, right?"

I let the question hang in the air as I wrestle with whether to tell him the truth. Deciding against it, I offer him a small smile. "I suppose you're right, but I guess I'm scared. What if I get hurt again?"

"Mia, I see the way he looks at you. That man, wooo, he's got it bad. Trust me."

"Maybe..."

"Okay, sure. Let's say you give it a try and it doesn't work out. What if you go for a drive and get in a wreck? What if you trip over that strand of lights and scuff up your pretty little nose on the pavement? You can live your life thinking through every possible what if, but then, are you even really living? Take a chance, Mia. Live."

I spot Preston across the square, laughing with Ernie, Tucker, and the guys as they argue about the height of the huge banner they're hanging at entrance of the festival. He catches my eye and flashes me that perfect smile, surrounded by deep dimples.

"James, how the hell are you so young, yet so wise?"

"I dunno, darlin'. Just lucky, I guess." He follows my line of sight and catches Preston and I staring at each other. He gently nudges me with his elbow, nodding to the pile of lights at our feet. "Come on. Let's finish these lights and then you go get your man."

Chapter 21

Preston

My afternoon began like a bad joke. *"How many men does it take to hang a festival banner?"* But that has been my reality for the last two hours. Since the inn was in pretty good shape for the upcoming Christmas festivities, I was voluntold by Mia to head into town and see what help I could offer the festival committee. Turns out, Ernie was heading up the committee and had a simple enough job for me—help him hang the banner his wife created for the entrance to the town square.

And it really should have been simple. I would climb up the ladder to secure one side and move to the other side while Ernie stood a few feet back directing me to make sure it stayed straight. Instead, before I could make it halfway up the ladder, everyone decided to huddle around us, offering their unsolicited opinions on how we planned to hang it.

Tucker was the first to appear, concern on his face as he looked disapprovingly at our pile of nails and string.

"Now, Ernie, I just don't feel good 'bout those wimpy little nails you're usin' to secure this. Here, let me go get my tools and we'll find something a bit sturdier."

"Tuck, I've been doing this for nearly twenty years, boy. I know what I'm doing. Trust me." Ernie folds his arms with a scowl.

"What you really need to do is add another pole down the middle. Otherwise, it's gonna sink right there in the middle," Richie shouts from across the street as he's caught sight of our attempt.

Fuck this, I mutter to myself as I grab one side of the banner, climbing up the rest of the way to proceed with our original plan. This banner is going to be up for less than a week and at this rate, that's about when this group will agree on how to string it up. They're so busy arguing with one another, they don't even notice what I'm doing until I shout to get their attention long enough to help me straighten it out.

I spot Mia as I'm tying off the final knot, almost dropping the rope in the process. She looks adorable in her bubblegum pink puffer jacket, her long hair hanging below a baby blue beanie, its fluffy pom blowing in the wind. Joy radiates from her as she smiles and laughs with Jimmy, working to untangle a mess of Christmas lights. The rational part of my brain knows they're just friends, but the baser part of me feels the irrational pangs of jealousy and before I realize what I'm doing, I've climbed down the ladder, headed in her direction.

"Wow, this place looks great, Mia. Hey, Jimmy." My voice goes up half an octave in an attempt to seem like I'm completely cool with the woman whose bed I've been occupying flirting with the man who *used* to occupy it. I don't know what the fuck is wrong with me. I'm never this possessive, but I really hope Mia doesn't catch on.

"Hey! James was helping me untangle this mess here. Five bucks says Chelsea put these away last year." She discards the ball of knotted lights, chuckling awkwardly while rocking back and forth on her heels, eyes darting between me and Jimmy.

"Oh, hey, uh. Look at that. Uh, do you think Ernie needs...yeah, I'm gonna, go that way." Jimmy comes to the rescue, breaking the unbearable silence, and points to, well, nothing as he makes his exit.

"Soooo...that was weird," she says with an awkward laugh.

"Yeah, a bit. So, uh, you're hanging out with Jimmy again? And you call him *Jaaames*. That's cool." I scrunch my face with embarrassment. What the fuck is wrong with me? Why am I acting like this?

"Oh my god! Preston! You're *jealous*!" Her eyebrows raise with realization, and she doubles over with laughter, crossing her arms around her stomach.

"Pfft. Jealous? Absolutely not. I don't get jealous. Should I be?" I'm joking, but a part of me wonders if I should be. Jimmy would be a fool to not be completely enthralled by this woman. Anyone would be.

She steps into my space, placing her hand on my chest, her big brown eyes gazing up into mine. "You are. But it's okay. I think it's kinda hot."

"Oh, you do, huh?"

"Kinda. Just don't do any of that alpha male bullshit and I can work with it." I can feel her smile through the soft kiss she places on my lips.

I yearn to kiss her deeper, to let everyone know that

she's *mine.* To let everyone know this woman has managed to do something I thought was impossible. She's made me feel, made me care, made me jealous. And that terrifies me because it could all go away.

"I used to come here with my mother when I was a kid." I take her hand in mine and turn to scan the square, which is coming together almost exactly as I remember it.

"Oh?" She sighs, a hint of sadness in her voice.

"Yeah. It's changed a lot, but there's so much that's the same." I point to a red and green booth nestled in the far corner of the square. "See that booth over there? That is the best cotton candy I've ever had in my life. Pumpkin pie flavored cotton candy? Who would've thought that up? My mother would try and warn me, but I always ate myself into a tummy ache." My eyes start to glisten at the memory and Mia's gentle hand comes up to cradle my cheek in comfort.

"You know, that's still Mr. Hogan's most popular flavor? You'll have to go get some once the festival kicks off."

"Come with me."

"To get cotton candy?"

"No, to the festival. Someone else can work the booth, right?"

"Oh, of course. Lizzy and Erik are scheduled to man the booth tonight anyway."

"So, is that a yes?"

"Sure. I'll hang out with you tonight at the festival."

Her flirtatious grin lets me know she's being purposely obtuse. She wants me to say it. No, she *needs* me to ask her properly.

"Mia," I say sternly. "You know what I mean."

"I do?"

"Mia, will you accompany me to the winter festival tonight as my date?"

She brings her pointer finger up to her chin, scrunching her face as if she has to ponder deeply before tossing her arms around my neck with a wide grin. "I'd love to go on a date with you, Preston."

⚒ ⚒ ⚒

IT TAKES ME ALMOST TWO HOURS TO GET READY FOR my date with Mia. I've always taken care to look my best on dates, but I've never been so concerned with my appearance before in my life. We did things a little out of order, jumping into bed before we even had a real date, but I want to make a good impression. This woman has seen me naked and undone, but I'm still desperate to impress her. I tried on at least five different outfit combinations before settling on a heather gray cashmere sweater over a white collared shirt, and khaki chinos.

I emerge from my room and spot Mia gliding on a subtle burgundy lipstick in the hallway mirror. She quite literally takes my breath away even in her simple maroon sweater dress, black wool tights, and black knee-high boots, her espresso waves pulled into a high ponytail with small curls framing her face. A small part of me wants to say "fuck it", skip the festival, and spent the entire night worshiping every curve of her body. But I couldn't derail our plans after the way her face lit up when I asked her on a proper date. Yes, being buried inside her is my new favorite activity, but I want more than that with her. She deserves better and I'm determined to be better. For her.

"Wow, you look beautiful." I place my hand on the small of her back and lean in, placing a light peck on her cheek. She looks me up and down with approval and I see her eyes darken with desire. Maybe she wouldn't be averse to staying home in bed.

"You clean up pretty nice yourself, Mr. Spencer." My cock twitches at the sound of her calling me *Mr. Spencer* and I fight to train my thoughts on anything other than the possibility of acting out all the filthy things she reads about in those billionaire romances I spotted on her bookshelves. Thankfully, I'm jolted out of this dangerous train of thought when my phone buzzes, alerting me that the car I've arranged for us has arrived.

The town square looks even more magical at night with all the twinkle lights on full display. The smell of funnel cakes and pine fills the air, the sound of carolers echoing in the open space. I silently applaud myself for choosing the festival as our first date and judging by the way Mia's face lights up as she takes it all in, I grow even more confident.

"What should we do first?" Between the food, the games, and the makeshift ice-skating rink, there's so much to do and I'm momentarily embarrassed that I didn't plan this out better. If I'm being honest, it's been a while since I've taken anyone out on an actual *date*. Usually, I take them to bed and forget about them in the morning. A grin spreads across her face, and she lifts her hand pointing to the center of the square where the ice rink stands. Dammit.

"Oh, no. No, Mia. I'm from LA. I don't know how to ice skate."

She gasps in mock horror and gives my hand a squeeze.

"Preston! You're a thirty-four year-old man and don't know how to ice skate?! How embarrassing for you." With a smirk, she tugs on my hand, dragging me to towards the rink.

"No, the embarrassing part will be me falling on my ass in front of the beautiful girl I'm trying to impress."

Her cheeks pink, whether from the cold or that absolute cheeseball comment, I'll never know. Still, I suck up my pride and follow her to the counter to rent our skates.

I stand unsteadily on the skates for the first time, waddling over like a baby deer to meet Mia at the edge of the rink. I brace myself along the makeshift railing, marveling at her, arms outstretched, eyes closed, a smile spread across her face in unrestrained joy as she glides around the rink. She holds out her hands to me and as I look her in the eye, I know right then this woman could convince me to do anything.

"Come on. Just keep your balance centered and glide your feet out in a V."

I take my first wobbly glide and manage to stay upright. Okay, maybe this won't be so bad.

"Yeah! You got it! See, not that hard?"

We barely make it one lap before I fall for the first time, face first, ice kicking up into my beard. As if straight out of a cartoon, each time I try to right myself, I slip back down, thrashing my arms wildly in a feeble attempt to regain my balance before falling at least four times on the ice. Mia has been doubled over in laughter at my first stumble until she notices my scowl. Even the small children speeding by me with effortless grace stop to toss a laugh in my direction. So much for impressing her.

I roll onto my back and lay on the ice in utter defeat,

grunting with frustration. Mia hovers over me with a kind smile and bends down, extending her arms to me as if to help me up. I make to accept her, but upon remembering her raucous laughter *at* me, I grab her arm, pulling her down on top of me instead, causing us both to erupt in laughter.

We lay there for what seems like hours, annoyed skaters mumbling their disapproval as they wiz by, before we finally catch our breath. With two quick pats to my chest, she helps me up and guides us off the ice.

"All right, maybe ice skating isn't your forte. How about we get off the ice and do something a little less risky, like hot cocoa?"

"I did try to tell you." We make quick work of returning our skates when her laughter returns, no doubt replaying my embarrassing display in her mind.

"I suppose you did. I didn't think you'd be *that* bad. Guess those muscles really are gym-made only, huh?" With a wink and a breathy laugh, she saunters towards the cocoa stand.

"109 different cocoa combinations?" I read the claim on the sign outside the booth skeptically.

"Oh yeah, it's kind of the highlight of the festival. We wait all year to see what flavor combination Bea decides to feature each year." She scrunches up her nose as she spots this year's signature flavor. Hot jalapeño cocoa. "I think we might pass on this year's feature and go for something a bit more traditional."

I nod in agreement before ordering two classic cocoas, exchanging pleasantries with Ernie and Bea who currently run the booth. Mia and I walk hand and hand, admiring the Christmas displays featured in the windows of the shops along Main Street, chatting about everything and nothing. It's amazing to me that I've only known this woman for a short time, but it feels like I've known her my entire life.

We stop at the center of the square which features a line of horse drawn carriages, and I extend my arm in a playful bow towards Mia. "Your carriage awaits, m'lady." I help her up and cover us with the fleece blanket as we take a ride back to the inn. The carriage ride loops around the tiny town, allowing us to admire how everyone has come together to transform their homes and businesses into a massive display of lights, creating a festive and romantic ambiance.

"It's been so good to see you smile again tonight. I feel like you've been...Is everything okay?"

I suck in a deep breath, debating if now is the time to tell her about the conversations I've been having with the board about shuttering the inn. But as I stare into the deep brown eyes that echo the well of emotion I feel for her, I hold back, unwilling to steal this bit of happiness from her. Instead, I give a dismissive wave and settle for half-truths, my stomach in knots as I do.

"Everything has been running on overdrive since Oliver and Stanley made me CEO. On the one hand, I feel like I've been preparing for this my entire life, but on the other, it feels like maybe I haven't prepared at all, you know?"

With a sympathetic smile, she brings my hand to her mouth for a comforting kiss and turns to face me. "You *are* ready for this. You're going to be great."

"If I'm great, it's all because of you, you know that right?" She looks at me, puzzled, still holding my hand in hers. "I was dreading coming back here. It reminded me of some of the worst times of my life, with my father abandoning us and my mother getting sick and..."

I trail off from the memory, catching Mia's gaze and see a flash of something that almost looks like guilt or shared sorrow, as if she too is remembering the same grief. I suppose she's thinking of that possibility with her own mother.

"I guess what I'm trying to say is, I kind of owe this change to you. Before I came here, my life was spiraling out of control. But then I met you and you just...you made me feel...like maybe I'm not the villain in this story."

"It's not. Because of me, I mean. And I don't think you've changed all that much," she says, snuggling into me as she pulls my arm over her shoulder.

"Oh, gee, thanks."

She giggles. "No, that's not—I didn't mean it like *that*. I just mean, you put up this facade like you're evil or something. I've never seen you that way. Sure, you've made some stupid mistakes. Like fighting with a construction worker in the middle of the foyer," she laughs into my chest. "You might play tough, but you're a big ol' softie." She tilts her head up, locking eyes with mine. "What you did for me with my mom, with the inn, I can't put into words what that meant to me. You're not a villain, Preston. You're...*good*."

She presses her lips to mine, not with lust or expectation, but as if she needs her body to tell me what her words cannot. It's over as soon as it began, and she snuggles back into my chest.

"Sometimes I don't feel that way. After Sadie, I was a broken shell of a man. I built up walls so thick that no one was getting through to hurt me that way again. I think back on how I used the parties, the women, to bury my pain and I'm not proud of the man I was then. The irony is that Sadie faked everything so spectacularly, she gave me the confidence to renounce my inheritance and focus on charity work, which ended up being the exact reason she left. She briefly made me feel like maybe I was worthy of love, despite the fact my father never showed me an ounce of it after my mother passed."

Placing my knuckle under her chin, I bring her face to mine, searching for any indication she's unhappy with this train of thought. Especially since Sadie is a sensitive topic with us, but all I see is compassion.

"Then I met you and you took a fucking bulldozer to those walls. With you, there's no doubt that you're seeing *me*. Or at least the man I want to become. And, yeah, I'm scared as hell, Mia. I'm scared of getting my heart broken again. I'm scared that you'll see how broken I really am and run away. For you, it's a risk I'm willing to take. I trust you and I know you'd never lie to me like that."

Her eyes glisten with tears and I worry maybe I fucked this all up with so many words. Talking about your ex on a first date is probably breaking some cardinal rule. But instead of being angry, she cups my cheek with her hand, inching her face up to mine.

"I see you—the man you were, the man you are, and the man you want to be. I like every version of you. You're not broken, Preston. Not any more than I am, anyway and I'm so grateful I get to be yours."

Mine.

She really is mine. She wants this as much as I do. I can't help but steal a kiss, pouring the emotions I can't say aloud into her lips, only stopping when I feel the carriage slow.

Snow begins to fall as we approach the inn. I exit first, coming around to her side, offering her my hand to help her down. My hands glide down her body, stopping at her waist as I guide her to the ground. Her jasmine and citrus scent is particularly intoxicating tonight as our faces remain mere inches from one another. Her eyes darken as mine roam her face, stopping at her full lips before crashing down again, claiming her mouth with mine. I don't care that we're out where everyone can see us as I pull her body into mine, opening her mouth with my tongue, eliciting a sinful moan from her.

"Preston," her voice a shaky whisper, "everyone can see."

"Let them. I want them all to know you're mine." As if to drive my point home, I cup her face in my hand, bringing her back to me, claiming her with another long, slow kiss before nearly dragging her towards the cottage in a sprint.

The second we close the door, we're a frantic mess of limbs, tearing off our clothes between kisses and gropes. I'll never get enough of this woman, and I need to feel her skin on mine now. Scooping her up in my arms, she wraps her legs around my waist as we leave a trail of clothes to her room.

I stand in utter disbelief as her naked body lays before me. She's perfection and beauty and need and, fuck, everything. I don't know what I did to deserve this, but I'm going to cling to her for as long as she'll have me.

Chapter 22

Mia

It's the day of our Christmas pageant and I wake up snuggled in Preston's arms. The steady rise and fall of his chest lets me know he's still asleep and even though I have much to do to prepare for this evening's events, I can't bring myself to get up. Selfishly, I want us to stay like this for as long as we can, knowing that once I tell him who I really am, this might never happen again. And I will tell him. Tonight, after the pageant.

"What's going on in that pretty little head of yours?" He runs his fingers through my hair, which is probably a horrific tousled mess from our enthusiastic sex last night, as he stirs from his sleep.

It would be so easy to blurt it out right now and part of me thinks how freeing it would be to just tell him and get it over with. The other part can imagine him shoving me off, glaring at me with utter hatred for being yet another manipulative liar in his life. But after everything we shared last night, how he opened up about his insecurities, and how we finally acknowledged our relationship, it's time for this charade to end. I tilt my head up to his, cupping his cheek with my palm.

"I'm just thinking about how incredibly proud of you I am for the way you're handling all of this, it's truly impressive. And I'm so glad you trusted me with everything."

"And the sex was fucking amazing," he interjects with a laugh, stealing a lazy kiss. My heart is racing, and I deepen our kiss, worried this might be the last time I feel his lips on mine.

"That's a given. But, Preston, there's something I have to tel—"

I'm cut off as my phone buzzes on the nightstand, the special ringtone I set for Dr. Sydek filling the room. I leave Preston's embrace, panic surging through my body as I answer the phone, every worst-case scenario flashing through my mind at the early call.

"Hi, Dr. Sydek? Is everything okay?" My voice is shaky, and Preston sits up straighter, rubbing my back comfortingly.

"Hi, Mia. Sorry to call so early. Everything's fine, I wanted to confirm some details for tonight. Is now a good time?"

I expel a loud sigh of relief and give Preston a nod, confirming everything is okay at the same time his phone starts blowing up too. He gets out of bed, placing a gentle kiss to my forehead before pulling on his sweatpants and going to the other room to finish up his call.

"Mia, are you there?"

"Sorry, I'm here. What details do you need?"

"About the timing. Is it okay if we arrive closer to the pageant start time? I'd like your mom to have as much time with you as possible, but as I'm sure you'll understand, she tires easily."

"Oh, yes! I completely understand. The pageant should get underway at six-thirty, so maybe get here around six, does that work?"

"Six is perfect. One more thing, I'd like to confirm the menu for the evening. The treatment has fairly specific dietary requirements and I need to make sure we don't need to bring a special meal down. Which, of course, I can do no problem."

We spend a few more minutes talking over the adjustments to mom's meal and he assures me I shouldn't worry. I know he'll be here to monitor her if anything goes wrong, but I can't seem to shake this feeling deep in my bones that something is going to go terribly wrong. And I can't help but think it has little to do with Mom and everything to do with what's going to happen when I confess to Preston.

⚒ ⚒ ⚒

Even though I had a hand in most of the preparation for tonight's pageant, I wasn't fully prepared to see everything pulled together so perfectly when I walk in an hour early.

Though we're serving a multi-course meal, determined to never let our guests go hungry, Chelsea set up a small buffet in the sitting room. Dozens of Christmas-themed sweet treats, coffee, and three different kinds of cocoa are stacked atop a serving table in the corner. The fireplace is roaring, and the scent of peppermint and pine fills the air as early arrivals grab plates of goodies, chatting away excitedly about tonight's event.

The twelve-foot Christmas tree is the focal point of our foyer, stopping right below the gorgeous new chandelier. Its bright light casts the room in sparkles, light reflecting off its glass and the ornaments of the tree. I follow the faint sounds of Christmas carols, and my eyes widen with glee at the sight of the finished dining room.

Perfectly pressed, white tablecloths adorn each table, a bouquet of freshly cut poinsettias in their center. In the corner of the room, a small stage has been erected, featuring a newly painted backdrop portraying a small Christmas-themed living room. It will be the stage for our main event, the town elementary school's production of The Night Before Christmas. To the left of the fireplace sits a beautiful red and gold throne, where Santa will take his seat and hand out gifts at the end of the night. Fake snow has been sprinkled throughout the room and dimly lit snowflake lights hang from the ceiling at varying heights, giving the illusion of a perfect snowfall.

"You did an amazing job, Mia. It's breathtaking. Like you," Preston says in my ear as he comes up behind me, his hand grazing the small of my back. I lean into his touch, savoring his smokey sandalwood scent.

"*We* did an amazing job. If it weren't for you and the boys this morning, we might have been in trouble!" Preston and Tucker's crew let me shove off a bit early to go rest before the party when exhaustion threatened to toss me off another ladder. The dining room was in decent shape by then, but this is even better than I could have imagined.

I turn around to look at him and my breath catches in my throat. Preston stands before me in a perfectly tailored black suit with a bright red bowtie sitting along his neck, a matching silk pocket square in his chest pocket. He's recently shaved the stubble that had been overtaking his face, leaving only a slight whisper of hair along his mustache and jawline. He flashes me a wide grin, dimples deepening on either side of his mouth, showing off his perfect white teeth, before scanning the room to make sure we're alone and bending down for a quick kiss.

"You look..." He looks so damn good I'm tongue tied, unable to finish my thought. My knees threaten to buckle beneath me. No one has a right to look *that* good.

He gives a light chuckle, stepping back to admire my look for the evening. Chelsea convinced me to choose a daring hunter green gown that I would have never picked for myself. The smooth satin hugs my every curve and is subtly adorned with silver beads, sparkling when the light hits them at the right angle. Its plunging neckline had me balk at first worrying my small breasts wouldn't fill it out properly, but with a little boob tape, even I have to admit, I look *good*. And judging by how Preston's eyes darken as they roam up and down my body, I think he agrees.

"*Fuuuuck*, woman. You're killing me with that dress." He bends in closer, his mouth brushing my ear. "How am I going to get through the night when all can think about is peeling this off you later and kissing every inch of your body until the memory of me between your thighs lingers for days? I can't have you forgetting about me when I'm in LA next week."

My stomach flips, heat pooling at my core, the images flashing vividly in my head. His words and the way he looks at me like I'm the last meal he'll ever devour sends a chill of anticipation down my spine. That is, until my brain reminds me that before there will be any peeling off of clothes, I have to tell him I've been lying to him for weeks.

"I can't wait," I reply, hoping the rasp of my voice comes out sultry instead of betraying my panic. Truthfully, I'd been so focused on what might happen after my confession, I completely forgot he needed to be in LA to deal with the transition. The thought of dropping this on him right before he leaves adds an extra layer of anxiety.

Fortunately, I don't have to dwell on that too long as the first crisis of the evening presents itself in the form of my head chef running out of the kitchen in a frenzy, stopping short before plowing into us.

"Oh, good. Preston, you're here. I have a prob—Holy hell you two look amazing!" She steps back, surveying us both intently. "Well, done. Mia, you sexpot! I knew that dress was the one." She winks at me and wags her eyebrows at Preston which receives an eye roll from my direction.

"Thanks. What's got you so frantic?" Preston pulls her back to the moment.

"Oh, right. We're fucked, basically."

"I'm sure we're not *fucked*. What is it?"

"Well, you know Erik, the new maitre-d we hired?" Preston nods as she throws up her hands in exasperation. "Well, he's sick."

Preston fights a laugh. "Is that all?"

"What do you *mean* 'is that all'?! Who's going to run dinner service tonight?"

"Well, I'm here, for starters," Preston says through a laugh, "and I *did* come up with the entire service plan and spent the past week training Erik. Will that work?"

Chelsea smacks her hand to her head. "Omg. *Duh*! Of course. Okay. Crisis averted!" She spins on her heel and goes back into the kitchen as Preston and I share a laugh.

He gives me a quick kiss on the cheek before following Chelsea to prepare for service.

An hour passes and I feel like I've greeted everyone in town, but I still haven't seen the only person I really want to to see tonight. I look down at my phone but find no missed calls or texts from Mom. As soon as concern starts to furrow my brow, I see Dr. Sydek holding her by the arm, guiding her through the door. She looks regal in her navy, floor length gown, cinched at the waist with a gold adornment that causes the skirt to pleat at the center. Her hair hangs in beautiful tendrils around her face, which shows none of the former exhaustion I saw the other day. She's walking with a cane, but judging by her spry jaunt, I assume the cane is more precautionary than anything.

"Oh, mija. It's beautiful." She stops in the foyer, taking it all in with a hand placed over her heart and tears pooling in her eyes. She motions for me to come hug her and I almost fall apart at her touch. I didn't fully allow myself to focus on how much I missed her until this very moment.

"Mamá, you look absolutely stunning!"

She does a cute little spin, brushing her hair over her shoulder with a laugh.

"Gracias, mi amor! I *feel* amazing. This one is a miracle worker!"

"I don't know about miracle, but I'm happy to report the treatment is working. We'll have another scan in a month, but preliminary results suggest your mother is responding extremely well to our efforts." Dr. Sydek smiles and shakes my hand in congratulations. "Anyway, I'll leave you two to catch up." He excuses himself and wanders into the dining area to mingle with the other guests.

Mom puts her hands on my shoulders, before bringing

them up to cup my face as she moves my head from side to side, checking for who knows what. I send up a silent prayer, hoping that my more amorous activities with Preston haven't left any visible marks.

"You look different," she says, flatly, but not cruelly.

"Um...thanks?"

"Not different, bad. Just...different. Qué te pasa?"

Shaking off her question, I offer my arm to take her to the table where we'll be sitting in the dining room. I glance over and my heart warms to see her beaming as she looks around the room.

"Well, he sure does clean up nice. Has something happened?" A knowing smirk spreads across her face as her eyes find Preston across the room.

"Um..." I struggle for an answer. Should I really tell her our relationship has progressed when it might well end tonight?

She rolls her eyes and huffs. "I knew that little pendejo couldn't keep his hands to himself after we talked at the hospital! Tell me you're at least being careful."

"*Mamá!*" I lower my voice, darting my eyes around the room, hoping no one heard that.

Instead, she waves her hand dismissively as if I'm not completely mortified by my mom giving me *The Talk* at thirty-two in my place of business.

"Oh, not like that! I meant with your heart. But now that you mention it..."

"You don't have to worry, Mamá. Preston has been, well, he's amazing. Trust me, okay?" I pointedly ignore the last part, determined to not speak of my sex life with my mom.

"How did he take the knowledge of who you really are?"

"I haven't told him yet. I meant to, but it got to the point where so much time had passed, I thought it would be weird if I told him. And then...we...kind of...you know." My cheeks redden at the thought of everything *you know* entailed.

She reaches up to cup my face, mercifully not addressing the "you know" of it all. "Ay, mija. That must be so hard for you. But you must tell him, yes?"

"He's constantly talking about how he can never forgive his father and his ex for their constant lying. What if he never wants to speak to me again?"

She considers this for a moment. "Hm, well, if he cannot accept that you are human and flawed, then he is not deserving of you."

"I don't think it's that simple. I..." I love him. I've been fighting the voice in my head that said it every time our eyes meet across the room. When our bodies accidentally brush against one another during our comfortable morning routine. As he's the last thing that crosses my mind at night before drifting to sleep. And when our bodies are intertwined, pouring all the feelings into each other that words could never convey.

But it must be far too soon to feel this way, right? Sure, I knew him when we were young, but I've only known this version of him for a little over a month. There's a part of me that worries I'm jumping in too fast with him like I did with Geoffrey, but everything with Preston feels so much deeper. Judging by the concerned look on my mom's face, I can tell she suspects it too.

"You love him, don't you?"

"I-I think I do. I *know* I do. Mamá, what am I going to do if this makes him hate me?"

"Oh, my Amelia, how could he ever hate you? I remember even back then he protected you with everything he had. Siempre tendrás su corazón."

You'll always have his heart.

I can't help but hope she's right. Maybe it doesn't even matter that he didn't recognize me at first. I've never believed in destiny or fate, but how can I deny that him coming back to me is a sign?

"Thanks, Mamá. I hate to leave you, but I have to go deal with a few things. Please enjoy everyone's company and I'll be back before dinner." I give her one last hug and break away as I notice our friends and neighbors making their way excitedly to the table as they spot her. I smile seeing her back in her element and start to think maybe everything will be okay after all.

⚒ ⚒ ⚒

THE PAGEANT AND DINNER SERVICE ARE PERFECT. Even the slight mishap as one of the kids forgot their lines and made up a completely different plot had the room erupting in laughter instead of disappointment.

As I walk out the last of the guests, I spot Oliver and a short, stocky man in a grey suit taking a drink near the fireplace in the sitting area. So, they did accept my invitation after all...

"Ollie! I'm so glad you could make it! Who's your friend?" I embrace him and place two quick pecks of air near each cheek.

"Miss Flores, you're looking quite fetching this

evening. This is Stanley Beck, lead counsel for The Spencer Group." He points to the man who acknowledges me with a curt nod. "The board sends their regrets that they were unable to accept your gracious invitation."

"Oh, well that's too bad. They missed one of our best performances." I plaster a sincere smile on my face.

"It was spectacular!" Oliver exclaims. His companion, Stanley, merely grunts in response as he continues to sip his whiskey.

"Preston had a lot to do with the planning and execution. You should extend your gratitude his way as well."

In answer, Stanley merely hands me his whiskey glass as he rises from his seat. "Yes, well, thank you for a wonderful evening, but we must be going. I'm glad to see the inn is doing well. It will go a long way with the fight with the board." He nods at Oliver, and they head out, leaving me standing there, confused.

Fight with the board? Panic creeps up my spine as I try to piece together what he could have meant by that. My mind flashes back to the man in the background of my FaceTime call with Oliver last week.

We are not continuing to pour money into a losing property!

Could this all be related? On top of my anxiety surrounding the looming conversation with Preston, I can't think of what it would mean if the company wanted to shut down the inn. I don't have too much time to dwell on it as Preston approaches the sitting room, a crooked smile on his face. He walks right toward me and wastes no time pulling me into his arms, breathing me in as if my presence sustains him.

"God, I missed you. I saw your mother and she seems to be doing so much better, doesn't she?"

I sigh contentedly, burrowing deeper into his arms. "Yeah, she's doing great. I was about to go find her."

"Oh, they had to head out. She and the doc told me to tell you they'd FaceTime you in the morning."

"Is she okay?" I push away from him, concern in my eyes, but he tugs me in closer.

"She's fine, Mia. She was probably just tired. Is there something else bothering you? You're so tense."

"Oliver and Stanley were here this evening."

"Oh?" His tone is clipped, as if he's holding something back.

"Yeah. They were quite impressed with the event, but that Stanley guy said something super weird and it kind of made me panic. He made it seem like the inn could be in trouble?"

"Fuck." Preston scrubs a hand down the length of his face in frustration.

"Look, Mia, I need to tell you something."

"We need to talk." My words come out over his. "Can we go talk in my office?"

As soon as we step into the room, I close the door, walking timidly to stand behind my desk, putting as much distance between us as possible, knowing that the second I feel his touch, I'll lose my nerve. Silence hangs heavy in the room until we both talk over one another again.

With a light chuckle, Preston tells me to go first.

"I just want to preface this by saying I promise you I had no ulterior motives, I just, well I wanted to tell you, but time kept getting away from me. There was the chandelier, then the electrical chaos, then you moved into my house, and I saw you walking around half naked, which was so not fair, by the way." I point my finger at him.

He laughs at me and walks around to where I stand, placing his hands on my shoulders.

"Mia, breathe. Whatever you have to tell me can't be that bad."

I wring my hands into the fabric of my dress as I take a deep breath and prepare to confess.

"Do you remember when you used to live here? As a kid, I mean?"

"Uh, do I remember the first twelve or so years of my life? Yeah. I think I remember that."

"Okay, so. You had a friend. A little girl."

A nervous laugh escapes me, and I notice his face is scrunched up as if trying to decipher what I'm talking about.

I clear my throat, willing myself to start again. "Well, I know all that because, um, I was here too. Living in the inn with my mom. Honestly, I was sure you'd recognize her when we went to visit. Not that you recognized me, so..." I trail off, the nervousness making my words come out like nonsense.

"Mia, what in the hell are you talking about? You're not making any sense." He doesn't look angry, just confused as he clearly hasn't connected the dots yet.

"Um...I thought...I mean, we grew up together. I thought you'd figure it out by now. But when you didn't, I couldn't figure out how to tell you and—"

I can't help the tears streaming from my face as my mind moves between memories of our youth and everything that has grown between us since his return. To the day I saw him pull away in the taxi, face and hand pressed against the window as he watched me sob on the front steps of the inn. And to present day, where he stands before me, a faint look of confusion on his face until a slight shift and his eyes go wide. I know then he's figured it out. He looks at me with recognition for the first time since his return.

"Amelia?!"

My tears stream out in a deluge as I hear my name on his lips for the first time in twenty-two years. I've waited so long for him to remember me. To acknowledge our connection meant something to him too. But the hurt on his face is so much worse than anything I could have imagined. I can't speak, so I nod, anxiously waiting for him to say something.

He takes a giant step back towards the door, rubbing at his clenched jaw as he considers everything I just said. I imagine he's thinking about the way he trusted me, confided in me about his mother's death. The way he let me see parts of him he's hidden away from the world for so long. The way our bodies confessed all the feelings our words could not and wondering how I could get so close when holding onto this secret. I only hope he'll understand I kept it out of fear of losing him.

Anger pours from him in waves, and I start to fear I've lost him forever. I struggle to say something, anything, but the words catch in my throat. If I could only explain, maybe I could make him understand...

"Let me see if I got this right—you let me bare my soul to you about my mother's death and my father's betrayal, all the while knowing everything? You let me confide in you about how much his lying, Sadie's lying, *ruined* me?"

He glares at me, the adoration he felt for me a few moments ago lost to the deceit as his eyes fill with anger.

"You sat there pretending you were hearing everything about my life for the first time. I opened up to you in a way I never have to *anyone*. God, Mia. I thought you were falling right alongside me, but I don't even know what was real. Was this all about the money? Saving the inn?" He continues pacing, shaking his head, fists clenched at his side.

"God, Preston, no. How could you think—"

"How could I think you're out to lie and manipulate me like everyone else? Mia, you had *weeks* to tell me this. Why now?"

I walk towards him pleadingly, but he stops me with his hands in the air indicating he wants me to keep my distance.

"Preston, please believe me. I'm so, so sorry," I choke out between sobs.

He scoffs and I hear him mutter something like "un-fucking-believable" under his breath as he turns to leave. I can't let him go. Not before I've had time to properly explain. If he could only listen. I move towards him again, slowly.

"You're just like *her*. Don't fucking follow me, Mia," he says over his shoulder as he exits the room, slamming the door in his wake.

Despair overtakes my body as I fall to my knees and lose myself to the tears.

Preston

Amelia fucking Aguilar is Mia Flores?! I suppose to anyone else, it would have made sense. Didn't she mention her mom ran the inn before her? Of course, my mother would have made sure the day-to-day operations fell to Amelia, ugh, *Mia's* mom. And how did I not recognize my former best friend the first time I stared into her kind eyes?

But I had, hadn't I?

I remember the first time I saw her here. How she whipped around to meet my gaze, all fury and wrath, ready to tear me a new one for being a dick to her receptionist. I felt something when she looked at me, but honestly, I thought it was my intense attraction to her. I never believed she could be my Amelia from all those years before.

But she's not *my* Amelia. My Amelia would never have been so cruel as to let me let my guard down like that. My Amelia was loyal and kind, truthful and genuine. My Amelia wouldn't have fooled me so spectacularly. You'd think I would have learned my lesson from Sadie, but I guess I have a type. I don't want to believe she was getting close for access to my money, but it's hard to ignore the way she let me foot the bill for all the repairs and renovations without offering me a shred of honesty.

My flight to LA to plead with the board to save this place wasn't set to depart until Sunday afternoon, but I need to get the fuck out of Stoney Ridge now. Gathering my things, I grab my phone and dial Oliver.

I don't even wait for him to answer before I begin barking orders at him. "Ollie, tell me you haven't left yet. I need to get back to LA. Tonight."

"Mr. Preston, sir, is something wrong? Miss Flores—"

"Nothing's wrong I just need to go. Have you left or not?"

"Erm, no, sir, we're not far. We'll be back at the inn momentarily to take you to the airport."

"Thanks."

I hang up and begin stuffing my clothes into my suitcase haphazardly. I've got to get out of here before Mia makes her way back to the cottage. If I have to look at her tonight, I don't know whether I'll end this thing between us for good, or cave as soon as she sets those doe eyes on me.

Shaking the thought away, I grab my suitcase as I see the black car pulling up the driveway to the inn. I waste no time as I virtually sprint outside without so much as a glance back. Everything I thought I felt with Mia is a lie. And this is why I never fuck a girl twice.

THE NEXT MORNING, I WAKE UP IN A PITCH-BLACK room, floating on a cloud soft bed, wrapped in buttery Egyptian cotton sheets. As my eyes adjust to the darkness, I see the familiar surroundings that indicate I'm back home in my LA penthouse. Everything has been put back exactly as it was before the nightmare that sent me to that godforsaken inn, and I can almost believe it was all a bad dream.

The scattered whiskey bottles next to my bed provide the why behind the searing headache I'm currently nursing and, at least partly, explains the nausea rolling deep in my belly. Mia's to blame for the rest.

Swinging my legs over the side of my bed, I wipe the sleep from my eyes and stretch deep, knowing there's a lot ahead of me over the next few days. On the flight back, Stanley went over the plan to fight the board, including everything we'd need to pull together before the final vote on Monday. I thank past me for having the foresight to grab my laptop and the briefcase holding all the financial data on the inn. We're going to need it. No matter how pissed off I am at Mia right now, the inn is my mother's legacy and I'll be damned if I'm going to let anyone take that away.

Squinting my eyes to focus, the clock on the nightstand reads six-thirty...p.m.

Fuck.

We got in early this morning and after my reunion with my old buddy, Johnnie Walker, I've managed to sleep the entire day away. At least I still have the rest of tonight, plus Sunday, to refine my presentation to the board and attempt to save the inn. Although, I really could use a night out to clear my head...

Now that he's back from Patagonia, I shoot off a quick text to Alexi to see what's going on tonight and hop in the shower to wash off the flight and the stench of whiskey. By the time I'm through, I have, no joke, twenty-five missed texts from Alexi. He has a line on some new club opening and we have VIP access.

I pull on an expensive suit as if it's battle armor and tell Alexi I'll meet him at his place with limo service. It's time to kick Vermont Preston to the curb and bring LA Preston back out.

On the way to Alexi's, I scroll through my old roster of girls, shooting off some texts telling them to meet us there. I couldn't be less excited about the prospect of seeing any of these women again, but the first rule of a new club opening is guys need to buy their way in with hot girls.

My thumb hovers over Mia's contact as I reach the M's, staring at the contact photo I snapped in secret. She stands at the reception desk, mid laugh, Chelsea and Lizzy laughing in the background along with her. My mind is at war with itself as part of me is dying to call her if only to hear her voice while the other part is ready to delete the number and all traces of her from my life.

Before I can take either action, Alexi's contact photo, face contorted in some dickhead expression, fills my screen indicating his incoming call.

"Yo! Preston, where you at, bro? I'm downstairs and there is no limo in sight. Hope you got that bottle service," Alexi shouts into the phone, competing with the noise of the city behind him.

"I'm pullin' up now. I got the Dom plus two shots lined up."

I'd hoped to have a few minutes with him in the limo to

talk about real shit before the booze and girls take over our night, but it turns out he promised some girls we'd pick them up on the way. Our limo is so full I have two randos sitting on my lap by the time we pull up to the club.

The club is the brainchild of some tech bro's kid and is the very definition of cringe. It stands out an obnoxious bright blue among the classier, muted establishments that line the street. If it weren't for his father, there's no way this douche would have been able to secure real estate here, but nepotism will get you everywhere as long as you're a rich, white guy.

Everything about this club screams tacky opulence. Its decor is chaotic, as if the kid couldn't decide whether he wanted to run a high-class night club or a frat house. Still, every one of its four floors is packed with social climbers looking to drown themselves in overpriced liquor and fake connections.

We bypass most of the chaos and head straight to a private elevator up to the VIP lounge on the top floor. Alexi pulls us to a back room, covered in semi-sheer red curtains, evidently the VIP area of the VIP lounge. Past Preston would have reveled in this shit but current me fights the urge to roll my eyes as I take a seat on the black leather couch in the center and order bottle service.

We share a few drinks with the girls, Alexi's tongue finding its way down the throats of a few of them, but I just sit there, nursing my drink. As I look around at my former life, I feel empty. I'm surrounded by beautiful women and some of my best friends, and yet all I can think about are the friends I made back in Vermont. And Mia. I catch Alexi staring at me, a puzzled look on his face. He lifts up the girl currently occupying his lap and shoos the rest of them out of the VIP area before taking a seat next to me on the couch.

"Dude. What the fuck?" There's an accusation in his tone as if he's upset with me for not having fun.

I answer with a shrug and down the remaining bourbon from my glass.

"No, seriously, man. I've watched you turn down at least seven girls tonight. Seven *willing* girls, man. Seven *hot* girls. I can't say I've ever seen you turn down one."

I catch the eye of a waitress walking by, holding my empty glass with a nod, indicating I need another one. She smiles and winks before heading off to the bar. "No idea what you're talking about. I'm fine."

"Oh, you're fine, eh? That's why you're sulking alone in this dark corner all by yourself? Because you're so fine? Look, man. I know we don't share our feelings or whatever," he waves his hands dismissively in the air, "but you can talk to me."

I let out an exasperated sigh. I guess I *did* want to talk to him about it, but part of me wanted to forget about everything that happened in Vermont and move the fuck on with my life. But maybe Alexi can give me a different perspective.

"Mia, man."

"Right, right. Mia. Who the fuck is Mia?"

The waitress returns with another drink and the rest of the bottle. I may not be having fun tonight, but I'll say this for the club scene, bottle service does not suck. I down the first drink in two sips and I tell him everything that went down in Vermont. But mostly about Mia.

About how I wanted her from the first time I saw her and how the shitstorm that Sadie brought with her during her wedding led to things heating up with Mia. And then I told him about those perfect nights where everything fell into place, and I thought we might be...before she confessed she'd been lying to me this entire time.

Alexi's face is utter shock as he takes in everything I'd just told him. He lets out a low whistle before asking, "Shit, man. What did you say?"

A sardonic chuckle escapes my mouth. "Say? I didn't *say* anything. I packed my shit and got on the next plane home. Fuck if I'm going to stick around and let her humiliate me anymore."

He remains uncharacteristically quiet for a long moment, his thumb absently moving around the rim of his glass. He sets his drink down and turns to me, sitting up straight in his seat as if he really means business.

"You know you're my boy and I'll support all of your choices, no matter how dumb, but this isn't like you. Letting yourself get torn apart over some girl. You *love* her, don't you?"

Shock steals my breath as I try to comprehend what he just said. *Love?* The word feels like poison in my mouth. I don't fall in love. What I had with Sadie, what I thought was love, was a lie predicated on her need for attention and desire for my money. Every other girl was only a body to warm my bed so I could ignore the loneliness. No, I don't fall in love. I don't even think I'm capable of love. My best example of "love" was a father who chose a hotel chain over his dying wife. Fuck love. I don't want it.

"Fuck that. You know I don't do that love shit. But I dunno, man. This girl is just..." I shake my head as if that will help purge her from my brain.

"Yeah, yeah. Not in love. Of course not. But, if you are,

or if you could be, shouldn't you hear her out? I mean, yeah that's fucked up what she did, no doubt, but maybe she had her reasons?"

I pause to consider this, trying to put myself in Mia's shoes, but I come up empty. Being too stunned to tell me when we first met is one thing. Dragging out this push and pull for over a month and then *fucking* me while still holding onto this was a deliberate choice. It reeks of the manipulative tactics I endured from Sadie. Not to mention the financial dependency aspect now that I'm CEO. I don't want to believe Mia's capable of that, but I don't have the best track record of seeing people for who they really are.

It's then the flaming auburn waves catch my attention heading in my direction. Sadie. What the fuck is she doing here? Alexi and I share a look, and he stands to block her path to me.

"Listen, Cruella, he doesn't need to talk to you right now, so turn that pretty little ass of yours around now and go crawling back to your meathead husband, okay?" Alexi folds his arms in front of him, planting his feet. Sadie tries, unsuccessfully, to push him out of her way with a jab to the shoulder. He's basically a 6'5 fucking viking and she thinks she'd be able to move him? I laugh into my drink.

"Oh, please. You don't scare me. I just want to say hello to an old friend," she says in a saccharine tone while batting her eyelashes.

Alexi scoffs. "You two were never friends. You'll never be friends. You're like a venereal disease that keeps coming back. You can go." He shoos her away, moving with her to stay in her way.

"Nah, man. Let her stay. What the fuck could she

possibly have to say to me?" I slur, the alcohol clearly taking root. I stare at her, eyes burning hatred in her direction.

She tosses Alexi a triumphant smirk and sideswipes him as he shakes his head before leaving us to our conversation. She slinks up next to me on the couch, curling her legs up behind her, resting one long, alabaster arm around the back of the couch behind me.

"What's got you in such a mood? The last time I saw you, you were running after that pretty little maid. How'd that work out for you?" Her condescending laugh as she sips her fruity drink only adds fuel to my rage.

"She's not a *maid*," I say through gritted teeth, filling my glass to the brim with another pour from the near empty bottle.

She waves off my comment with the hand that holds her drink, spilling a little on my jacket in the process. I scowl at her lack of awareness, but she doesn't even seem to notice.

"Whatever. In any case, you're back here and we find ourselves alone in another dark corner. Interesting, no?"

"Where's your husband, Sadie?"

She runs her hand along the back of my neck, leaning in close so her mouth is inches from my ear. "Not here."

I turn to face her with an annoyed glare. The look on her face a clear indication she wants something. Wants me, most likely. But not for me. For the attention. She drags her teeth over her bottom lip, her eyes roaming along my face, stopping at my lips. Before I even have time to think, she closes the gap between us, pressing her lips to mine.

It's nothing like kissing Mia. I try to force myself to feel something, *anything*, other than this ache in my chest, but all I can see is Mia.

This shit with Sadie has to stop.

I push away from our kiss, pressing my hands into her arms a little roughly. She runs a hand down my chest, stopping above my waistband, trying to slip beneath my pants. My entire body tenses, filling with disgust at the thought of ever taking this woman, any woman, who isn't Mia to my bed. I grip her wrist tightly, stopping her motion.

"Stop." I push her off me, standing to leave.

"What the fuck, Preston?" she shouts from behind me.

"Sadie, what the fuck do you want?"

"I thought that was pretty obvious. I want you, baby."

"Oh yeah, what about Everett?" I snap.

"He's...he's not what I thought."

"And I suddenly am? Why? Because I have my father's money back?"

"Well, yeah. I mean, no. But now things can go back to normal." She sits up on her knees and takes my hand in hers.

"It was always meant to be you and me, Natalia even said—"

"I'm sorry, what? You spoke with Natalia?"

She lowers her eyes, realizing she wasn't supposed to say anything. "Um, well, yeah. How do you think Everett and I found that little inn? Then she called to let me know you'd be back in town. Said I could catch you here and maybe convince you to come back to me. To come back to who you were before that sorry little stint in Vermont."

I clench my fists at my sides, my jaw flexing so hard I feel like I might shatter my teeth. Natalia and I are going to be having a talk, but right now, I need to get away from the vapid socialite in front of me.

"My 'little stint' in Vermont?"

"Preston, come on. You can't be serious. That small town girl? She's not right for you. You need someone who can thrive in the spotlight. You need me."

Like a fucking hole in the head. This conniving bitch is once again using me to stay relevant and I almost let her. I lean in close, glowering at her, seething with anger.

"Let me make something abundantly fucking clear, Sadie. I don't ever want to see you again. I don't want to hear your voice; I don't even want to know you still fucking exist. And if you ever speak about Mia that way again, I will fucking bury you so far into obscurity you'll be lucky to have the relevancy of a discarded condom. You got me?"

For the first time possibly ever, she looks genuinely shocked, but I can't muster up an ounce of sympathy as I toss the curtains out of my way and storm out of the VIP.

Pushing my way through the crowd, I breathe in deep once I finally reach the exit, taking the cold night air into my lungs. Alexi's right—I love Mia. Distracting myself with some other girl, especially Sadie, isn't going to change that. I have to get back to Vermont. But first, I need to make sure the inn is safe.

Mia

I spent the night in the only vacant room in the inn, the formerly decrepit nightmare room where Preston spent his first night. It's now fully renovated, complete with functioning electricity thanks to James, and as I look around shaking off sleep, all I want to do is call Preston. To beg him to hear me out. But he made it crystal clear that he wants nothing to do with me and, if I'm being honest, how can I blame him?

His words echo in my head on a loop since they left his mouth.

Don't fucking follow me, Mia.

And so, I didn't. I wanted to give him some space, so I stayed here. Now in the harsh light of day, I'm determined to get him to talk to me, even if he doesn't want to.

I stop by the kitchen, grabbing a couple donuts, swiping a jelly for Preston, his favorite, and fill two large to-go cups with fresh coffee. I don't expect it to fix anything, but it's an olive branch I hope he's willing to take. But when I burst into the cottage, it's bathed in complete darkness.

"Preston? You here?"

Silence.

"I come in peace. And with jelly donuts."

Still, no response.

I set the donuts down on the table, turning to the hallway that leads to his room, when my eye is drawn to a single manilla folder sitting in the center of the table. A sticky note stuck to the front with my name in Preston's messy handwriting.

Flipping the folder open I see a stack of papers, the title page reading, *The Early Bird Inn Fiscal Analysis and Budget Plan.* I nearly gasp as I look through the pages, seeing the level of thought he's put into this proposal. He's drafted a comprehensive business plan for the entire upcoming year, complete with full budget approval from The Spencer Group. A single message scribbled at the bottom of the title page reads, "Please contact Oliver for any questions or change requests."

A pit forms in my stomach as realization sweeps over my body. Even though this sick feeling tells me exactly what I'll find, I sprint to his room, throwing open the door, hoping to find him snuggled under the covers. But, of course, that's not what I see. Tears well up in my eyes as I take in the empty room before me. The bed is perfectly made and not a single trace of him remains. He's gone and all he left me is a budget report and a broken heart.

My phone's alarm pulls me from sleep, and I realize I passed out on the couch last night after a bit of drinking. *Lots* of drinking, if the open wine bottles scattered around the room are any indication. Once I understood that Preston was gone for good, I wallowed. *Hard.*

Though the wine dims my recollection a bit, I vividly recall sobbing on his bed for a solid hour, curled up in the fetal position. It barely smelled of him anymore because he spent the last few weeks occupying mine.

How did everything go so wrong so fast? I pulled myself together enough to go swipe multiple bottles of wine from the inn's cellar and proceeded to drink until my body finally gave in to sleep.

It's eight a.m. and I really should head into the inn, but I can't bear the thought of plastering a fake smile on my face as I try to avoid the evidence of him everywhere. But as I look around the cottage, my former safe haven, it's also tainted with the ghost of him everywhere. I see him standing in the kitchen, shirtless, making me breakfast while I sit at the table sipping coffee. I hear the sound of his god awful, off-key rendition of my favorite Taylor Swift songs. I feel his breath on my neck, the weight of his body on mine as ours connected for the first time.

Defeated, I wrap my blanket around my shoulders, grabbing the remaining two unopened bottles of wine and retreat to my room to get re-drunk and sleep until I can no longer see his face every time I close my eyes.

⚒ ⚒ ⚒

A faint pounding drums in my head, emphasizing the throbbing now forming there. I blink away sleep and the pounding gets louder and louder. It's pitch black in my room, save for the yellow lights of my alarm clock, which informs me it's nearly seven p.m. I managed to sleep the entire day away.

It hits me then that the pounding is actually my front door as I hear Chelsea screaming threats and obscenities about how if I don't unlock it now, she's going to kick it down. Knowing her, this is far from an idle threat, so I haphazardly pull my robe on over my wrinkled pajamas and shuffle towards the door. One look in the entryway mirror and I visibly cringe at my hair, giving new meaning to the term "messy bun" and the giant red jelly stain running down the front of my oversized t-shirt from the donut I inhaled between sobs last night. I swing open the door to find Chelsea standing impatiently, holding a stack of food containers obscuring her face.

"Uh, care to help a girl out here?"

I scoop a few containers off the top and head to the kitchen without a word, the open door the only indication of an invitation.

"Jesus fuck Mia. What the hell happened here?" Concern spreads across her face as she looks at the evidence of a night of heavy drinking strewn around my usually tidy home.

"Had a bad night," I shrug, ignoring the feast she's brought over to take my place back on the couch. I pick up a partially emptied glass of wine, giving it a quick sniff before downing its contents and pouring myself another hefty serving from the open bottle beside it. I've been awake for mere minutes, and I already want to drink myself back to sleep.

"What happened? I've never seen you like this and

when you didn't show today, I got worried. Where's Preston?"

"Preston's gone." My words come out muffled as I try to suppress the emotion building up inside me. It's no use, though, because with one concerned look from my friend, my body dissolves into agonizing sobs.

After a few moments, I manage to regain a little composure and finally get the words out. "I told him. Everything. Who I am. How I recognized him instantly and hadn't found the words to tell him the truth. He left, Chels. He left me."

"Oh, honey. I mean, are you sure he *left* left? I mean he had to go to LA for the board stuff, right?"

I shake my head, leaning out of her embrace to pick up my wine glass and take another sip. "No, he's gone. All his things. He's not coming back, Chels. I fucked it all up."

"I don't accept that! Mia, that man is crazy about you. It's so incredibly obvious. He has been since the moment he saw you. There is no way this can ruin what you two have."

"You didn't see his face when I told him, Chels. He was utterly betrayed. He couldn't even *look* at me. And, honestly, he has every right to be pissed. The things he shared with me about his past, I mean, I already knew, and I sat there and let him be vulnerable as if I had no idea who he was. And after his father, and Sadie. No. He'll never forgive me. He said he was falling..." I choke on the last words as if I don't have a right to say them.

"Mia, he *was* falling. He *fell*. We all saw it. You don't just fall out of love with someone that quickly. Trust me. Did I tell you about me and Katy's first real fight?"

I shake my head waiting for her to continue.

"God. I was so fucking pissed at her. We'd been dating for about a month, exclusively, or so I thought. We were laying in bed after an evening of intense feelings and many, many orgasms, when her phone dinged with a text. Without thinking, I picked it up off the nightstand to hand it to her and saw an incoming pic from her ex. A very *suggestive* pic.

I lost it. I screamed at her and told her I never wanted to see her again. I wouldn't let her explain. My insecurities overpowered my rational brain. I *knew* she was cheating. I didn't need to hear her words.

Of course, she *wasn't* cheating. Her ex was drunk texting. She didn't know Katy had moved on because they hadn't even talked since they broke up."

"Yeah, but you at least went back and let her explain. He wouldn't even *look* at me. He left without giving me a chance to say anything."

"Okay, true. But I *didn't* give Katy a chance. Not at first. I ghosted her for a week, if you recall. I was done. Until I wasn't. The more I thought about my life with her, how every day I spent with her was made a little bit better because of her, I knew I had to make it right. I can't tell you when he'll have that revelation, but I can tell you that not a single moment went by when I wasn't deeply, hopelessly in love with her, even when I hated her. Give him some time." She gives me a squeeze and heads into the kitchen to bring out the platters of comfort food she brought over.

We spend the next few hours drinking, eating, chatting, and watching bad movies. By the time she leaves, I feel a little lighter, no doubt in part to the amount of wine currently occupying my bloodstream. But I still see his face behind my eyes with each blink. So, I grab the rest of the bottle and make sure to get well and properly drunk. Which, as it turns out wasn't my best idea, given my propensity for drunk dialing.

Before I can stop myself, I'm clicking the call button on his contact. I'm greeted by his generic voicemail as the robotic voice instructs me to leave a message at the tone. I take a final swig to drain my glass and prepare to lay into him...on his voicemail.

"Ha! I shoulda known you wouldn't answer. That's very, very rude of you, Preston Daniel Spencer." My words are slurred, bordering on incoherent, but that doesn't stop me.

"Yes, I know your middle name, because yes, I know you. But do I? You left and didn't talk to me for, like decades, and then just show up at my inn all hot and acting like you don't even remember me? What the fuck, Preston? That hurt to know you were such a big part of my life and I meant nothing to you. And, yeah, okay maybe I shouldn't have slept with you without being honest about who I was, but, pfft, god you're so...you know what? Never mind. I thought we had something...something...more deserving of you leaving a stupid note saying you left. But, wait! It didn't even say that, did it?

You know what? Fine. I'll be fine. I have the New Year's Eve party to plan and, I had planned on going with you, but you left me alone all these years, so what's one more? So I guess I'm calling to say, good. It's good you left. Because maybe I thought I was fa—"

A loud beep cuts me off before I can finish that sentence, which is probably for the best since what I wanted to say was, "*I was falling in love with you.*"

⚒ ⚒ ⚒

If I thought yesterday's hangover was painful, it doesn't hold a candle to the way I feel today. In addition to the unwelcome pounding in my head, waves of nausea war in my belly, and my throat is so dry it feels like I'm swallowing knives. That's when I vaguely recall scream singing to breakup songs all night.

I'm dreading heading into the inn, but there's still a lot to do to prepare for the New Year's Eve party and I can't push all that off on Chelsea. I pick up my phone to text her that I'll be in late, but see she's beaten me to it.

> **Chels**
> Mia - take the day off. Think about things.
> We got this. Text me if you need anything.
> I LOVE YOU! 💗 😘

The warmth from her kind text is short lived as holding the phone in my hand triggers a most unwelcome memory.

Fuuuuck.

I called him, didn't I?

I frantically swipe over to my outgoing call log and nearly throw my phone across the room. FIVE TIMES?! I called him FIVE TIMES?! In a row, by the timestamps. Try as I may, I can't remember what I said. Maybe I just hung up? But knowing me, at least one of those was some long, incoherent diatribe.

Fuck. Me.

I toss the covers over my head, burying my face in my pillow before falling back asleep for the rest of the day.

⚒ ⚒ ⚒

THE NEXT MORNING, I'M UP BEFORE MY ALARM. I still have no idea what atrocity I left on Preston's voicemail, but I feel a hell of a lot better after nearly twenty-four hours of sleep. I'm refreshed and determined to put everything out of my mind. I have to believe Chelsea's right and Preston will come to me when he's had time to cool off. Until then, there's work to do and I can't—I *won't*—leave my staff hanging for another day.

Freshly showered with a steaming mug of coffee in hand, I head over to the inn, the barest hints of dawn peeking through the still moonlit sky. My sole focus today is on our end of year New Year's Eve bash. While the entire town is invited, the party is supposed to be a thank you for our staff, but for the past few years, we've been so broke, it ended up being more like any other event where the staff worked throughout most of the evening. I want this year to be different and if I can, I'll give them a much-deserved break.

I have a bit of time to review the packet Preston put together, hoping to find some additional funds to hire proper outside staff for the party. My jaw drops open when I see the profit summary for the last few months alone. The inn was finally making money for the first time in a long time, and we finally have enough to properly give back to the team who's worked so hard this season.

Still, I can't help but worry as I consider the comment Stanley made before leaving after the Christmas pageant. He mentioned a fight with the board and, perhaps taken by itself wouldn't be a cause for alarm, but then there's that comment from that guy in the background call with Ollie. If the inn's in trouble, maybe now isn't the best time to be throwing a party.

But the team deserves this, and, dammit, so do I! Even so, I have to call for budget approval and while I'd usually call Oliver for this, maybe Preston...

I scold myself for even thinking about calling him again. He sent not even so much as a text after my embarrassing five calls to his phone, so I'm not sure how he can make it any clearer that he doesn't want to talk to me. Determined to take Chelsea's advice and give him space, I suck it up and call Oliver to get approval to hire a band and a catering company. And if he happens to tell me about Preston, well, so be it.

I'm surprised when Oliver picks up on the second ring with all the drama surrounding the scandal keeping him busy, but I'm just grateful at least someone at The Spencer Group seems to be taking my calls.

"Miss Flores, how lovely to hear from you. What can I do for you?" There's something fake about his tone, but not in the way that would indicate he isn't pleased to hear from me, but in the way that suggests he's hiding something.

"Hi, Ollie. Thank you so much for coming to the pageant. Some of the team mentioned you and Stanley extended kind words to them and it meant so much to have corporate take an interest."

He sounds genuinely surprised at the compliment. "Oh, well, erm, thank you. But you didn't have to call and thank me. You know the company will always support the inn and it was a joyous occasion!"

"Right. Well, I have a bit of a favor to ask. I've been going over this year's projections and it looks like we're ending with quite the surplus. As you know, we wrap up the year with a New Year's Eve soiree, and this year I'd like to hire a band and give the staff a break by bringing in a proper catering company. We should have more than enough from our profits to cover it, but especially with everything going on, I wanted to check in and make sure to get budget approval."

"Ah, yes, well, erm, I'm not quite sure I'm going to be able to approve that. You see, we're undergoing some, erm, leadership changes right now and it seems I'm no longer responsible for budgetary decisions."

"Oh, okay. Well, no problem! Could you give me the name and number of the new person in charge?"

He's silent for a beat longer than normal. "Erm, I guess, well, that would be Mr. Spencer. That is to say, Preston."

Oh. Right. I guess as CEO he would be in charge of these decisions. I'm suddenly nervous at the thought of speaking with him again, but this would be a perfect opportunity to call him. My heart beats rapidly at the thought of hearing his silky smooth voice again.

"Um. Great! I'll give him a call then, I'm sure—" I stop as I hear his voice in the background asking Oliver about some board meeting.

"Miss Flores, Preston is here if you'd like to speak with him, I can, oh, no, no, wait. Erm...never mind. Let me ask him."

Okay. Apparently, he still doesn't want to speak to me. That's just...wonderful. Oliver attempts, poorly, to cover the microphone, but I can make out their entire conversation.

"*Miss Flores is asking to speak with you regarding a budgetary request for a New Year's Eve party?*"

"*I don't need to speak with her. What does she want?*"

"*It appears they would like to hire staff for the event. A band and a catering company. It does seem as though the inn did quite well this year. I'm certain Miss Flores can explain it better. Are you sure you wouldn't like to discuss this with her?"*

"That won't be necessary. Give her whatever she wants."

I hear the door shut in his wake and I didn't miss the terseness in his voice. I fight the urge to fall apart again at his dismissive attitude towards me. If he can't even speak to me about work, how can I ever begin to hope he'll reconsider us?

Oliver fumbles with his phone, returning his attention to me. "Great news! Mr. Spencer has approved the budget for additional staff. Please send over the invoices as soon as you have them."

"Sure thing!" My voice comes out an octave too high as I try to mask my disappointment at Preston's dismissal.

"Oh, yes, sir. I will let her know," Oliver responds to someone in the background I can't quite hear. "Oh, Miss Flores, before you go, Mr. Spencer would like you to know his presence can be expected at this party."

"Oh. Sure. Well, we look forward to seeing him again." I stammer before ending the call.

Great. Good. Preston will be here in a few days. That means I have time to come up with a way to explain why I wasn't honest with him. And maybe earn a place back in his life, in his heart.

Chapter 25

Preston

Mia's slurred speech echoes off the walls of my bathroom as I replay her drunk dial while I knot my tie in the mirror. I can't help but chuckle at her wine addled soliloquy, but she's not wrong.

Running away was probably the least mature thing I could have done, and yet, it was as natural as breathing. If I'm truly committed to becoming the man she believes me capable of, I need to own up to my own shitty behavior and hear her out. But first, I need to make sure the board doesn't follow through with their plan to sell off the inn to the highest bidder.

I stayed up the entire night drafting a compelling presentation that even this greedy board can't refuse. So, when I arrive at the office, my confidence doesn't waiver for a second. Even at the sight of the board sitting in their swivel chairs, their lack of faith in my ability to serve as CEO written across their faces.

"Thank you for your time this morning and for your warm welcome as I transition into this new role. As you know, despite the fact that the firm was absolved of involvement in the unfortunate scandal, we're still responsible for restitutions. The search for a new CFO is underway, but until that time, I'll be accepting those responsibilities."

A large man with sparse, silver hair, scoffs from under his bushy mustache, interrupting me. "Where do you get off thinking you're qualified for any of this? Last month your face was plastered all over the gossip pages downing booze while your father's company crumbled. Just because you share his DNA doesn't make you qualified to run a multibillion-dollar company." With a mocking laugh, he looks around at his peers for support, though to my relief, he seems to come up short.

Doing my best to channel my father, I walk towards the man, a look of icy defiance trained solely on him. "Look —*who* are you, again?"

"Paul Irving, sir, um Mr. Spencer, sir." All previous insolence seems to leave his tone, and I allow a satisfied smile to spread across my face as my intimidation has landed. As much as I hate to admit it, there's something to be said about my father's favored tactic. I don't necessarily feel good about being an asshole, but right now saving the inn, and Mia's livelihood, is the only thing I care about.

"Well, *Paul*, would my MBA from Stanford, where I graduated in the top five percent of my class, coupled with the fact that I've been primed for this role since I was eighteen years old be enough qualifications for you?"

He sinks down into his chair, embarrassed. "Y-yes, sir. Apologies, I meant no offense. It's just that, well, you haven't exactly been active in the day-to-day operations."

"Well, you got me there, Peter. But the way I see it, all

of you acted with gross incompetence when you allowed one man to nearly topple the entire company. So, really, it's you all who should be worried about your continued existence on this board, not whether I'll remain in charge, am I right?" I pause for a response that never comes and take that as a cue to continue.

"Now, as I was saying, in my capacity as CEO, I've become increasingly focused on our historical financial data to ensure we approach this new phase responsibly to avoid something like this happening again. After reviewing Stanley and Natalia's recommendations on property liquidations, I'm in agreement with the majority of the plan. However, The Early Bird Inn will not be closing and that is not up for discussion."

"With all due respect, Preston," a deep gravelly voice speaks up from the corner of the room. My eyes catch on the man who has now stood from his chair, his imposing frame dwarfing those around him. "I'm Dennis Tully and I've served on this board for the past fifteen years. This inn is a money pit and has brought in no new revenue in the past decade. Your first act as CEO cannot be to make such a costly, and frankly, irresponsible, decision to keep a property that would bleed us dry when we're trying to recover from the last bad decision your family made." He folds his arms over his chest as the rest of the board murmurs and nods in agreement.

"Darius, I'm glad you brought that up because I spent quite a bit of time with the inn's records, and you know what I found?" I pause for dramatic effect, slowly picking up the presentation clicker from the table to move through a few slides until I find exactly what I was looking for.

"It's Dennis, actually," he interrupts.

"Right. *Dennis*," I snap, my tone conveying my unhappiness for the interruption. "Anyway, it seems that Winston was targeting the inn as the source of most of his embezzlement. For nearly two decades, he has increasingly taken more from the inn, which absent that theft, you can clearly see has managed to be one of the *only* properties consistently growing year over year. In fact, the projected surplus from this year alone will cover the renovations I've already authorized, as well as operating costs for the first quarter of next year."

Nearly every board member sits forward in their chair, grabbing their individual copies of the report that sits in front of them. The room is filled with excitement as they pour through the detailed projections I've laid out for the next ten years. As they debate the value of keeping the inn, relief sweeps over me as I realize I've won. We shift into planning mode, laying out a detailed plan for the upcoming liquidation.

Once the last of the board leaves the room, Stanley approaches me with a look of sorrow on his face, instantly darkening my mood.

"Preston, good job out there. Your father would be proud. But we need to talk."

At the other end of the room, Oliver shuts the door before taking a seat at the table next to Stanley. Stanley takes a deep inhale, placing his hands on the table.

"The case against your father is...damning. He maintains his innocence, but the emails on Winston's computer depict discussions with your father directing the transfer of funds. Now, I'm doing everything I can, but without a confession from Winston, it's going to be quite difficult to prove your father was not involved."

"So, he *is* responsible?" My heart sinks into my stomach, my voice coming out like the whisper of a terrified child.

"Not necessarily. Oliver combed over the correspondence, and he doesn't believe your father wrote any of it. I've sent the computer out to a digital forensics team to see how Winston may have compromised your father's account to falsify a paper trail. There's more."

I exhale a sigh as Stanley pauses, an uncharacteristic look of trepidation on his face.

"What we haven't told you yet is two days ago, the prosecution filed a petition to withdraw bail, and it was granted. Your father is currently in custody until his trial. And he'd like to see you. Today."

Words fail me as I process this new information. My father is in prison, and no one bothered to tell me. I tamper down my rage at this deception and give Stanley a slight nod, following him down to the car. Neither Stanley nor Oliver says another word the entire drive to the correctional facility.

⚒ ⚒ ⚒

THE METROPOLITAN DETENTION CENTER IS NOTHING like I had expected. As I empty my pockets and prepare to cross the metal detectors, I'm faced with the reality that the notion I'd held of a cushy white collar resort style prison was nothing but lies brought on by numerous Hollywood films. No, my father was in *prison* prison, complete with lifeless concrete floors, brick walls, and shouts coming from the prison guards, all of whom look like they've seen some shit.

I'm led into a private room with one small table and two metal chairs. I anxiously wring my hands together since they confiscated my phone at security, robbing me of the solace doomscrolling might bring as I wait. Fortunately, within fifteen minutes, the door is swinging open, my father in tow.

And he looks like shit.

It's like he's aged twenty years in the few weeks since I've seen him. The fight in his eyes has dimmed, the man before me a broken shell of the ruthless businessman I've known my entire life. His hands hang low, cuffed together at his hip and he wears a light gray jumpsuit that fits baggily off his thinning frame. A guard cuffs him to the table, which I find completely unnecessary, after guiding him to sit in one of the metal chairs opposite the one I occupy.

"You've got ten minutes, Spencer," the overweight guard informs us, shutting the door behind him.

Not one to waste time, my father leans forward, the commanding look in his eye back, ready to speak. "Thank you for coming, son. There are some things I need to tell you," he looks around the room, spotting the camera, "but I need to be careful, you understand." He nods his head in its direction, a not-so-subtle attempt to inform me he'll need to be careful with his words.

"I want to tell you how proud I am of you. Stanley and Oliver filled me in on the transition and how you dove in, headfirst and for that I'm grateful. But mostly, I'm grateful for what you did for the inn. For Gab—your mother's inn." His voice quivers as he stumbles over her name, and I think I see a tear threatening to fall down his cheek.

"It was my home too," I say, my voice coming out more

timidly than I had intended. This is the first time we've spoken about my mother since she died.

"I mean, thank you for preserving her memory. She always was the best part of me." He stares into the distance as if he can picture our life before. Before his ambition and pursuit of wealth overpowered his love for his family.

"I'm sorry you're in here, but why am I here?"

He sinks back in his chair, the chain from the cuffs preventing him from getting fully comfortable. "I need you to know, to understand, that while it may not seem like it, everything I did, everything I will ever do, is for you. This is no different."

It takes everything in my power not to return his sincerity with a sarcastic laugh. "For me? You abandoned me, leaving me to care for my mother while she was dying not even so much as sending a card for her funeral, 'for me'? Then decades later, stole millions of dollars from a company you promised I'd inherit 'for me'? I'm failing to see how any of your actions helped anyone other than yourself."

"I imagine it's hard to understand my actions. Believe I never wanted to hurt you in the process."

"You did. Hurt me. But more than that, you hurt *her*. And for that I will *never* forgive you." My words spit out like venom and for a brief moment, I feel bad as the look of unrestrained grief overtakes his features. He hangs his head in his hands, and for the first time in my life, I witness my father cry.

"I will never forgive myself. *Never*." His shoulders quake with emotion I never knew he could possess.

"Why, then? Why didn't you come back for us? For her? For me?" The tears I'd worked so hard to hold back fall from my face as I finally get to say all the things I've wanted to say to him for so long. "She cried out for you every night in those final days. She never stopped loving you, even though you didn't deserve it. I needed you, Dad. You left me to bury her by myself."

"I KNOW," his grief-stricken yell reverberates along the prison walls. "I couldn't face her. By the time she was diagnosed, I'd already broken my vows. Looking back, I don't even have a good reason. I got caught up in the lifestyle and longed for what I thought I missed out on because we married so young. The both of you deserved so much better than this cowardly, greedy asshole I'd become, and I thought the best thing I could do for you two was stay far the fuck away. Nothing I can do will ever make up for it, but this is me trying."

"What do you mean?" I look at the clock and notice our ten minutes is almost up.

"We have no line on Winston. He's in the wind and Stanley isn't optimistic we'll ever find him. Even if we can somehow prove he faked the emails, it's going to be nearly impossible to convince a jury I had no knowledge of the bank accounts he opened in my name, especially since the withdrawal slips had my signature. If they keep digging, they're going to question the penthouse, your security detail, how I paid for your education, how you manage all these trips and nights out. This can't blow back on you. I won't let it."

I finally understand what he's implying. He's going to take the fall in order to protect me. He's going to stay in prison for something he didn't do, for me. To atone for his biggest regret.

"No, we can find him. Make him confess. I have

evidence that he was skimming from the inn for decades. He won't get away with this."

A weary smile passes across his face as he reaches for my hand. "It's okay, son. This is what I deserve. And if it means you're safe and cared for, it's worth it. This has always been for you. Don't say another word. It's all yours now. I know you can do this."

Before I have time refute, to beg him to fight, to see reason, the guard comes storming back in the room. "Times up." His gruff, authoritative voice balks no argument as he quickly uncuffs my father, pulling him towards the door.

"Wait!" I cry and the guard stops, looking annoyed.

"I'm sorry, Preston, for being such a fuckup. I hope one day you can forgive me." He gives me a strained smile. "I love you, son," my father says, with one final look over his shoulder as he's guided back to his cell to serve out a sentence for a crime he didn't commit. For me.

Whatever the cost, I will not let my father rot in prison. Maybe it's the reality that he may be forced to live out his final days in a grimy prison cell, or maybe he's carried the weight of this guilt the entire time. Either way, the man in that room was changed and I owed it to him, to myself, to clear his name. Maybe out of prison, we can repair our relationship and be a family again.

I storm out of the room, running into Stanley and instruct him to ramp up the search for Pickering. This man will not get away with destroying my company and imprisoning the only family I have left. He assures me they will stop at nothing and that he already has his people heading to the UK, where they assume he fled.

In the meantime, I have a girl to win back.

Mia

Tonight's the New Year's Eve party and my stomach has been in knots with the knowledge Preston will be here. It's been a week since I left that drunken message and the closest we've come to talking is when he relayed his budget approval through Oliver, refusing to speak directly to me. While the memory of my drunk dial hasn't fully returned, I have a dim recollection of almost telling him I was in love with him. At least I *hope* it was an almost.

The inn should be quiet today as most of the preparations for tonight are in place, so I take a little extra time to sleep in. I grab a cup of coffee and snuggle up in my favorite blanket on the couch to catch a glimpse of the news. A perky meteorologist stands in front of a large green screen, cracking bad puns about this weekend's weather conditions before kicking it back to the main anchor for this week's entertainment news. I sit up a little straighter in my seat hoping to catch a bit of titillating celebrity gossip, a guilty pleasure that always reminds me of Mom. My jaw drops at the sight of a familiar face.

A semi-candid photo taken of Preston fills the screen. He appears to be at an old event for one of The Spencer Group's resorts, and *god* he looks good. He's adjusting his cuff while smiling his genuine smile, dimples prominent on either side of his perfectly white, toothy grin. My heart tugs as I remember what it feels like to have those hazel eyes trained on me, to be the cause of that grin. It's a stark contrast to the contorted look of resentment on his face the last time I saw him.

> *"Preston Spencer, LA playboy and newly appointed CEO of The Spencer Group, found himself in hot water when his father was named in an embezzle-ment scheme earlier this year. The infamous heart-breaker was seen partying it up at expensive night clubs with an entourage of socialites the same night massive layoffs were announced, earning the ire of thousands of online commenters.*
>
> *One comment read, 'These one percenters are so out of touch! My father worked for The Spencer Group for fifteen years and without so much as a recom-mendation letter, lost everything. In an email! While this [expletive] gets bottle service?'"*
>
> *Mr. Spencer was not available for comment.*

A photo collage of the comments keep flashing on the screen until they switch to a photo from this past weekend in LA. Preston, getting quite cozy with a redhead in the middle of a night club. Although I'd only met her once, I'd recognize that blazing red hair anywhere. Sadie Perkins. No. Sadie *Townsend* because she's married.

The news anchor goes on to explain he was spotted canoodling with her and their friends as they celebrated his new role as CEO. The news report ends with the announcement that Roman has been officially charged on multiple counts of theft, fraud, and breach of fiduciary duty. He's being held in a minimum security prison until his trial begins after the new year.

Disappointment, betrayal, anger, and extreme sadness, both at seeing Preston with Sadie and for the news of his father's fate, swirl inside me. I guess this explains why he hasn't contacted me. He's gone back to his old life.

I click off the TV right as they cut away to a podium, presumably for a press conference about the trial. Vowing to put this out of my mind, I refuse to let the tears fall and turn my attention to tonight. This event is important to me and my staff, and I refuse to let my sadness ruin this night for them.

⚒ ⚒ ⚒

AFTER A LONG SHOWER AND A CATHARTIC CRYING session, I'm ready for the party. This year we've opted for a masquerade, so I decided to treat myself to a new dress. The calf length black dress fits daringly tight against my curves, its neckline scooping low to reveal enough cleavage to be a little scandalous. A sad sigh escapes my mouth when I remember Preston was my motivation for buying this dress. Pathetic, I know, but a part of me always hoped he would have reacted differently to my confession. Before he went crawling back to Sadie. At least the accompanying black and gold mask will hide my face enough to cloak any emotions I may be feeling when I see him tonight.

The professional event staff we hired has transformed our dining area into what can only be described as opulent elegance. Black and gold accents dominate the room, our cozy cottage decor tucked away somewhere in our storage shed. I look around grateful for the increase in funding, made possible by Preston, which allowed me to go all out this year. My shoulders sink in despair as his name brushes against my thoughts, but I steel myself with a deep breath and prepare to meet the guests as they arrive.

I flitter between the mass of people congregated around the room, spending time thanking everyone for coming. Ernie and Bea regale me with their plans for a post-holiday cruise. Mrs. Sinclair raves about the improvements to the inn, making sure to take credit for most of the ideas. Benny apologizes to me profusely about the altercation with Preston, asking where he is tonight to extend his apologies. I give what I hope is a sincere smile as I tell him that while I haven't seen Preston yet, he's expected to be here tonight. I spot Chelsea and Katy chatting across the room and make my way to them for a reprieve from the small talk.

"Mia! The place looks great!" Katy leans in for a quick hug as she gestures to the newly renovated dining room. "Chelsea hardly shuts up about the new kitchen you got her and now she won't shut up about upgrading ours at home. Thanks for that," she says with a teasing wink.

"It was, well, I had some help." My smile doesn't quite meet my eyes and Chelsea notices immediately.

"Have you seen him yet?"

"Is he here? He said he was going to come, but, well, we haven't talked." Her eyes widen in surprise.

"You haven't spoken to him since Christmas?!"

"I might have left a stupid message on his phone. After you left, I finished the wine and saw five outgoing calls the next day. One was three minutes long, so I can only imagine what damage I did in that time."

She shakes her head with a light laugh. "I knew I shouldn't have left you alone. Well, look on the bright side. At least you'll have something to talk about."

"Oh, we'll have something to talk about, but it's not that voice message. Did you see the news?"

She exchanges a worried look with Katy. Of course she saw. I must have read dozens of headlines going over his scandalous reunion with the newly married socialite.

"Well, I don't think he could have made it any clearer that he's done with...whatever this was." My voice quivers and I shrug in defeat.

"Maybe not..." Chelsea says, pointing to the entryway.

Preston stands tall in the foyer, dressed impeccably in an all black Italian suit. Even through his golden mask, I would know those hazel eyes anywhere. I can't stop myself searching the space behind him for Sadie, my stomach churning at the thought of seeing them together in the flesh. Before our eyes can meet, I spot James chatting with a few guys from Tucker's shop. I make a b-line towards him, if only to distract myself from learning whether Preston is alone. James beams at me with a nod and a wave as he excuses himself to meet me halfway.

"James! You sure clean up nice!"

He stands tall in a navy pinstripe suit, a copper mask accentuating the blue in his eyes, his hair pulled back in a half bun. He spins around, followed by a bow as he returns his eyes to me.

"Thank ya, darlin'. But you...damn, Mia. Respectfully, you look..." His eyes roam the length of my body, his Adam's Apple working as his gaze lingers a bit too long at the neckline that stops below my sternum.

A low laugh escapes me. "So, you approve, then?"

He awkwardly adjusts his tie, which was perfectly in place, but now hangs slightly askew at the gesture. "Um... y-yes. You know you're—is it hot in here?"

I lower my eyes with a small smile as my cheeks heat at the compliment and seeing him flustered. The feeling, of course, is fleeting as I remind myself the man I really wish would be complimenting me will probably never speak to me again.

"Well, thank you, James. And thank you for coming. And, of course, for all this." I gesture around to the impressive temporary lighting he supplied for the party.

"Oh, it was my pleasure. I was dying to do something more creative than fixing fuses. Preston and I talked about me maybe doing a few pieces for the inn. Where is he tonight?"

I take a deep breath and try to keep the emotion from showing on my face. By the way his brow furrows with concern, I can tell I failed. "Um, I'm not sure. I think I saw him, but we haven't...we aren't..." I clear my throat, my voice breaking, and I bite my lip to focus on anything other than the stinging behind my eyes. "We haven't spoken since the Christmas pageant, but I did see him arrive a few minutes ago."

"I see. I don't wanna pry, but I thought you two were headin' towards something. You don't have to tell me, but

I'm here for you, Mia." He pulls me in for a hug, holding me tight to his chest until I'm ready to answer.

"We were, but...We fought the night of the pageant, and he went back to LA, without a word. And now...I think, well, the news...he's back with his ex."

"You sure 'bout that? I've seen how you look at each other. There's something real there, Mia." He pulls me back from his chest and locks his eyes on mine. "I don't think—"

"Mia" My body tenses at the familiar low hum of Preston's voice coming from behind me. I slowly turn to face him, his hazel eyes locked onto mine and I almost feel like I can see...sadness.

"Hey, Preston," James interjects when we've let the silence drag on for longer than comfortable. "Good to see you man! Say, I was won—"

"Good to see you too, James. If you don't mind, I'd like a word with Mia," he speaks to James, but he doesn't take his eyes off me. My heart races as he extends his hand to mine, his eyes begging me to take it. But I don't move.

My mind flashes back and forth between the photos of him with Sadie and the hurt in his eyes right before he left my office. There's a part of me that wants to hear him out, but the other part is afraid of what he might say. Maybe he regrets whatever happened with her in LA and they're not together after all. But then there's the possibility that he might be here to tell me it's over between us. That we can't come back from this deception and it's that possibility I'm not sure I can survive right now.

"No. I-I can't do this. I have to—" I say as I rip off the now suffocating mask and flee the party.

Chapter 27

Preston

I watch as Mia tears out the back door, heading straight for the cottage. Immediately after the press conference announcing my new role as CEO, I hopped on our private plane, singularly focused on making things right with Mia. My talk with Alexi unveiled the truth I know I've been denying for quite some time now. I love her. I'm *in love* with her and all I want to do is tell her that, but somehow, I've already managed to fuck it up.

Tossing my mask on a table, I sprint towards the direction she fled, finally catching up to her in the garden. "Mia, I—"

At the sound of my voice, she picks up speed, but I close the distance in one stride. Grabbing her wrist, I gently tug her in my direction until she spins around to face me, tears streaming down her face. My heart shatters at the look of anguish that rests there. At the undeniable knowledge that it's there because of me.

"Why are you here, Preston?" Her words spit like venom and who can blame her after my cowardly escape? I scrub my hand down the length of my face and try to come up with a way to defuse this situation.

"Didn't Oliver tell you I'd be here?"

She scoffs. "Why didn't *you* tell me? You could have called. Texted. Emailed for all I care, but all I got was silence. After we—" Her tears are falling steadily now, and I can barely restrain myself from reaching forward to wipe them from her cheek. "And where's *Sadie*?"

Truthfully, I had completely forgotten about running into Sadie. It seems so inconsequential when I think about how that awful kiss spurred on the realization that I'd accidentally fallen in love with the girl I once called my best friend.

With everything that happened with my father and the board, I've barely had time to sleep, let alone care about what the tabloids were saying. A pap must have snapped a photo of us and plastered it all over every gossip site. The old me wants to lie, to play dumb until she reveals exactly what she knows, but lying is precisely how everything got so twisted between us.

"Sadie's not in my life anymore. Whatever the media reported, they have it wrong. I-I was so fucked up about everything. About us. I stupidly thought that I could forget about it all. When she kissed me, I thought you and I were done, but the second her lips landed on mine, I saw you. She tried to take it further, but I stopped it before anything happened. I'm so fucking disgusted with myself. I never wanted to hurt you."

Her eyes narrow to slits, a humorless laugh expelling from her mouth. "Yeah well, you did. Never mind the temporary lapse in judgment that led to kissing your *married* ex, which is an entirely different conversation by the way, you just *left*. You didn't even give me a chance to explain. You abandoned me—" She stops short, her voice catching on the surge of emotion. But I understand the implication.

Just like I did all those years ago. Logically, I know it wasn't my fault that I had to leave, but that's irrelevant. She was still hurt and once again I failed her, broke her trust and I don't know how to earn it back. Or if I even deserve to. Nervous energy spreads through my body, threatening to explode. How did I fuck this up so spectacularly? I had a plan. I thought I'd apologize, confess my love, and we'd be able to continue building on this thing between us. I drag a hand down the length of my face with a frustrated sigh.

"There's no excuse for the way I walked out. None. But please believe me when I say I went to LA *for* you as much as to get some time *from* you."

The faint tilt of her head is the only indication I have that she's heard me.

"Explain," she demands, folding her arms over her chest with a defiant glare.

"For the past week I've been fighting the board to keep the inn open. They—"

"What exactly do you mean 'keep the inn open'?" She huffs out, worry written all over her face.

"The board wasn't impressed with how much money the inn was losing. They wanted to hold a vote to close it at the end of the year. But—"

"And you didn't think to tell me about this?!"

"Fuck. I'm doing this all wrong. Could you chill out and listen for a second?"

"No, Preston, I will not 'chill out' when you're telling

me that the inn is, or was, in trouble and you held the truth from me."

"Not to be that guy, but you're one to talk about withholding truths." I wince. That was the exact wrong thing to say, and I knew it the second it left my mouth. Her face flushes with anger, taking a step closer to me.

"That was low," she says, her voice eerily calm, "I know I was wrong to keep my identity from you. You'll never know how much I regret it. But this, your ex, the way you so easily walked away from everything we had built. It's too much."

From the deflated tone of her voice, I know I'm losing her, and I scramble for the right thing to say. The words that will wash away all the bad that has transpired over the past few days. I step a fraction closer, the distance between us so infinitesimal that I can feel her breath. My hands clench at my side as I fight the urge to reach out and touch her because I haven't earned back the right to do so yet.

"I'm so fucking sorry, Mia. I've replayed that night in my head a million times. What I would have done differently. What I would have said to comfort you instead of being a prideful asshole. I would have taken you in my arms and told you how much I—"

"Don't," she interrupts me, finality in her voice. "Preston, this is...us...I need time to think. I'm going to stay with Chelsea tonight. You can stay here."

Then she turns and walks back towards the inn and as much as I want to follow, I have to respect her need for space. But that doesn't stop my stomach from dropping at the thought that maybe she's walking away for good.

Chapter 28

Mia

When I ran back to the inn, it took Chelsea all of two seconds to spot me and take me back to her house. It took the entire twenty-minute car ride, plus an additional fifteen minutes to finally calm down enough to tell her about my interaction with Preston and how the inn was, or maybe still is, in trouble.

"Do you think maybe that's what he was trying to tell you the night you told him about your past?" Chelsea asks, pulling a platter of sweet treats from the refrigerator.

"Yeah, I do. But he'd known for a week by that point and, frankly, I'm pissed that he didn't tell me about it. And that he had the nerve to basically say I had no right to be mad since I lied too." Katy and Chelsea share a look, their faces conveying they don't necessarily agree with my line of thinking.

"What?" I ask, impatiently.

"It's just...didn't you kind of do the same thing?" Katy's voice is soft and empathetic.

"Ugh. That's exactly what he said."

"He has a point, Mia," Chelsea starts, "I'm not judging you. I understand why you were nervous to tell him, but from his perspective, you both held onto these secrets, despite the impact they'd have on one another."

"It's not the same! This is my business, my livelihood. I should have told him, I know that. But he said they considered shutting us down. What if—"

"But they're not and it's all because of him. You have every right to be upset, but, and I say this with love, you're being a little hypocritical. You two need to talk to each other, air it all out."

I huff, folding my arms across my chest, but I can't even muster up any anger because the fact is, she's right and she knows it.

"I guess. I just...I can't. I'm so emotionally drained anything I say to him tonight will end badly."

"I get that. The guest suite is always yours when you need it, so why don't you go get some rest and talk to him in the morning, okay?" Chelsea shoves a cookie in my mouth as she gives me a quick hug and she and Katy head up to their room.

⚒ ⚒ ⚒

Despite the softness and warmth of Chelsea's guest bed, I slept fitfully. My mind wouldn't shut off, going over her words and the look of torment on Preston's face when he realized I wasn't ready to forgive him. The more I thought about why I was upset, the more I realized how stubborn I'm being and at the very least, I should talk this out with him. The truth is, I'm completely in love with him and there's no going back now.

I head downstairs to the sounds of sizzling bacon and brewing coffee. I stop on the stairs with a smile as I admire Chelsea and Katy sharing a kiss as they maneuver around the kitchen making breakfast.

"Morning," I say, taking a seat on one of the high-back chairs at their massive kitchen island.

"How'd you sle—" Chelsea stops short, her eyes wide when she turns around to look at me. I didn't bother checking my appearance, but as I run my fingers through my unruly waves, I can only guess how much of a mess I look after all the tossing and turning.

"Uh…not good, evidently."

Katy sets down a large envelope in front of me, my name scrawled across it in Preston's familiar handwriting. "This was taped to the door this morning."

I stare at it for a moment. The last time Preston left me something, he took off. I can't imagine he'd do that again, but perhaps my unwillingness to hear him out made him think I'm not worth the trouble.

The envelope contains a stack of legal papers and a handwritten note. I take out the note first and read what Preston had to say.

MIA,
INSIDE YOU'LL FIND THE DEED TO THE COTTAGE. IT'S MORE YOURS THAN MINE AND I WANT YOU TO HAVE PEACE OF MIND KNOWING THAT NOTHING WILL EVER TAKE THAT AWAY FROM YOU.
THERE'S SO MUCH I NEED TO SAY TO YOU AND IF YOU'RE WILLING TO TALK, PLEASE MEET ME AT THE

ENCLOSED ADDRESS AT 2PM. I HOPE I SEE YOU
SOON.
   I LOVE YOU
    -P

"Holy shit." I pull out the deed as I sink back in the chair in disbelief.

"What's going on?" Chelsea whips around, holding a spatula covered in pancake batter.

"Um, Preston gave me my house. And he wants to meet."

"Whoa! That's...wow. You're going, right?"

I pause, unsure of why I'm hesitant to say yes. This man essentially bought me a house and is only asking for me to hear him out. Wasn't I ready to admit that I owe him a conversation? Haven't I been dreaming of him coming back to me since he left?

I know I'm in love with him, but I'm still so hurt that he was able to so easily walk away from me, from us, when I made a mistake. I don't know if my heart can take him walking away from me again.

"I'm not sure," I finally answer, earning a glare from Chelsea.

"You know I love you, but you're a fucking idiot." I balk at her frustrated tone. "He *loves* you. It says it, right there!" She points emphatically at the letter sitting on the counter. "More importantly, *you* love *him*. I don't know why you're being so stubborn about this."

"I don't know either! I'm just—I—he—"

"Ugh. Get over it already. He fucked up, you fucked up, everybody fucked up. But, Mia, he's made you happier than I've ever seen you before. This shit is once in a lifetime." She moves closer to her wife, wrapping an arm around her waist, adoration filling their eyes that are now locked on each other. "Trust me, Mia, when you find a love like that, you hold for dear life."

Katy brings her hand up to cup Chelsea's cheek before leaning in for a sweet kiss. I sit there, admiring their love, easily imagining this being me and Preston one day. Once again, Chelsea's the voice of reason, and I know what I have to do.

"Okay. I'll go."

"Damn right you will."

Chapter 29

Preston

Signing over the deed to the cottage to Mia was always my plan the second I was promoted to CEO. Even though everything's okay with the inn, I know she was upset with the knowledge that something was wrong, and I didn't tell her. I needed her to know that no matter what happens with the inn, she'll always have her home.

The letter, well, that was something I turned over in my head. The evidence of the dozens of bad drafts lay crumbled in the kitchen trashcan as I check my watch for the millionth time today. It's barely past noon and I'm desperate to see her, to touch her, to say all the things I didn't get to say before she ran off last night. I only hope she's willing to show up, to let me explain, and that what I have planned will be enough to win her back.

I arrive at the cemetery a few hours later, standing nervously at the gates with a bouquet of fresh flowers.

My mother is buried right behind these gates, and I haven't returned to her grave since the funeral. Over the last month in Stoney Ridge, I've debated coming here a thousand times, but I could never muster up the courage. It's like saying goodbye all over again, and the truth is, I can't imagine doing this alone and Mia is the only person I trust to see me this vulnerable.

As her Mini Cooper pulls up the hill, I momentarily begin to doubt my decision when I see the apprehension on her face. Admittedly, it's a little weird to invite a woman to a cemetery to express your love and beg for forgiveness, but it's the best way I know how to make her understand I need her and trust her completely.

"Um, Preston, what the hell are we doing here?" Her eyes dart around the space with trepidation.

"Thanks for coming. I know I don't have a right to ask, but can you trust me?"

With a deep breath, she finally nods, walking in front of me through the gates. I lead her down a walkway to a large headstone covered with a light dusting of snow from this morning's snowfall.

"Hey, ma," I say, placing the bouquet at the front of the headstone. "Sorry it took me so long to make it back here." I don't bother to stop the emotion building up inside. I need to release the hurt I've held onto for all these years.

"I wish you were here. I wish you could see how beautiful the inn has become. I wish you could see how hard dad is trying. He misses you so much and regrets being such an asshole. I really think he's trying to be a better man and I'm just so sorry he couldn't be that man for you when you needed him."

I pause, wiping the tears from my eyes that are freely falling down my face. Warmth spreads through my body when I feel Mia's hand on my back, rubbing gentle, comforting circles as I finally have a long overdue conversation with my mother.

"I miss you so much. I haven't always been the man you raised me to be, but I'm trying to be better. For you, for dad, for myself, but most of all, for her. There's someone I want you to meet." I beckon Mia closer, and she takes my hand to stand next to me.

"This is Mia. The woman I love." I turn to lock eyes with hers that now glisten with unshed tears. "You knew her as Amelia, and I think you'd really love the woman she's grown into. She's fierce, but kind; stubborn, but compassionate; and she's so fucking gorgeous." I wince, imagining my mother balking at the curse. "Sorry for the language. Anyway, she's perfect and without her, I don't know if I'd be half the man I am standing before you.

But, Ma, I'm hoping you can help me, because I think I messed up with this girl. She made a mistake, but instead of being the forgiving boy you raised, I was immature and prideful. I turned my back on her when she needed me, and I don't know if she's going to forgive me. And while I've made a lot of mistakes in my life, loving her was never one of them."

I lock my eyes with Mia's, tears streaming freely down her cheeks now.

"So, do you think you can help me convince this beautiful, perfect woman to give me another chance?"

"Preston..." Mia whispers, bringing her arms up to embrace my neck. We don't say anything, just stand there holding one another as we cry until she breaks first, taking my hand in hers as she steps back.

"Let's go home."

✦ ✦ ✦

THE DRIVE BACK TO THE COTTAGE IS SILENT, BUT MIA allows me to hold her hand the entire time. Not knowing whether she's forgiven me is killing me, but I don't want to pressure her and end this delicate truce we've entered. I don't have to wait long, because as soon as I shut the door behind us, she speaks.

"We still need to talk about a lot of things."

"I agree. So, let's talk." I guide her by the arm over to the couch, sitting so close to her that our legs touch.

"You really hurt me, Preston. I know you said...I mean...last night...you implied you l—"

"I love you," I blurt out. "Yeah, I said that, and I didn't imply, I meant it Mia. I've been falling for you for a long time now."

"Right. Well, I guess I don't understand how you can say that and still turn your back on me and run back to your ex."

I sigh in frustration, but not at her words. "Because I'm a fucking idiot." That earns a light chuckle from her, but her smile fades quicker than I'd like. "My traitorous brain kept telling me that you were like Sadie, manipulating me and using me for my money, but that argument fell apart the second I calmed down and thought about it for more than two seconds. When you told me who you are, I should have immediately grabbed you and held on for dear life, reveling in the fact that I get to be in love with my best friend."

Her face is unreadable as she lowers her eyes to her hands, which wring nervously in her lap. We sit in silence until I can't stand it and break first.

"Mia, I love you so fucking much. I can't think when I'm around you. I left because I wanted to be angry, and I knew the second I looked into these beautiful brown eyes that would be it. I'd forgive you anything." I shift to sit on the coffee table in front of her, taking her hands in mine as I beg her to hear my words. "Please...tell me I didn't fuck up the best thing that's ever happened to me."

Her face softens and she brings my hand to her mouth, placing a soft kiss to the back of my palm. "You didn't ruin it. I'm in love with you too, Preston."

Before I can stop myself, my lips crash down on hers, not desperate with lust, but with the need to pour every bit of emotion I'm feeling directly into her and make sure she never again questions my love for her.

She parts her lips, matching my urgency, our tongues dancing with each other, only breaking to stand, bringing our bodies closer together. I tilt her head backwards to deepen our kiss before slowly stealing my lips from hers, peppering kisses along her jaw to her neck. I'm rewarded with the softest, breathy moan of my name and I nearly come at the sound. God, I've missed her.

Grabbing her head between both hands, I kiss my way back up to her mouth, tasting tears as I reach her cheek. My eyes blink open and I see the streaks of tears marking up her perfect face. Worry floods my body as I can't decipher the expression she wears.

"What's wrong?" I keep my hands on her face, but pull back, giving her room to react.

She shudders a sigh, bringing her hands up to clasp mine. "Nothing. I just...thank you for coming back to me." Relief warms my heart as I realize her tears match what I've been feeling—overwhelming love, desire, and devotion.

"No matter what, I'll always come back to you. I'm quite literally yours, Mia. Always have been. Always will be. For as long as you'll have me." I lean down, pressing my forehead to hers.

I can't contain the need running through my body and evidently, she feels the same as she claims my mouth with hers, running her hands along the base of my neck, pulling me closer.

"Preston I...I *need* you."

The hungry desperation of her tone is all it takes for me to cup her ass, wrapping her legs around me as I take her to her bedroom. Every nerve in my body feels like it's about to explode, screaming with the need to bury myself inside her. But I want to savor this moment, to take my time showing her exactly how much she means to me.

I slowly release my hold on her, allowing her feet to touch the ground. She moves quickly, her hands shaking as she begins to unbutton my shirt, placing kisses along my chest and stomach as each patch of skin is revealed. My head tosses back in ecstasy as she runs her tongue along my nipple, slowly grazing her teeth against it.

"*Fuuuuuck.*" It comes out as little more than an exhale as I run my fingers through her hair.

Her hands slide down my torso until she stops at my belt, looking up at me with a wicked grin. Her mouth is swollen from our urgent kisses, her lipstick smeared in a beautiful mess. I'm about to lose all control as I watch her drop to her knees in front of me. She expertly unfastens my belt with one hand, the other palming me through my pants right before she unzips them, pulling my cock free.

She brushes a light kiss to my tip and grips her hand around my shaft, pulling down to its base. A low growl escapes me, spurring her on as she parts her lips, taking the head of my cock between them. I see stars behind my eyes when she pulls me back out to run her tongue along the base, pulling me in deeper until I'm touching the back of her throat. If she keeps this up, I'm not going to last another second.

"Fuck, Mia. That feels so goddamn good."

She moans, sending vibrations all along my cock and I know I'm done for. She feels it too as she moves a hand down to grip my balls and locks eyes with mine, her silent consent urging me to let go. I can't help myself thrusting forward as I come undone and spill into her mouth. She clamps her hands on my ass, pulling me closer so she can take in every inch of me as I find my release in her. She runs her tongue along the tip of my cock, making sure to get every last drop of my cum. It's the hottest thing I've ever seen.

I offer my hands to help her up and before she can even fully right herself, I'm pulling off her jeans, peeling them down her curvy body until she stands before me in nothing but a thin pair of lace panties and her crop top. It's not until now that I notice she's not wearing a bra. My eyes roam over her body, her chest heaving with anticipation, her pert nipples straining against the thin fabric of her shirt.

Reaching my hand behind her, I place one hand on the small of her back, the other on her opposite hip, and lean in to whisper in her ear. "My turn." It comes out more like a hungry growl and I feel her entire body shiver beneath me as I gently lead her down to the bed. I stand above her, admiring her body illuminated by the soft glow of the sun peeking through the window before settling on my knees in front of her. I pull her towards me slowly, poised to worship every inch of her, running my hands along both of her legs until I reach her hips, tugging her underwear down, tossing them across the room.

"Fuck, beautiful. Is this all for me?" I groan as I slowly run a finger up and down her soaked center.

She squirms, letting out a low moan and I can hardly take it. Hooking her knees over my shoulders, I place my face between her legs and breath in her heady scent, parting her with my fingers so I can run my tongue from her entrance to her clit. The taste of her is better than any drug and my cock is quickly growing hard again. I now understand what the gods meant when they spoke of ambrosia—it's pussy, more specifically, Mia's pussy, and I would gladly give my life if it meant one more taste of her.

Her hips buck against my face and she cries out as my lips close around her clit, sucking and teasing her with my tongue. Her breathy moans beg for more as she runs her fingers through my hair, pulling me closer. Desperate to give her everything she needs, I place one arm over her stomach to hold her in place, allowing me to steady her, pushing two fingers inside, softly curling against her inner walls. A satisfied moan turns into screams that fill the room as her back arches and her eyes snap open at the sensation of me hitting that coveted spot.

"That's it. I want to taste your cum on my tongue."

Her breath quickens and her hips buck wildly, the walls of her pussy gripping my fingers as I pump in and out of her until a powerful orgasm rips through her entire body. When the flutters stop, I pull my fingers out of her, softly kissing her clit one more time as she rides out every last second of pleasure.

"Preston, I need you inside me. *Now*," she whimpers, grabbing at my shoulders to pull me towards her.

I stand up, quickly pulling my pants off the rest of the way. I lean over to grab a condom from her nightstand, ripping it open and sliding it on frantically. Tonight is so much more than lust, it's *need*. The need to claim her. To feel her surrounding me. To give her all of me, mind, heart, body, and soul.

I position myself over her, hovering for a moment in awe that this woman chose me, despite every reason to walk away. I brush her hair from her face and place a slow, languid kiss on her lips. "God, you are so fucking perfect. I love you so much, Mia," I say slowly pushing into her, feeling her stretch around me.

Her kiss confirms the depth of her feelings that match my own. We aren't merely chasing pleasure, though the way her pussy clenches around me, wet and hot, is a pleasure I hope I never forget. Tonight, we've declared ourselves to one another. As if we've tumbled off a cliff and are frantically grasping each other before we crash into the waves below. Out of all the women I've had, nothing prepared me for the way I feel having given myself completely over to her.

Our bodies move in perfect harmony, responding to the push and pull of our need. Her fingernails dig into my back as I feel her getting close. I open my eyes to look down at this amazing, beautiful, intelligent woman, captivated by everything she is. Emotion floods my chest, and I feel my own release building. I reach my hand between us, caressing her sensitive clit, coaxing out another orgasm. She wraps her legs around me as she cries out in pleasure, and I follow her over the edge.

Chapter 30

Mia

My body is sore in the most delicious way as I wake in Preston's arms. Yesterday was emotionally and physically exhausting, but despite that, I've never been happier than I am now, safe in the arms of the man I love.

The low grumble of hunger from my stomach demands that I get breakfast now. I gently slip out of his arms, pulling on my robe as I walk out to the kitchen, suppressing a startled scream as I spot Chelsea, her head resting on her hands with a giant smirk on her face.

"Jesus Christ! How long have you been here?" I walk over to the table to inspect the box of donuts she's brought, grabbing myself a chocolate and setting aside a jelly for Preston.

"Oh, don't worry. I didn't hear anything important. I've only been here for, like, five minutes."

"So, what are you doing here?" I say around a mouthful of donut.

"Yeah, as if I was going to miss the big day after the

reunion. I knew the second you left to meet up with Preston that you'd be in for some god-tier makeup sex, so I figured I'd bring some refreshments to replenish your electrolytes...or something."

I shake my head but can't suppress a laugh. "You know, for a chef, you know surprisingly little about nutrition."

She shrugs and takes a bite out of a pink frosted donut. "Hey, I just make shit taste good. I don't really care about the rest. So..." She looks me up and down and it's then I remember I'm wearing a skimpy robe that barely leaves anything to the imagination. I absentmindedly tighten the belt, as if that'll do anything to help.

"I guess by the state of things, you two reconciled?"

A wide grin spreads across my face. "You could sa—" I cut myself off as I see Preston stumbling out of the bedroom, completely naked.

"FUCK!" He scrambles to cover his cock with his hands when he sees Chelsea, who now sits at the table cackling.

"That you did, amiright?" Chelsea says suggestively with a wag of her eyebrows.

Preston runs back to the bedroom to get clothed as Chelsea mouths 'Oh my *god*'.

I nod, raising my eyebrows knowingly, my grin widening.

"What on earth are you doing here at," I glance at the microwave clock, "6:30 in the morning?"

"Well, *some of us* work for a living. In case you forgot, it's breakfast service. And also, I'm nosy as fuck and wanted to know how last night went. But mostly I'm here to talk about the plans for the inn and the restaurant."

I shoot her a quizzical look as Preston joins us, placing a kiss to my forehead before grabbing his jelly donut.

"Wait, how do you know about that?" Preston asks, leaving me confused as to what either of them is talking about.

"Well, after you two sprinted out of the party like she was Cinderella at midnight, I got to talking, specifically to Ollie and Stanley. They spoiled your little plan, and frankly, I think it's amazing! Congratulations, Mia!"

"Um, thanks?" My brow furrows as I dart my eyes back and forth between Preston and Chelsea. "But I honestly have no idea what you're talking about."

Chelsea chucks a balled-up napkin at Preston.

"Hey! What the hell?" he says, tossing it back in her direction and missing.

"You didn't tell her? I mean, surely you didn't dick her down that long!"

"Tell me what?" I direct to Preston, his face showing nothing.

"It's good news, I promise. You're gonna love it!" Chelsea claps her hands together excitedly. "Sorry, go ahead." She gestures to Preston to explain.

"It is good news, I hope. You know all those financial records I was pouring through?"

I give him a small nod, encouraging him to continue.

"Well, it turns out Winston was stealing an obscene amount of money from the inn, more than any other property. We assume he thought it would go undetected, and I guess that proved to be true since no one at HQ noticed. But, Mia, the work you and your mom have done here is nothing short of amazing. You've managed to create a staple of the community while drawing in repeat business from all across the eastern seaboard."

I place a hand over my heart, surprise and horror filling my body in equal amounts. "So, all this time...we weren't failing?"

"Far from it. Here," he grabs his laptop and pulls up a chart which appears to outline the last ten years as well as projections for the next ten, "if you look at the actuals versus reported, the inn has grown by at least ten percent each year. That's crazy good in this industry. Yes, there are some issues we need to address like pricing. You've been severely undercharging for *everything*."

"And you think we can really stay afloat?" My voice comes out hopeful and I sit up a little straighter.

"More than that, you can thrive." He digs in his brief-case, pulling out a stack of papers, placing them in front of me.

"I worked with Stanley on the flight over to finalize this. Basically, you and your mother kept the inn running, profiting, even, despite the lack of support from us. I made sure the new agreement reflects that."

Confused, I thumb through the paperwork, my eyes going wide when I spot the change. "Preston...this is..."

Chelsea's bouncing in her seat, unable to contain her excitement. "I know, right? Mia, you're a partial owner of the inn!"

And she's right. I flip through the rest of the paper-work, confirming a twenty-five percent stake in the inn assigned to Paola and Amelia Flores. Tears well up in my eyes as I consider what this will mean for me and my mom. Her medical expenses will be easily covered with this new cashflow.

"Tell her about the restaurant!" Chelsea demands.

"I'm getting there," he admonishes. "Chelsea and her menu have already been drawing attention, but we believe we can bring in a whole new clientele with the full support of The Spencer Group's marketing.

Gone will be the days of buffet style service. We want to focus on getting Chelsea a Michelin Star by the end of the year and transition to a full-service restaurant open to the public. If you agree, Chelsea will become a partner, with her focus being on this new endeavor."

"It's not even a question! Of course, Chels, you deserve this so much!"

She stands up, running over to me, squeezing me tightly. "Fuck, we're in our boss bitch era now!"

I laugh as she sways us back and forth almost pulling me out of my chair. When she exits our embrace, I jump into Preston's lap, placing my lips to his.

"Welp, that's my cue. I do *not* need another eyeful of what went on last night, but damn. Good job, both of you. Toodaloo!"

I roll my eyes as she gives a dainty waive with her fingers and leaves us alone.

I shift to face Preston, bringing my face flush with his. "I don't have the words to thank you enough for this. For believing in me. For giving me my..." I choke back a sob, "for giving me *your* home."

He shakes his head. "After one night here, I saw the love you and your mother poured into this place. It's been yours for a long time, I only made it legal."

I bring a hand to caress his cheek and lean forward, planting another soft kiss to his lips. "So, what will you do now that you're president and CEO?" A part of me worries that his new position will separate us just when we've finally reconciled.

"Well, the way I figure it, president is kind of more of a figure head. And Ollie and Stanley have been handling things so well in my father's absence that I gave them Co-CEO titles. I thought I'd let them run things in LA so I can stick around Stoney Ridge, run the company from here. That is, if you'll have me?" He flashes me a wide grin which I mirror with an excited squeal.

"Of course, I'll have you! I'm yours, Preston. Always." He pulls me in tight, placing his mouth next to my ear.

"You're mine, Mia. And I'm yours. You're my home and I'm never leaving you again."

BREAKING NEWS

Roman Spencer cleared of all charges while his son, Preston, ushers in a new era for The Spencer Group

STONEY RIDGE, VT (NYT) — The Federal Bureau of Investigation has officially cleared Roman Spencer of all charges pertaining to the $500M embezzlement investigation into his company, The Spencer Group.

Early last week, agents apprehended former CFO, Winston Pickering, in Brussels. Pickering confessed to orchestrating the scheme, spanning nearly two decades, and will face extradition for his trial, scheduled for next month.

Roman's only son, Preston, will retain the position of President, which he accepted during his father's incarceration, with long time executives Oliver Hughes and Stanley Beck serving as Co-CEOs of the company.

The youngest Spencer, meanwhile, will continue to support the company from their first property, The Early Bird Inn, located in Stoney Ridge, Vermont. The inn, which is a popular upscale dining destination ran by renowned chef, Chelsea Taylor, earned its first Michelin Star earlier this year.

In other news, Preston recently announced his engagement to his childhood best friend and partial owner of the inn, Mia Flores. They're expected to wed this December on the grounds of the inn where they met.

Acknowledgments

No one tells you how many people will be involved in publishing your first book. I'm so grateful for the support I've had from everyone as I worked towards realizing a dream I've held my entire life.

To the community I found on Bookstagram, Booktok, and Bookthreads, I owe you my sincerest thanks. For the feedback, tips, funny memes, comments, and likes, you've helped me have the confidence to share this story with the world.

To every single alpha, beta, and ARC reader, thank you for reading the early stages of this book, helping me to refine the story and give Preston and Mia the ending they deserved.

Most of all to my friends and family whose unwavering support and encouragement helped me push through when I was sure my writing was shit and publishing would never happen for me.

I could never list them all, but special shout outs to Audra, for patiently reading all the shitty first drafts, Raquel, for your mentorship on self-publishing, and Taylor, my emotional support extrovert, for being my biggest cheerleader throughout this entire process!

To my bestie, Brittany, for always believing in this crazy dream of mine and for listening to me yap endlessly about this book. To my parents, Steve and Sheri, for starting my reading obsession early, without which I'd never try to write my own stories.

Special shout out to my cover artist, Kristina Fostovets, who brought Mia and Preston to life so perfectly. I really couldn't be happier with this cover and the character art you nailed.

Last, but not least, to you, dear reader, for taking a chance on an unknown indie author who just wanted to write cute little love stories. I hope you enjoyed your time in Stoney Ridge as much as I did.

Thank you all for believing in me and helping me share my voice.

- S.V. Lynn

About the Author

S.V. Lynn is a Midwest girl at heart, but now spends her days in Dallas, Texas. An avid bookworm and storyteller, it was only a matter of time until she put pen to paper and shared the stories floating around her head with the world.

Holiday Handyman is her debut novel. When she's not writing, you can find her with her nose stuck in a book or fueling herself on espresso at one of her favorite Dallas coffee shops.

Connect with her on Instagram, Threads, and TikTok at @author.svlynn.